EXOS  I

EXOSKELETON

A Novel

Shane Stadler

A Division of New Street Communications, LLC
Wickford, RI

Published 2012

Dark Hall Press
A Division of New Street Communications, LLC
Wickford, RI

Acknowledgements

I would like to express my thanks to the many editors and agents who have given me useful feedback on this novel in its early stages, and for their general encouragement.

I'd like to thank William Greenleaf for a very helpful critique of the early manuscript.

Finally, I am grateful and indebted to William Renehan, Editorial Director at Dark Hall Press, for taking a chance on *Exoskeleton*, and its first-time author.

CHAPTER I
Day Minus-One

Innocence or guilt is irrelevant.
To William Thompson this was no epiphany, but an unwilling metamorphosis to acceptance. He reminded himself that *he'd be free in a year*, but it did little to temper his anger.

The frigid air in the dark helicopter cabin continuously drained the heat from his body, and he clenched his jaws to keep his teeth from chattering. But a deeper coldness, a weave of anger, fear, and sadness, encroached upon him as they neared their destination. It was this edgy foreboding—and the intuition that time was running short on something—that had disturbed him ever since the sentencing.

Far below, streetlights twinkled like stars as tree branches and other obstacles flickered through his line of view, and frozen lakes appeared as voids of black in an otherwise glittering landscape of life. The cars on the streets seemed to crawl from that altitude, and Will found himself wishing he was in one of them—*any* of them—and that he was another person...

From five thousand feet, the building that was their destination resembled a colossal computer chip embedded in a matrix of illuminated streets, and it loomed more and more menacing as they approached the landing pad on its roof. Will wrung his numbed hands, relieved that the four-hour journey was finally coming to an end. He then scraped frost from the window, and looked closely as they circled to come in from the north. The color of the building was a deep red—a blood red.

Will rested his forehead against the cold, vibrating window, and wondered if he could get himself to jump from the roof of the building if the opportunity arose. Never in his forty years of life had he considered suicide, but he now understood how humiliation and shame could drive a man to such an extreme. His leg suddenly twitched, causing his foot to kick the seat in front of him. He knew it wasn't the cold that triggered the spasm, but rather the anxiety that bound him like a coiled spring. Even though he knew no *specific* details, he was convinced that the "treatment" would be unpleasant.

Will's head jerked sharply as the chopper bounced down on the roof of the thirty-story building. Once the aircraft settled, the pilot shut down the engines and tapped the copilot on the shoulder. The man responded by pushing a button on the control panel, and cupping the helmet-mounted microphone in front of his mouth. "Marion Prison, this is MP-101," he said. "We have arrived at the Detroit facility; the package will be delivered shortly. We'll fuel up at Detroit Metro for the return trip. Our ETA is 04:20."

"Roger that, MP-101, keep us informed," a man's voice replied over a background of scratchy static.

Will heard the chopper's rotors slow down to what was probably a safe speed. The four men who comprised his escort detail opened the sliding doors on the starboard side of the passenger cabin, and climbed down to the roof. The largest of the prison guards reached back into the cabin, unlocked one side of Will's handcuffs from a steel eyelet on the seat, and clamped it on his own wrist.

"Let's go, asshole," the guard ordered over the decaying whine of the engine.

Will said nothing. The anxiety for what was coming, that which had caused his muscles to tremor like high-tension cables, was stronger than any anger those men could summon in him. Besides, he was so cold he wasn't sure whether he could get his mouth to form words—his jaws seemed to be locked in the closed position.

Will stood up slowly, ducked his head and shoulders under the doorframe, and jumped to the ground three feet below, where he landed heavily. The rest of the men immediately surrounded him—acting with extreme caution, as they always had when handling him. They were larger, both individually and in number, but Will sensed they still felt threatened. He didn't blame them; he'd nearly killed a giant-of-a-man while in prison. Until a little more than a year ago, he reflected, he'd never assaulted anyone.

Will realized that being handcuffed to the oversized guard, whose badge read *Hank Tritt, MP#: 2119*, extinguished any hope of running for the edge of the roof. Although he could probably drag the Neanderthal over the edge, he hadn't reached the point where he'd be willing to take an innocent man down with him.

The guards led him out from the shelter of the helicopter, and Will's feet were so numb he couldn't sense the ground beneath him. The only indication of his own movement was the squeaking sound his shoes made on the hard-packed snow—a noise that made him feel even colder—like that made by rubbing together two pieces of Styrofoam. After just a few steps, they were fully exposed to the weather, and Will thought the December wind might blow right through him. The guards shielded their faces with thick coat sleeves to protect against the whirring ice crystals. It was a luxury Will wished he had; he still wore his short-sleeved, prison-issued jumpsuit.

A hundred feet in front of them, a red hutch protruded from the flat roof of the building like the conning tower of a submarine. They waited on the landing pad, and just as the gusting wind, engine exhaust, and a stench that Will thought must have been coming from the city sewer system were becoming intolerable, a door on the protrusion opened.

Light spilled out and into the night, producing a dim, red hue on the roof. A stocky figure emerged, looked in their direction for a moment, and walked towards them with some difficulty. The man obviously had problems with his legs or hips, his hobbling amplified in his silhouette. The guards remained still as he closed the distance, and his rough face finally came into view. He was at least in his mid-sixties, Will estimated, and reminded him of some of the civil service employees who worked at his former university: old, weathered, and angry.

The old man stopped just a few steps away and yelled to the security guards through the cold wind. His words emanated as white puffs of breath blown through jagged, black-yellow teeth. "I'm Ruggins. Welcome to the Red Box... This must be Thompson." He nodded towards Will.

"Yeah, here's the paperwork," Tritt said as he handed Ruggins a clipboard, its papers crackling in the wind. "We can finally detach ourselves from this piece of shit." He looked around the roof. "You've got a nice color scheme going here."

Ruggins ignored the comment, flipped through the papers he'd been handed, and signed one of the documents with a gloved hand.

Tritt turned to the other men in his detail as he pulled some keys out of his jacket pocket. "All right, let's get outta he—"

"—What are you doing?" Ruggins cut in. "You never un-cuff a patient on the roof. And you're not done: an admissions officer has to sign off on some of these forms. You can't leave until this guy is *behind the door*." He pointed to the entrance of the hutch, and led Will and two of the guards to it. Tritt ordered the third guard to inform the pilots of their delayed departure.

Will burped silently and winced as bile stung the back of his throat. He felt his stomach worsen as he got closer and closer to the punishment he had chosen.

Richard Greene shifted in his seat and tried to remain calm as an itchy sweat broke out on his back. It seemed to him that all government buildings had climate control problems; in this case it was too hot even though the weather outside was frigid—a nasty December night in Washington, DC. He knew, however, that his discomfort was not driven by temperature alone. Although he wasn't overtly sweating, like the man sitting in the center of the stuffy room, he was sure he was just as nervous—and wondered if he might be sitting in the same chair someday soon.

His colleague, Heinrich Bergman, seemed to ponder as he paced back and forth and rubbed the dark stubble on his chin. He stopped in front of the man in the chair, dropping his hands to his sides. "Come on, Frank," he said. "You've already admitted to selling the technical designs. Why not fess up to the missing project files, and we can put all this behind us?"

"I already told you," Frank replied, rubbing beads of sweat from his balding head with a thick hand. "I sent the files to Langley to be digitized as I was ordered, and they were sent back. But I never saw any backup copies—"

"You're responsible for *everything* that's shipped to and from this site," Bergman said. "The originals and the backup copies made it back here. The backup copies have disappeared. For God's sake, Frank, it was a *crate* of files. Where is it?"

Frank only shook his head and looked down to the floor.

"Lenny," Bergman said as he turned to the man sitting to Richard's right. "I think we need to enhance this man's desire to cooperate."

The wooden chair under Lenny creaked as the large man stood. He put on a pair of thin, black gloves, and produced four pairs of plastic, zip-tie handcuffs out of a leather satchel. The man's mere presence in a room made Richard nervous. Lenny wasn't very tall—maybe five-foot-nine—but he was as wide as a Volkswagen Bug, and his giant, catcher's-mitt-hands hung from unusually long arms.

Lenny walked over to Frank and cuffed his wrists and ankles to the arms and legs of the chair, despite the man's resistance.

"What are you doing?" Frank asked nervously.

Richard heard a hollow cupping sound as Lenny hit Frank's head with an open hand.

"Shut up," Lenny ordered.

Richard always heard a subtle accent in Lenny's voice, on the rare occasions that the man spoke, but could never place it.

"Why are you doing this?" Frank cried. His eyes darted back and forth, still reeling from the strike. "I told you, I don't know anything about missing files."

"I *want* to believe you, Frank, I *do*," Bergman replied. "But you lied to me about the technical plans already." Bergman shook his head in disgust and then asked, "You have a kid in college, don't you Frank?"

After some hesitation, Frank nodded.

"I'd hate it if our problems here had to spill into your private life," Bergman said.

Richard shuddered as his prickly sweat suddenly turned cold. *What about his own kids?* He thought of his two girls. They were a year apart—first grade and kindergarten—but practically identical. *But Bergman wouldn't hurt little kids, would he?* Richard already knew the answer: Bergman might even *eat* little kids, if that was what the project required.

"Are you threatening my family?" Frank asked.

"Just thinking about why you might need the extra cash," Bergman replied. "I've got two in college right now—love'em to death, and always worrying about them—but not enough to sell out my country."

He turned to Lenny. "Get what you can out of him—the usual treatment. I'll be back in a half hour."

Lenny nodded.

Bergman looked to Richard and gestured toward the door.

Richard followed the long-gaited man into the hall and around a corner where Bergman turned to face him. Richard always thought Bergman looked hungry and desperate, but his voice didn't match his appearance; he always sounded confident.

"Sorry to keep you here so late," Bergman said. "I needed you in there to estimate the damage of the leak. But I don't think he took the project files. What do *you* think?"

Richard was taken aback by the question. He felt Bergman's dark, beady eyes staring at him, searching for any indication of deception. He knew if he could convince Bergman that Frank took the *project files* as well as the technical plans the poor bastard would probably end up as fish-food. The heat would be off for a while, but he didn't want to be responsible for harm coming to the man. "I don't know about the project files," Richard responded, "but the technical plans he sold were old—we don't even use that technology anymore. Minimal damage, if any."

"Even if he leaked the most current technical plans, of the device, or the facilities themselves, it wouldn't matter anyway," Bergman said. "Only our contractors have the resources to produce any of that stuff. But the missing *project files* are damning—they reveal everything. If they were made public, the project would be done for—as would we." Bergman pulled a cell phone out of his pocket and looked at the screen. "It's getting pretty late. I don't want to delay your work on the upcoming presentation. You'll need some time to put a positive spin on the report. All of the big players will be at this meeting." He put the phone back in his pocket and clapped Richard on the shoulder. "Good luck."

Bergman walked down the hall and turned a corner. Richard went over to a large window and peered out, trying to collect his thoughts. He was sure Bergman would eventually figure it all out. He just hoped it wouldn't happen too soon—not before the files got into the right hands.

He stepped closer to the window; the nighttime view of DC was always impressive. He saw it often as of late, and once again he wouldn't be home until well after midnight. His wife and girls had missed him many nights over the past year. They thought he was a hard-working engineer, and that's what he *was* at the beginning. But they had no idea of what he was currently doing, or more importantly: what he was *going* to do. And they didn't know how they were unknowingly involved. His heart ached with guilt: *What was he risking?*

As Will had suspected, the hutch was an entrance to an elevator. He and the other four men crammed in, and he felt the guards' shoulders press tightly against his as the doors slid closed. His face was so close to the back of the man in front of him that he could smell the residue of cigarette smoke embedded in the canvas of his jacket. On the verge of breaking into a claustrophobic fit, he concentrated on being sheltered from the wind, and on absorbing the warmth from the bodies around him. After a few seconds of deliberately obstructing his thoughts of panic, he had calmed himself enough to survive the elevator trip.

About a hundred buttons of various colors arrayed the elevator control panel, which Will found strange as he estimated the building to be about thirty floors. Of the three buttons labeled with a 5, Ruggins pushed the red one. The elevator quickly descended, beeping its way down the levels, and Will felt it decelerate as they approached the fifth floor.

"Hang on," Ruggins said as he grabbed a handle on the wall.

Will felt the elevator stop its descent, and then accelerate *horizontally*.

"What the hell is this?" a guard asked, pushing against a wall to maintain his balance.

"Strange, isn't it?" Ruggins said, grinning.

"I've heard rumors about this place ... don't know if I *want* to know much more," the guard replied, winking at Will. It wasn't a friendly wink.

"I've been here since it was built—about two years now—and I *still* get lost," Ruggins grumbled.

The elevator decelerated, making everyone teeter again, then came to a full stop. The doors opened, and new air filled Will's nostrils with the smell of fresh paint. He peered around the shoulder of the bulky guard in front of him, surveying the layout of the room outside. It was reminiscent of the lobby of a medical clinic, complete with institutional-style furniture and a clerk window.

The mass of men piled out of the elevator, and Ruggins approached the window. It was made of bulletproof glass, as indicated by a small sticker, and had a metal drawer beneath it to pass things back and forth. The only door in the room, other than that of the elevator, was located to the right of the clerk window. It looked massive—like a door to a vault—but devoid of any visible hinges or handles.

Ruggins tapped his key ring on the glass, producing a sharp sound that made Will's muscles twitch. A moment later, a large woman with thick glasses appeared on the other side whose name tag read *Darlene Jackson, Admissions Officer*. She spoke into a microphone, the noise spilling out of a speaker in the ceiling with the sound quality of a drive-through intercom. It seemed only Ruggins understood what she said.

"The patient is here to in-process," Ruggins yelled back into the window.

The woman collected some items, put them in the drawer on her side of the glass, and pushed the contents out to Ruggins, who scooped them up and replaced them with the paperwork the guards had submitted to him. He handed some of the papers to one of the guards and said, "Fill these out. And give me your prison ID's, I'll need to make copies." He hobbled over to Will and Tritt, the guard to whom Will was cuffed. "Release him—he ain't going anywhere now." He handed a clipboard and a felt-tipped pen to Will. "Fill out these forms."

Will clutched the clipboard and pen while Tritt removed the cuff from his right wrist.

Ruggins squared up to Will and pointed to a chair. "Sit down," he ordered. "Check and initial where indicated, but don't *sign* anything yet—I have to witness it to make it official." He then turned to Tritt. "What we got here anyway, drug dealer? Murderer?"

"Child rapist and *attempted* murderer," Tritt hissed. "What's going to happen to him here—hard labor or something?"

Will listened carefully to Ruggins' response.

"I have no idea," Ruggins answered and grinned, revealing his stained and cracked teeth—this time in bright fluorescent light. "And if I did, I couldn't talk about it."

The three Marion guards chuckled nervously. Will made eye contact with the one closest to him—*Donny Anderson: MP#: 2187*—and didn't break it until the man looked away. The others became silent, seemingly wondering what Will might do now that he was no longer cuffed. Will waited to see if Donny would reestablish eye contact—he didn't—and then turned his attention to the paperwork.

Some of the information was already filled out: *Name: William Dale Thompson, Height: 5 ft. 10 in., Weight: 215 pounds, Hair: Brown, Eyes: Blue, Race: Caucasian.* They had the blood-type wrong, so he crossed it out and corrected it. One of the forms asked for former addresses, employers, education, etc., like he was getting a background check. Others were release forms of all types: general medical care and first aid, implementation of various medical-related procedures, minor surgery, a feeding tube, intravenous medications, various scopes, X-rays, and for recovery procedures, in case of "cardiac arrest or obstructed breathing." All of the releases were riddled with fine print that he had no desire to read. Other forms indicated the forfeiture of all of his assets, and the release of all medical, dental, psychological, and financial records. Another was a release for the implementation of psychological treatments, including psychotropic drugs and electroshock therapy. Finally, there was a consent form for the application of a biomechanical interface system.

Will had no idea what the last one was for, or why they wanted many of the other releases, but he'd sign them anyway. He wanted no delays—no time for them to change their minds.

Will's life had started to take a downward turn a few years before the "incident" that led him to the Red Box. It began with his philosophical outlook, which took on a complexion of impending doom, along with a sense of indifference towards many things that had once been important to him. Even his value of life—his own life—had diminished. Maybe the death of his grandmother a few years earlier had started it—a reaffirmation of his own mortality. It had been his only encounter with death; he had been there when she died.

Maybe the depression had emerged because he felt a lack of purpose: he'd already accomplished most of the major tasks in his life, and no longer had any goals—nothing more to dream about. There was one exception: he *had been* looking forward to starting a new life with his fiancee. But he knew now it would have been a mistake; he'd wasted four years of his life with her.

He shook out of his depressive trance, finished reading, and signed all of the forms in front of Ruggins, who initialed "JR" next to each signature.

Ruggins walked the paperwork to the window and sent it through to the Admissions Officer. She paged through the stack, verified each signature, then signed and stamped a form and sent it back. She leaned to her right and pushed a button on the desk. Her voice crackled over the speaker, "Please escort the patient to the door."

Patient? Why are they calling me that? Will wondered. It was the third time he'd heard himself referred to that way. He shifted in his seat and prepared to stand up. The Marion prison guards stirred nervously—a reaction that Will had observed often.

He knew the guards' uneasiness could be traced to a single event. Ronald "Rocco" Ballistreri had been a convicted murderer housed in the Marion maximum security facility during Will's time there. The hairy man was a giant; over six feet four and nearly three hundred pounds. On Will's third day in the pen, the brute had walked up to him during lunch and knocked his food tray to the floor. Rocco, who didn't perceive Will as a threat at his size, was surprised to have his own tray of food suddenly mashed into his face. Will followed with a right that struck Rocco square in the nose, sending him to the floor. He leapt on the man and felt his bottled rage release, pummeling him with a flurry of strikes. The next thing he knew, the guards were pulling him off by his arms ... but not before Rocco had been rendered unconscious on the floor with mashed potatoes, gravy, and blood embedded in his beard. Will could have killed that man, and they all had known it—inmates and guards alike; hence the reputation that had protected him.

Rocco had been killed a week later. Will figured the fight had emboldened some of the other inmates who had been tormented by the man. They had done it with a large zip-tie in the laundry facility—zipped it tightly around his neck, and left him to strangle. Will later found himself feeling pity for him; it must have been a horrible way to die.

On another level, the guards' reactions deeply *disturbed* him. Will was horrified by how much he had changed in the last year: from a professor who had hated to fail students—even if they'd deserved it—to a convicted felon who summoned fear with mere eye contact. From someone who had abhorred violence, to a man who embraced it, and used it to his advantage. He had done things he was sure he'd regret one day, when the ugly head of conscience emerged from the murky waters of circumstance. Maybe it was already time for him to pay for some of those things; it was time for him to enter the Red Box.

It was time to go through the door. Will dazed when he stood up, and his vision turned to white, TV-like static for a few seconds.

"Let's go," Ruggins ordered, taking hold of Will's upper arm. He handed the signed paperwork to Tritt, and then escorted Will to the door.

Will noticed the Marion guards watching with curiosity. He appreciated the meaning of the moment: He was going through a one-way door that would take him away from his current world; his past life could never be recovered.

Darlene Jackson nodded at Ruggins, then pushed a button on the wall. Will felt the floor rumble beneath his feet as the massive steel door slowly lowered through the threshold. His chest seemed to rumble along with it, but he wasn't sure whether it was the mechanical grinding of the door mechanism, or the rapid pounding of his heart, that caused the deep vibration.

The door took a full minute to recede, after which Ruggins led him over the threshold and down a short hallway to an open elevator. Will turned in the elevator to face outward, and saw the three Marion guards watching him as the large steel door slowly raised again.

The elevator doors slid closed with a loud clank, and they descended. After what seemed like an eternity, the elevator came to an abrupt stop. Will was certain they were somewhere far below ground, and the doors opened to a hallway illuminated with caged, red bulbs.

Will was surprised Ruggins was allowed to escort him alone—he could have easily overpowered the old man and attempted escape. He realized what this implied, and shuddered; there *was no escape*.

Ruggins led him down a long, dimly-lit corridor, and finally locked him in a room that resembled Will's former prison cell—except this one had a private bathroom and shower.

Will was nervous, exhausted, and starving. What he wanted much more than food or sleep, however, was to find out what the "treatment" entailed—hazardous labor, or whatever it was—he needed to know. But he knew that that would not happen until the next day, or perhaps later. Fully dressed, he stretched out on a small cot that took up most of the floor space. He noticed a clock on the wall above the door, protected by a thick wire mesh. It was 11:15 p.m. on December 30th. He felt himself quickly succumb to exhaustion.

CHAPTER II
Day Zero

Will opened his eyes and looked up into the bearded face of Rocco, the thug from prison. Startled and confused, he sat up quickly and stared in the direction of the large man while his brain underwent an accelerated "boot-up" process. He quickly realized where he was, and that the events of the previous day had not just been fragments of a nightmare. This wasn't Rocco.

"Get up," the man said.

Will heard a Midwestern accent in the man's voice, and his red scrubs made him look like a giant male nurse.

The man put a towel, red hospital gown, and paper slippers on a chair next to the bathroom entrance. "Shower and get dressed," he said, pointing to the clock on the wall above the exit. "You have fifteen minutes."

Will noticed a plastic, engraved tag on the man's coat that read, simply, *Orderly*. He watched the orderly leave, and heard the door lock click as it pulled shut.

Will showered and put on the disposable garments. At 6:15 a.m., the large orderly and a smaller, identically dressed man entered the room. The smaller man, whose rodent-like features seemed to match well with his dark, slicked-back hair, spoke first. "You'll now be referred to as *Number 523*, understand?"

Will shrugged and nodded. The depersonalization seemed to work in his favor. Maybe it was best to not associate his name with any of this experience.

"Let's go," the larger man ordered. Will noticed that both men avoided making eye contact, even when they spoke to him, and that their overall body language was impersonal. It made him feel cold and uneasy.

The orderlies approached Will, and each man tightly clutched one of his arms. He found this strange, since the night before he'd been escorted by a decrepit old man. They steered him out of the room, turned right, and walked him down a long, well-lit corridor. The bright fluorescent light made the place feel much less ominous than it had the night before, when it had been illuminated in dim red. The air carried a scent reminiscent of wet cement.

The corridor sloped gradually downward and then upward again a long distance away, so that Will could not see the end. After they had walked at least two hundred yards, they finally arrived at a door identical to that of the steel vault design, through which he and old man Ruggins had gone the night before. The larger orderly retrieved a card from his pocket, swiped it through a slot, and punched a code on the number pad located next to it. Will heard a motor hum. The door took a minute to recede, after which they stepped through.

They entered what looked like a wing of a hospital, with high ceilings, and bright, recessed lights. A waxy chemical odor wafted from the shiny tiled floor, which gleamed as if it had recently been buffed and waxed.

There were doors on both sides of the hallway, and they stopped at the first one on the right, on which there was a sign that read: *A-Level: Rm. 1 Orientation*. The smaller orderly knocked, opened the door, and led the way into the room. A woman in her late forties or early fifties with short, gray-speckled hair, narrow glasses, and a blue suit-skirt sat on a leather chair next to a coffee table. She pointed to another chair directly across the table from her.

The orderlies brought Will over, pushed him down roughly into the chair, and walked out of the room, closing the door behind them.

The woman stood, retrieved a thick file-folder from a desk behind her, and returned to her seat. "Good morning, Mr. Thompson—uh, Number 523," she said. "My name is Dr. Smith, I'm a psychologist and Orientation Administrator. My job is to tell you what's going to happen *today*—your actual treatment will start *tomorrow*."

Will noticed an underlying smirk on the woman's face, and something about the tone of her voice annoyed him. He nodded, acknowledging that he understood.

"Here's the itinerary," she explained. "After our meeting, you'll undergo a series of evaluations and tests." She proceeded to summarize the details of the appointments scheduled for the day, two of which caught Will's attention more than the others: a *financial meeting* and something about being *fitted for equipment.*

"The process takes the entire day," Dr. Smith continued, "and it won't end until ten or eleven this evening. Your first *real* treatment session will start tomorrow morning at 6 a.m." She seemed to be having more difficulty holding back the smirk. "Do you have any questions?"

Will stayed calm, but the woman's smugness was wearing on his fragile disposition. At least, he thought, he might get more insight into what was to happen over the next year, but his words reflected his discontent. He looked up and made eye contact with Dr Smith. "I have many questions. But there's something disturbing about your attitude. Are you enjoying this?"

The woman raised an eyebrow. "I'm here to answer whatever questions I can—or that I'm allowed." Her face became serious, the smirk hidden. "So ask specific questions, and I'll do my best." She didn't answer his question.

She leaned back and crossed her legs, which Will interpreted as a defensive posture. People immediately assumed he was an animal, and there was nothing he could do to correct it; mere words could do nothing if they weren't believed. Dr. Smith's behavior angered him, but his need for information quelled his temper, and he proceeded with a question. "What do you mean I'll be 'fitted for *equipment*'?"

"That's a common question." With a rehearsed tone she explained, "It's a device that's used to administer various treatments, and it monitors your vital signs. It's made from stainless steel and titanium, and the more *intrusive* parts are made from surgical quality materials. The motors and electronics are all corrosion-resistant and waterproof and, of course, biocompatible when they need to be."

Intrusive parts? Motors? Biocompatible? "I still don't understand. What is it? What does it do?"

"It gives us complete control." She looked at him as if the answer should have been obvious.

"Control of what? I'm *locked up*—don't you *already* have control?"

"There are … *features* … the system provides that are unique. That's all I can say about that," she said and then looked at him for the next question.

Will swallowed hard. He wasn't satisfied, but decided to move on. "What does this program involve—hard labor? Hazardous duty?"

"You could say that the activities are somewhat hazardous," she replied, "but you can rest assured that your health is important to us."

"I'm not sure what you mean."

The woman squirmed a little in her seat before she replied. "Let's just say that it's hazardous, okay?"

"What's hazardous about it?"

"Let's move on."

The exchange made Will's anxiety redline. He knew his choice to take the Compressed Punishment sentence had come with risks—he just hadn't known what they were. It was a decision made on incomplete information, but it had to be better than the alternative: being locked up for twenty-five years would be like burning away the rest of his life—he'd be near retirement age by the end—if he survived, that is. Chances are he wouldn't last very long in the general prison population, considering the nature of the crimes of which he had been convicted.

"And the financial information?" Will inquired.

Sustaining a blank smile, Smith replied, "Did you think the *tax payers* were going to pay for your treatment costs?"

He practically *felt* the adrenaline inject into his bloodstream, and was unable to control the volume of his voice, "How much will it cost?"

"Everything you have, most likely." She smirked openly now.

"Are you enjoying this?" He heard a near breach of his temper in his voice.

The woman reversed her crossed legs and shifted away from him slightly. She pulled a key ring out of her breast pocket, and pushed a red button on a small device that hung from the ring by a short chain. While maintaining her condescending expression, she replied, "Just doing my job."

Will wanted to slap the woman, but maintained his composure. "How do you live with yourself?" His neck muscles tightened like cables in a winch.

A few seconds later the door flew open, and the two orderlies rushed into the room. Both men stopped a few feet inside the doorway, their heads swiveling about, their wide eyes assessing the situation. They both fixed on Will, and rushed towards him.

Will rose instinctively to defend himself from the advance, shoving the larger orderly hard enough to lift him from the floor and send him stumbling back a few feet. The man looked stunned, and the smaller orderly froze in confusion behind his partner.

"Stop," Will said to the larger orderly. "There's no problem." Will glared at him and then at the other one: *relax*.

Both orderlies backed off slowly, seemingly confused about what to do next.

"I thought he was getting out of control," Dr. Smith explained.

"Do I look out of control to you?" Will shot back, but in a restrained tone.

"I think I've given you all the information you need," Dr. Smith said and moved away quickly. She spoke to the larger orderly, "You can take him to the next meeting." She walked towards the door, and dropped the file folder onto the desk as she walked out of the room.

As the click-clack of her heels quickly faded down the hall, the orderlies approached Will slowly. Will stuck out his arms in a gesture to indicate that he was going to cooperate—he just wanted to get things going. Both orderlies seemed to relax a bit, and took his arms.

"You shouldn't resist when we try to secure you," the larger man said.

Will shrugged and responded, "I didn't feel like ... being handled." He found himself becoming more and more nervous as they proceeded towards his next appointment.

Stadler

Jonathan McDougal gazed through the window of his office as he savored the first sip of his morning coffee. Sunlight beamed through an eastern window and reflected from the large wooden table in the center of the room, illuminating the tall bookshelves that lined the perimeter. Jonathan did his best thinking in his office; the morning light produced a soft wooden hue that felt nice on his eyes. At night his gaze would sometimes wander to the high, coffered ceiling, lit by the stray incandescence of the floor lamps. It was a place for reflection and contemplation.

His joints ached as they always had when he'd gotten too little sleep. The dull pain in his sixty-four-year-old knees was becoming the norm, and the Chicago winter wasn't helping. Being on sabbatical this semester only made his work habits less structured, and he couldn't help himself from working past 2 a.m. most nights. He thought coming to the office without having teaching duties was enjoyable, but being on campus had its disadvantages. Today, it was an early-morning committee meeting. He was supposed to be exempt from such things, but he was sighted, and then "invited" to join the meeting by the Dean himself. Now he was *obligated*. He decided that it was okay, just this once, since it forced him to get an early start on his work.

His involvement in the DNA Project had been a boost for his already successful career in law: it had led to him being offered the directorship of the DNA Foundation. But now he thought he might be starting to spread himself too thin. It wasn't easy to teach law *and* run the Foundation, although the conflict would be delayed for the time being. But sabbatical would end before he knew it, and he would need help.

The real impact of the Foundation was on his *ambition*; he now had the means to affect true, positive change in the legal system. His early efforts with the DNA Project contributed to the moratorium on the death penalty, and that was certainly something of which he could be proud. But the next thing, and his central goal as the leader of the DNA *Foundation*, was to expose the Compressed Punishment program.

Two CP facilities were already active; one in Detroit, and another on Long Island—but a third was under construction in Baton Rouge, Louisiana. So it was clear that they—whoever ran the shadowed government program—had the plans, and funds, to expand... What bothered Jonathan deeply was that he couldn't find *anyone* who fully understood what *happened* in these places—or at least no one who would *tell* him. There was some publicly disclosed information, but it was completely useless.

He'd been able to get some basic statistical data from one of his former law students who had worked at the Long Island facility for a short time. However, all Jonathan had been able to extract from it was that the program suffered from an unusually large number of inmate suicides, and murders—and even *this* information was outdated, and unreliable.

He'd located a few of the former inmates, but they had all refused to talk. He knew of others who were confined to mental institutions after being released from the program, but he'd not been granted access to them.

Being a renowned expert on the subject of corrections, Jonathan knew that his public opposition to the CP facilities, or at least to their *secrecy*, carried some weight with both the media and the public. He'd debated on many of the major television networks, including CNN, but the topic never gained traction. His reputation, and the public exposure, had probably helped their effort, but he did *not* have the power to change anything directly—that is, until the DNA Foundation had blossomed. It was a mechanism of action, a resource that he could now employ to attack the system, or at least to force them to open up to the public.

The circumstances of William Thompson's case—his refusal of a plea bargain in the face of a twenty-five year prison sentence, asserting his innocence to the last—had peaked Jonathan's interest immediately. A man with no prior criminal record, a professor no less, decides to rape a fourteen year old girl on a whim in a highly public setting? It didn't sit right, and Jonathan desperately hoped the case would prove useful. After many months of research, it was the only potential chink he had found in the Compressed Punishment System's armor of secrecy.

A knock on the door disrupted his thoughts. "Come in," he said loudly.

The door opened and a slim woman with long, dark hair walked in and closed the door behind her. It was Jonathan's intern, Denise Walker—a promising young law student. Over the past few months, Jonathan and his wife, Julia, had grown very fond of Denise. She was warm and intelligent, but it was probably her resemblance to their daughter, Laura, that had drawn them closer. At five-six, she was a full two inches shorter than Laura, and she had a darker complexion, but her mannerisms and willowy body were a perfect match, as was her smile.

"Good morning," Jonathan said. "I suppose you're here for the case file. It's out for delivery—should be here by 10 a.m." He held up a carafe. "Coffee?"

"No thanks," she replied and held up her travel mug.

He topped off his own cup and stirred in some cream. "I dug up some background info on the witnesses in the Thompson case. Turns out his ex-fiancee is here in Chicago."

"Really? It would be useful to talk to her."

"I agree," Jonathan replied. "I've heard her testimony didn't help his case very much, but we'll have to see the transcripts to know exactly what went down during the trial. Anyway, I'd like you to contact her and see if she'll talk to us. I want to know if we're wasting our time on this case."

"Where is she?"

"She's in the MBA program at Loyola. She transferred from Southern Illinois after the conviction."

"I'll get on the computer and search for her right now," Denise said as she put her knapsack over her shoulder.

"No need," Jonathan said. "I know a good way to find her information quickly. I'll let you know when the files arrive, and we'll dig up her info after we've had a look at them."

"Sounds good," Denise replied.

Jonathan heard the door close as she left for her office down the hall, and he turned once more to the rising sun beaming through his eastern window.

The orderlies brought Will to a door with a sign that read: *A-Level: Rm. 2 Psychology*. The larger orderly lifted his arm to knock, then looked at Will and said, "Better behave."

Will shrugged. He knew he couldn't guarantee *anything*.

The orderly rapped loudly on the metal door. A moment later it opened, and a tall man with a brown, well-groomed beard stepped out. He pulled on a tweed jacket with elbow patches, and reached behind his neck with one hand to free his gray-streaked ponytail from under the collar.

The quintessential pseudo-academic, Will thought.

The man looked at his wrist-watch. "7:15. You're early, but I suppose we can get started. Put him on the couch." There was a tone of irritation in his voice. "Have his file?"

"No, sorry Dr. Cole, it's in Room One—I'll go get it," the smaller orderly said and scurried away.

The larger escort directed Will to a couch and told him to sit, then stood next to him as they waited for the smaller orderly to return with the file. A half-minute later, the little man returned, and both orderlies walked to the exit.

"Come back at 11:45," Dr. Cole said, and closed the door behind them.

The room was well-lit and comfortable. The leather couch and three leather chairs surrounded an oval coffee table that stood in the center of the room. The furniture was of higher quality than the institutional-style furnishings to which Will had become accustomed over the past year.

Cole sat down on a chair directly across the coffee table from Will, opened the file-folder and a notebook, and pulled a pen out of his shirt pocket. He then retrieved a cylindrical case from the breast pocket of his jacket, and popped open the top. He slid out a pair of half-rimmed reading glasses, placing them on his face such that the rims were halfway down the bridge of his nose.

"Let's see here ... William Thompson, *number 523*, I'm Dr. Cole," he said as he read the first page of the file. "I'm actually a *psychiatrist*—even though the sign on the door reads *psychology*. I'll cover a lot of ground with you in the next few hours, and your job is to answer my questions the best you can. Understand?" He looked over his glasses for a response.

Will nodded.

"First, you need to know this is *not* going to be a cake-walk," Cole said in a serious tone. "People are usually concerned about the *physical* discomforts of the treatment—and they're not going to be pleasant, let me assure you. But there are numerous uncomfortable things to which you'll be subjected—psychologically, emotionally, etcetera..."

Will felt his heart pick up pace.

"What the hell are you going to do to me?"

"Please," Cole said as he took off his glasses and rubbed them with a cloth. "Be calm... What happens to you after you leave this meeting is out of my hands, and I certainly don't have the full picture." He put his glasses back on and put the cloth in his pocket. "But I *do* know the program has *many* purposes. To start, our prisons are overcrowded, and this is one way to expedite the corrections process. Second, the program has very few, if any, repeat offenders, which is another goal of our penal system. Finally, this facility is full of inmates—*patients*—who are here by their *own choice*. And *you* are one of them: you *volunteered* for this."

Will's temples pounded. Of course he'd *chosen* this option, and he assumed it wasn't going to be a boatful of laughs, but now the unknown was starting to become unbearable. "It was this or twenty-five years of my life being burned away. I didn't have much of a *choice*; I would've been killed in the general prison population for the nature of the crimes of which I was convicted."

The psychiatrist popped his pen and grabbed his notebook.

"Good—that brings us to our first question: do you know *why* you are here?"

Annoyed, Will shook his head and replied, "Of course."

Cole nodded for him to continue.

"I was convicted of rape and attempted murder." His annoyance grew but he maintained composure.

"Don't you mean that you *committed* those crimes?" Cole asked in a corrective tone.

"No. I was *convicted* of those heinous acts, but I did not *commit* them."

"I see, still in denial then," Cole said, and scribbled something on the file.

"I am *not* in *denial*," Will retorted. The last year had been hell, and now he was reliving it, yet again. He'd probably have to tell the story many more times—even though no one would believe him.

"Okay … okay," Cole replied. "Can you explain to me *how* you were convicted—I mean, what exactly happened that led up to it? It's here in the file, but I need to hear your perspective."

"This is not my *perspective*—it's what *happened*," Will said. He took a deep breath and began. "It was a Friday night. I was driving near a local high school and saw the stadium lights. I hadn't seen a live football game in fifteen years, so on a whim I decided to go. I drove towards the lights, found a parking spot about a quarter-mile away, and walked to the stadium. I found the entrance gate where some students were tending a cash box, paid the entrance fee and got my hand stamped—"

"That's right, the stamp was evidence," Cole said, seemingly proud that he'd remembered a detail from the file.

"Sure, that was *evidence*," Will replied with sarcasm. "I *admitted* to being at the game. They didn't need *evidence* of that, but they made a big deal about it during the trial. It was a ridiculous—"

"Please move on," Cole interrupted.

Will changed his position on the leather couch, producing a skin-on-leather squeak. "There were no seats left in the stands. Evidently it was a big game, so I had to stand on the east side of the field—on the south twenty-yard-line. There's a hill there that slopes up from the sideline to the parking lot, and into a patch of pine trees about fifty yards further south. The hill was a nice place to watch the game—a good view of the field, and the trees blocked the wind. It was a cool night for August."

Will adjusted his hospital gown and repositioned himself, again making the leather squeak. The clothes, topic of conversation, and extreme anxiety made it difficult for him to keep his line of thought, but he continued. "At halftime I bought a large coke and went back to the same spot where I had watched the first half. After a while, I started to get a little chilled—the cool weather was getting to me by the end of the third quarter—and I had to go to the bathroom badly about halfway through the fourth. They only had three outdoor toilets, and there was a line about a mile long at each one. *Three* bathrooms for a crowd of two thousand people ... so I went to that grove of trees, instead. I walked away from the crowd, snuck into the pines about fifteen feet, and relieved myself."

"You were all alone at this game?" Cole asked.

"Yes."

"Why?"

"Do I need a reason?" Will responded defensively. "My fiancee was visiting her family during that time, but she probably would've passed on going to the game, anyway." Will's mind conjured up an image of Pam, and he was instantly reminded of the betrayal.

"Her testimony worked against you," Cole said and waited for a reaction.

Will made eye contact with Cole and nodded.

"What was it about?" Cole asked.

"Our relationship, and our so-called *sex life*," Will replied. He clenched his jaw and ground his teeth together before continuing. "She took the side of the prosecution when she learned about the *nature of the case*. Never gave me a chance—"

"Please, we have limited time," Cole said, cutting him off. He motioned with his hands to get going.

Will squeezed his fists in frustration. By now he should have been used to people not listening to him; it had been that way since he had been arrested. He opened his fists and loosened up his hands by wiggling his fingers. "On my way out of the trees, a student saw me and reported me to one of the cops standing near the crowd. He must've thought that I was sneaking in from the parking lot without paying. It was already the middle of the fourth quarter, so I don't know why they were so worried about it. The cop approached me and asked to see my hand, so I showed him the stamp. He asked me what I was doing, and I told him I was stretching my legs—taking a walk. I really didn't need a citation for urinating-in-public, getting written up in the paper for the people in my department to see."

"That's right, you were a college professor."

"Yes, an *untenured* professor, and I didn't need any negative publicity. It's hard enough to get tenure as it is," Will said.

"And what were you a professor of, Mr. Thompson?"

Cole's head tilted slightly to one side as he asked, and Will noticed a hint of a condescension in his expression, a smugness in his voice. "Actually, if you're going to be formal, you should call me *Dr. Thompson*. To answer your question, I *was* a physics professor."

"Well … I think I'll just refer to you as *523* from here on out."

Cole's look became distant, and there was a moment of awkward silence. Will watched the man's face, but Cole didn't make eye contact, and gestured for Will to continue without looking at him.

"The cop asked for my ID," Will went on, "and then told me to stay out of the trees. I'm sure he knew what I did, although his later testimony was embellished. I went back to the game, the home team was winning big, so I left early to avoid traffic. After that I went to a local cafe to warm up. That was at 10:00 p.m., and the place closed at eleven." Will shrugged his shoulders. There was nothing more to say about that.

"What happened *after* you left the cafe?" Cole asked.

Will shifted in his seat again. This was a part of the story that truly bothered him. "It was about 11 p.m. when I drove home—about ten minutes away," he explained. "When I got to my house, there were four squad cars there—three parked on the street and one in my driveway. Two cops were on my front porch, knocking on my door, and I saw three or four more walking around the back. Two more were standing by their cars—one was on the radio. I pulled up behind one of the squads parked on the street, got out, and walked over to one of the officers."

"What did you think was happening?" Cole asked.

"I thought someone must've broken into my house," Will replied. "When I approached the cop, she told me to get back in my car. So I asked her what was going on, and explained they were at *my* house. Her eyes about popped out of her head, and she asked me if I was *William Thompson*. I said 'yes,' and she immediately got on her walkie-talkie to summon the other officers. I had no idea what was about to happen." Will shook his head and looked down at his trembling hands. Thinking about being violated in such a way always brought him to a nearly uncontrollable rage—it was something he had to fight against endlessly.

"Continue," Cole said, halting Will's digressive thoughts.

"The other cops showed up, and the one I talked to told the rest of them who I was. Next thing I knew, I was being tackled to the ground. I took a boot to the head and to the face—I should've had a few stitches under my right eye." Will turned his head so that Cole could see the scar.

Cole glanced at the scar, seemingly as a courtesy. "Did they tell you *why* you were being arrested?"

"Sexual assault of a minor, indecent exposure, and something else—I don't remember." Will shook his head. "They took me to the police station, and then to a more secure facility the next day."

Cole looked up from his notebook. "The charges changed to rape and attempted murder later, and you were convicted of those charges."

"Yes."

"So let me see if I have some of these details summed up correctly: a fourteen-year-old girl, Cindy Worthington, was raped, and nearly killed—beaten into a coma—in the very grove of trees in which you went to relieve yourself that night. A cop placed you there—and even looked at your ID." Cole waited for an affirmative response.

"Yes."

"The cop testified that you looked a little flustered after coming out of the trees, and that you were adjusting your clothing."

Will nodded.

"So then," Cole paused to look down at the file, "the barista at the café said she noticed the stamp on your hand, and that you'd arrived at the café just after 10 p.m.—which was before the game was even over." Cole looked up from his notebook.

"Again, I admitted I was there, and that I had left early." Will tightened his fists and released them. "I have been through this a thousand times already ..."

"Please, I need to know what you know. Let's see ... they asked you *why* you were at the game. The prosecution made the argument that you had no reason to be there: you didn't have kids at the school, you weren't invited by anyone, and you didn't know anyone who was playing, etcetera ... and your fiancee was out of town. The argument was that you were there as a sexual predator."

"That was their argument." Will explained, "I don't think anyone needs a *reason* to go to a football game other than to *watch it* ..."

"I understand, 523, but now you're *here*," Cole cut him off. "It's strange how one seemingly minor decision can change everything."

Will tried to recall how he had come to that 'minor decision' … *what was he even doing in that part of town on that night?* He remembered: *there was no reason.* Sometimes he drove around to relax, and to *think.* It was a small town, and he'd seen the stadium lights before. But that was the first time he'd gotten close enough to be drawn in.

"There were other things," Cole continued. "Your fiancee testified for the prosecution. Why again?" He had a perplexed look and shook his head slowly.

Will sighed. "She testified regarding the status of our relationship, and our sexual activity." Will flushed and put the palms of his hands over his eyes as he continued to speak. "She claimed that I was avoiding having sex with her, and that I would go out at night to avoid it."

"Was that true?" Cole asked.

"The *truth* is that the woman never wanted to have sex," Will replied. "Her saying *I* was avoiding it was bizarre."

"But there was more to her testimony," Cole continued.

"Yes," Will replied. "She told them that I often went out late at night without telling her where I was going."

"So? Why was that significant?"

"There were other attacks—rapes and murders—that had occurred in the town during that time—at least two of which coincided with my late-night drives," Will explained.

"But you weren't charged with those other crimes?"

"Surprisingly, no."

"Why *surprisingly*?"

"Because the whole case was conducted like a witch trial—someone was going to hang. Ended up being me… I was convicted on circumstantial evidence, alone." Will was angered every time he thought about it—*circumstantial evidence.* They were essentially calling him a liar: he'd been an upstanding member of society his entire life, and it didn't even earn him the benefit of the doubt.

"Happens all of the time."

"Yes, it does. But they had physical evidence that could have exonerated me," Will said.

"What do you mean?"

"They'd recovered DNA from the girl's body immediately after the attack."

"What happened with that?"

"It was *misplaced*," Will replied.

Dr. Cole's eyes widened. "Hmm … no physical evidence, the girl in a coma … the rest must've come off as pretty convincing."

Will nodded his head in recognition, and then shook it in disgust. It seemed to him that Pam's testimony might have tipped the scales with the jury. He'd worked himself into a rage many times thinking about it, but he was now helpless to release it.

"No matter how you got here, you're *here now*," Cole said with a tone of depressing finality. He stood and poured himself a cup of tea, the fragrance of Earl Grey permeating the room.

"I'd offer you some," Cole said, "but you can't have *anything* today—medical tests and procedures in the afternoon." He sat down and put the steaming mug on the coffee table.

Will felt the weight of the situation increasing—the stress was getting to him. He thought he had held up fairly well through the past year; his mind was strong, and he knew it would get him through this, too—if he could keep it on his side.

"Let's move on," Cole said. "I have many questions. Some may seem irrelevant, but I assure you, they are all significant. So answer them the best you can. My positive evaluation of your mental state is required for you to continue in this program. If we find that you don't qualify for some reason, mentally or physically, you'll be removed, and you'll have to serve the conventional sentence. Is that clear?"

Will nodded. It was the last thing he wanted.

Cole clicked his pen a few times. "Who are the most important people in your life? Give me five or six."

Will thought for a few seconds and recited a list that included his parents, his sister and her family, his best friend Matthew, and his ex-girlfriend Danielle. Pam didn't make the list. Hearing the names of his loved ones conjured up a deeply disturbing feeling; a convalescence of guilt, shame, and nostalgia. If he spent the next twenty-five years in prison he would essentially be *dead* to those people. And they'd be dead to him, too. They'd probably come to visit him a few times a year—at first. But then they would just fade away into the past. *Maybe he was already dead to them. Maybe they thought the real William Thompson was the rapist—not the scientist, son, brother, friend. Maybe the good William never existed.*

"*523,*" Cole said, interrupting his thoughts. "Let's move on."

Will regained his focus.

Cole asked numerous questions, and as he had warned, many seemed irrelevant. What was his favorite color? Favorite food? If he could design his own world—his own heaven—what would it be like, and what would he be in that world? Similar questions about Hell. What things in this world, the real one, could make him happy? That was a question Will had frequently asked himself—and one he had difficulty answering, even before the horrific situation by which he was now consumed. He was asked about his childhood, and his best and worst memories. Lastly, he was administered an IQ test.

After the test was completed, Cole collected the exam and pencils and told Will to relax for a minute. "For this last part, someone else needs to be here," Cole said.

Will couldn't believe there was *more*—he was already mentally and emotionally exhausted. And now there would be *two* people interrogating him?

Cole walked over to his desk and picked up the phone. "Bring in Mr. Jones."

Heinrich Bergman stood next to a large window in his office, shielding his eyes from the late morning sun as he spoke into his mobile. "Go ahead, Lenny."

"I found out who's prying into the Thompson case," Lenny said. "It's a lawyer in Chicago—one Jonathan McDougal."

"That's just fucking great."

"It's about the lost DNA evidence, as you expected," Lenny replied.

"Thompson has already been inserted, and I'll be damned if we have to dispose of a perfectly good test subject because that fool McDougal wants to play detective. That son of a bitch has been making waves for too damn long," Bergman said.

"I know."

"Get out to Illinois and look into it," Bergman ordered. "They won't have justification for a retrial unless the missing DNA sample miraculously turns up. Make sure that doesn't happen."

"I'll arrange a flight out tonight," Lenny said.

Bergman flipped his phone closed and slowly paced back and forth. He trusted Lenny. It wasn't only for the man's decades of loyal and competent service, but more for what he *had* on Lenny. Bergman knew every operation the thug had carried out—and many of them hadn't been pretty. Of course, Bergman knew, *he* had given Lenny the orders on most of those operations. Their trust was symbiotic.

His relationship with Richard Greene and many of the other high-level engineers was different, however. They knew everything about the project—everything that was on paper, anyway—enough to sink the entire program. In the case of Richard Greene, Bergman knew he could count on three things to keep that from happening. First, Richard was an expert in the technology—he'd be throwing away his life's work. Second, Bergman had more than hinted at the fate of those who tried to sell out the program. His latest exhibition was Frank Weiss; this was the real reason he'd asked Richard to be present for the man's interrogation… Finally, if the program was sunk, Richard would undoubtedly go down with the ship: he was as culpable as anyone in the program.

Bergman's thoughts turned back to the lawyer. The unplanned release of an *inserted inmate* would be a complete disaster—sure to draw a whirlwind of media attention. This he did not need—his contributors were already nervous. Such a situation was a vulnerability for which there was no solid contingency plan. There was only *prevention*; they would head McDougal's investigation off at the pass. As a last resort they could terminate Thompson, though that might draw even more attention.

Bergman tried to remember exactly when he had lost his conscience. He was sure it hadn't happened all at once. He recalled when he'd been promoted to head of the project some twenty-five years ago, and the week afterwards when he had proposed to his wife. Life had been good for a while. At the time, he had no idea of what he was getting himself into—but now he was in as deep as one could get, and the walls were closing in. *But we've come so far,* he thought. They'd finally worked most of the bugs out of the treatment, and if their predictions were correct, a positive result was imminent. Such an event would *change the world*, and everyone would see it was well worth the cost in lives.

Explaining the lack of progress was going to be difficult, but Richard Greene would handle that. He trusted him for those types of tasks—the man could really bullshit when he needed to. The problem with the Chicago lawyer trying to reopen the case was again, difficult, but solvable. On the other hand, finding the missing project files, and the *source* of the leak, was daunting. If they failed, and the files got into the wrong hands, the project would be *crushed*. They outlined every action, technical detail, and motivation for the project. He couldn't let that happen.

Will nervously rubbed his knees as he and Cole waited for Mr. Jones. After a few minutes, someone knocked at the door and Cole let him in. The man who entered maneuvered his large, athletic body around the chairs, and stopped in front of the coffee table, where he rubbed the stubble on his chiseled sandstone face.

Will's eyes were drawn to something on the man's head: two bony knobs bulged out of each side of his forehead—near the hairline. They were the diameter of a quarter and raised a half an inch from his skull, as if ping-pong balls were cut in half and place under his skin. In the middle of each was a circular indentation, about a quarter of an inch in diameter. Will tried not to look, but he couldn't help it. *Horns?*

"I'd like you to meet a former patient; this is Mr. Jones," Cole said.

Jones walked closer and nodded to Will.

Will responded with a nod, and said, "Mr. *Jones.*"

Jones shrugged and smiled in recognition of the alias. "I'm *Number 112.*"

Will noticed the man's voice was a bit slurred, like he'd had a minor stroke. And he quickly did the math: if they put one person in the system each day, *number 112* should have been through the year of treatment and out for weeks. *Why was he still here?*

"We're going to explain a few things, and get your take on what you think this next year is going to bring," Cole said. "Have a seat—both of you."

Jones sat in the chair next to Cole, across the coffee table from Will.

"523, I assume you've already been informed that you could die here," Dr. Cole said.

Will was shocked by the words. "What do you mean?"

"The death rate of this program is about twenty-seven percent," Cole replied.

Will's heart sank. "I don't understand, what do you mean *death rate*?" His attention was momentarily distracted by the hideous cackle of Jones, who Will believed to be mentally damaged.

Cole shook his head at Jones, then answered Will's question. "The extreme stress that patients experience during the treatment can sometimes precipitate a physical failure, such as a stroke, heart attack, etcetera."

Will glanced at Jones, and again wondered if he'd had a stroke.

"We try to choose healthy people, of course," Cole continued, "but there are always a few fluke things that can happen. The point is: there's a fair chance you won't leave this place alive."

"I wasn't told any of this before," Will responded. He was shocked—*what type of risk was he taking*? "They didn't tell me anything about this place!"

"Then why did you agree?—you had to *choose* this," Jones said.

"You were also given a plea bargain," Cole added.

"The plea bargain would have been for *twelve years*—still too long for a crime I didn't commit," Will retorted. "The one-year option was the right choice—guilty or not. This is the only way I can recover my life—"

"You'll *never* recover," Jones cut him off.

"Oh, that's not true at all," Cole contradicted emphatically, and spoke to Will, "It depends on the individual. Look at Jones here—he's a new man. He's a survivor, and he'll be released into the world again soon." He turned back to Jones. "And you'll be a good boy out there, won't you Mr. Jones?"

Jones flushed and looked down, and Will noticed one of the man's eyes was slow—a lazy eye. Will was feeling even more frightened: *what had they done to this man?*

"You see," Jones said, "once you get through this place—*if* you get through—they'll monitor you very closely. Any crime you commit from that point forward could land you back in here. You won't want to come back."

"We've only had one graduate of this facility called back so far," Cole added. "And he managed to kill himself before being ... readmitted."

"What do you *do* here? What are you planning to do to me?" Will was starting to feel the way he did when his claustrophobia would act up. He edged forward in his seat and pointed to Jones. "And what did you do to this guy?"

Jones must have sensed Will's nervousness. His eyes dilated and shifted back and forth, the slower one now dragging more noticeably. He moved to the edge of his seat and tucked his feet beneath him as if he were going to stand.

"You gotta get the hell out of here man," Jones said, his voice a little slower now, but louder. He lifted his hand, and Will noticed it trembled. "They're going to ..."

"112, tell your orderly to take you back to your room," Cole commanded.

Jones stood, his eyes wide—one locked on Will, and mouthed the words, "*run ... run,*" as he slowly shook his head.

"*Go, 112,*" Cole ordered, more forcefully now.

Jones maintained eye contact with Will as he maneuvered around the couch, and then turned and walked out.

"*That* never happened before ... last time we'll do this with *him*," Cole said under his breath as he scribbled something in his notebook.

"What the hell was he talking about?" Will asked.

"It's not a secret that the treatment isn't going to be pleasant," Cole continued, "but it is impossible to convey to you exactly how stressful it will be."

"Why don't you *try*."

"I only know *generalities*," Cole explained. "There are physical, psychological, even spiritual aspects."

"What do you mean by *spiritual aspects*?"

"Well, if you're religious, imagine questioning your deepest beliefs—even your very *existence*."

"I don't see how anyone could touch that," Will said with some defiance.

"Now we're digressing into things of a more philosophical nature, and we're nearly out of time," Cole said, looking to Will. "My job is to evaluate your state of mind—and I find that you are sane now, and were of sound mind when you made the decision to enter the program. You are therefore cleared to proceed." He took off his glasses and put them back in their case.

"Barring a physical condition that precludes your continuing," Cole explained, "you're at the point of *no return*." Cole glanced at his watch and looked startled. "Oh, we have to wrap this up. You have a few more meetings today."

The orderlies escorted Will down the hall and to another door, on which there was sign that read: *A-Level: Rm. 3 Finance.* The larger orderly knocked before ushering Will in, then closed the door behind him as he left.

The room was small and carpeted, and Will detected a faint scent of perfume in the air. It was a fragrance that on another occasion might have been pleasant. In his current state, however, it was only nauseating.

A man and two women sat at small desks working on computers. "Please sit down," one of the women instructed, as she pointed to a chair next to the man's desk. Her green suit-skirt strained as she tied her red hair into a tight bun, wrapping a rubber band around it. The other woman, tall with olive skin, kept her eyes on her computer monitor as she rapidly typed.

On Will's right, near the wall, the man casually stroked his black goatee while glancing back and forth between a file on his desk and the screen in front of him. His pin-striped suit looked like it was tailored to fit his thin frame. Will sat in the wooden chair next to his desk.

"This shouldn't take long, *523*—you don't have many assets," the man said without looking up. "I'm Mr. Redd. We're going to run through your possessions. Please verify each item I describe, and let me know if there are any mistakes."

Will nodded. *All business, no small talk.*

"You have a house at 104 South Glenview in Cordova, Illinois?" he asked.

"Yes, but it's not paid off," Will responded.

"I see; you have $125,320 in equity, and owe another hundred thousand," Redd said, flipping to another page in Will's file. "You have a bank account at University Federal Credit Union through your former employer, with $14,345 in funds—including savings, checking, and money market accounts?"

"That sounds right."

"And I see $121,872 in an online banking and trading company called ElectroTrade. Looks like you could've paid off that house if you wanted to."

Will nodded. Sure, he *could* have. But he was going to wait so that he and Pam could pay it off *together,* after they got married; then the house would be *theirs.*

"You own a Toyota Four Runner?"

Will nodded.

"A vintage classical guitar?"

"Yes, how did you know—"

"Just answer the question," Redd cut him off rudely.

Will felt his face flush. His temper was getting more and more difficult to manage as the day progressed.

"Look," Redd said without looking away from his monitor. "You're in a new world now, and your new existence doesn't include you owning anything you had before this point. You won't even be able to cover the total cost of this program with everything you own anyway. You'll be given a government loan to cover the difference."

Will processed the information. He wondered how someone with a job like Mr. Redd's could sleep at night, or even sit quietly with his own thoughts. "What if I refuse to sign everything over?"

"I don't know what they'll do, but we'll still get it," Redd answered. "Now, do you have any other assets besides those I just mentioned?"

If he didn't survive the program, Will thought, it didn't matter what assets he had. And if he *did* survive, he'd have to start completely over with life, which he'd already accepted. What did he want from his former life anyway? Even if they released him immediately, there was nothing to salvage. "I have assets in the house: a computer, entertainment system—big screen TV, etc., some metal and wood-working tools in the garage, and some—"

"Anything very valuable?" Redd cut in.

"Not really."

"Then that's good enough, we don't care about the small stuff," Redd said. "Those items will be auctioned off later, and we'll have an itemized total for you during your exit interview in a year—if there is one. Another question: are you in line to inherit any money or property—are you in anyone's will?" Redd turned and made eye contact with Will for the first time.

Will thought for a moment and figured he probably *was* in line for some inheritance—but that would be years down the road. "I'll be in my parents' will—along with my sister—but I wouldn't expect to have to worry about that anytime soon."

Redd nodded and then responded, "If anything else comes up, you'll find out in the exit interview. Now, we need to complete the transfers and close out all of your accounts." He tapped on his keyboard for a minute. "What's the password for your ElectroTrade account?"

Will was silent. The shock of his new reality was setting in—he stared in a daze for a few seconds.

"Mr. Thompson ..." Redd prodded.

The words just wouldn't come out—it took Will thirty more seconds to override the mental safety switch before he responded. Slowly, he began to list the password characters, "*w, m, *, 3, s, 7, j, 5, T.*" It was complex, and he was surprised he remembered it after more than a year.

Redd nodded to the dark haired woman, who had been writing down the characters as Will recited them, and she went to work on her computer.

After surrendering all of his usernames and passwords, the red-haired woman pulled up a chair next to him and sat down. She opened a manila envelope, removing some papers and placing them on a clip board. "This one is a *Transfer of Title* document for your car, and this one's for the house," she said, handing him a pen. She pointed out multiple places to sign and initial.

Will signed and initialed.

From her desk behind him, the olive-skinned woman reported, "The transfers have been authorized, and the requests for account closures have been submitted."

Mr. Redd nodded and tapped on his keyboard with more vigor, as if he was completing a big assignment. "... and ... *Enter*," he said with a final tap of the button. "Okay, that's it for the financial part. Now we need some identity info." He opened a cabinet behind him and lifted out an apparatus that resembled a microscope. He plugged the cable from the device into the computer on his desk, turning it on. Next, he retrieved a flexible pad with the outlines of two hands on it, plugging this into the computer as well. He nodded and turned to face Will. "Look into the eyepieces and place your chin on the bar—don't blink."

Will did as instructed. He heard Redd tap a button, and observed as a thin vertical line scanned across his field of vision. This was followed by a flash of white light, which quickly faded to black. The process had finished.

Redd clicked his computer mouse a few times, then looked again to Will. "That looks good. Now place both palms on the pad, inside the hand outlines."

Will pressed lightly into the spongy surface of the device.

Redd pushed a button, which produced a short beeping sound.

"Good enough for government work," he said, motioning in the direction of the women. "Bring in the DNA kit."

The red-haired woman walked over to Will carrying a gun-like device with a hypodermic needle protruding from the barrel. She latched a narrow, cartridge-like piece into the bottom of the handle, as a clip would be inserted on a pistol. Four clear vials shined in the light.

Before Will knew what was happening, the woman plunged the needle into his arm.

He flinched, hissing at the pain.

The woman pulled the trigger on the device. It hummed softly, and he watched the vials fill with blood, each having a capacity of a few cubic centimeters. They were filled less than a minute later, and she extracted the needle.

The women left with the blood, paperwork, and an electronic storage device that carried his handprint and iris pattern information. Mr. Redd pulled a form out of a printer on a small table behind him, handing it to Will along with a felt-tipped pen. "This is a nondisclosure form. It states that you'll be prosecuted for treason if you reveal anything that you see while you're at the Red Box. Sign and date it."

Will did it, even though he was certain he'd reveal *everything* when he got out.

If he got out.

Mr. Redd rattled and clicked on the computer for a couple more minutes, before turning his attention back to Will. He glanced at his watch, then said, "This is what we've done: we have all of your belongings and your identity— basically, you are now government property."

Will felt as if he had just jumped off of a cliff—there was no going back. *Still,* he thought, *forfeiting all of this—his identity, his money, his possessions—had to be better than spending twenty-five years in prison.* He had to constantly remind himself of that.

"Do you have any questions?" Redd asked.

"No." He had a million questions.

"Okay," he said and looked at Will's itinerary, "hmmm ... off to medical next. We're running a little late." He picked up the phone and summoned the handlers, then stood up from his chair, motioning for Will to do the same.

Will heard the orderlies knock, and they were soon on their way.

The morning sun brightened Richard's office to the point of obscuring his view of the computer monitor. He knew it would only last for a few minutes, so he took a break from the work on his upcoming presentation.

He swiveled his chair over to small table at his right, opened a thick envelope and removed its contents. It was a binder containing the weekly Red Box patient reports. He looked at the summary: the first thing he noticed was that two patients had died in the past week. It was not out of the ordinary. The summary also had a section for 'Number of Incidents' but it was empty.

Richard paged through the individual patient reports, *NTR* on the top line of every one: *Nothing to Report*. Although they were probably correct, he was skeptical about the quality of the personnel running each experimental room. Each treatment was conducted by two controllers, one technical, and one medical. The techs had engineering degrees of some sort, and the meds had either gone to medical school, dental school, or had psychology degrees, depending on what the specific treatment entailed. The problem was that people who held those degrees could make a lot more money in their respective fields, so the CP facilities had to settle for the bottom of the barrel. Richard wondered if they had been missing some of the more subtle signs.

Other than a few misdiagnoses that had been quickly corrected, it had been only NTR's on the reports since the project had begun. For a scientist who had no moral issue with the project, the constant flow of negative reports would certainly be disheartening. But Richard *did* have moral qualms with the project. His change of heart had started two years prior, when the Red Box began treating subjects—*real people.* Up to that point, it had only been a bioengineering project for him.

He speculated it had been the same way for the scientists who worked on the Manhattan Project. That had been quite a scientific feat, rivaled only by the moon landing, in his opinion. But after they had succeeded, and their breakthrough had transformed into a devastating military tool, many of them had moral objections to its use. *Too late.* Richard felt it might be too late for him, as well. But still, he would try to redeem himself.

He noticed the sun was off of his monitor, and he put the report binder back in its envelope. There were no incidents, so it would be easy to work up the weekly summary for Bergman. The presentation, however, presented a challenge: no positive results, again. He turned his chair back to the computer desk, and went to work.

The orderlies directed Will into an elevator, which moved them up a floor. They stepped out into a large hall, similar to one they had just left, and shuffled to a door that read: *B-Level: Rm. 1 Medical.*

The larger orderly knocked loudly and stepped back as the door opened. A woman stepped out, rolling up the sleeves of her red scrubs. She was in her mid-thirties and she wore her dark, curly hair in a long ponytail. Her black-rimmed glasses contrasted sharply with the bright red lipstick that glistened on her full lips; it was the recent application of the latter that made Will uneasy—it seemed out of place.

"I'm Dr. Johnson," she said as she guided Will into the room, closing the door behind the exiting orderlies. "Step over there, and remove your clothes." She pointed to a medical table.

Will looked around as he walked to the table. The large size of the room surprised him, as did the number of people in it—nearly ten, all dressed in red medical scrubs, and scurrying about. Some moved carts and hooked up electronic devices, while others sat at tables and typed on computers.

Will squinted due to the bright, fluorescent light that reflected from the numerous stainless steel tables. The place was illuminated like an operating room, and each table had an apparatus next to it with accompanying electronic gadgets. His eyes were drawn to two red, illuminated signs at the far end of the facility: one read *Strong Magnetic Fields*, and the other, *Danger: X-rays.*

"Number *523*, this is Dr. Poliakov and Dr. Noh," Dr. Johnson said, gesturing to each. She put her hands on her hips and shook her head. "Now, am I going to have to call the orderlies back here to undress you?"

Will found it strange the orderlies weren't constantly present to assist with some of the physical situations that could develop. Although *he* was smart enough to understand his chances of escape were negligible, he was sure they'd dealt with less astute patients before. He untied his hospital gown and disrobed.

"Good, now lie down," Johnson said, pointing to a stainless steel table covered with a large sheet of wax paper.

As his back made contact with the table, he felt the cold steel through the thin sheet, and goose pimples broke out all over his arms and legs. His testicles felt as if they'd moved all the way up to his throat. He noticed now, too, that the air in the room was too cold to be comfortable without clothes.

To Will's left, Dr. Noh rolled up a cart with a stack of tubes, bunches of hypodermic needles, and electronic components. Poliakov rolled a similar collection of medical gear to the other side. Both wetted gauze pads with alcohol, filling the air with the aroma of discomfort, and rubbed down parts of his body; Noh his left bicep, and Poliakov his right inner thigh. Next, each produced a needle-terminated tube, patting around on Will's skin with their free hands. Noh started first, and Will felt the cold steel penetrate his flesh, probing around. Poliakov followed with the same on his inner thigh—which was much more sensitive—and Will gasped.

Dr. Johnson pulled out a small syringe, filling it with pale-blue fluid from a small, glass bottle. She flicked it a few times, then squirted a little into the air before injecting the concoction into Will's shoulder. "This will take a few minutes to take hold."

"What is it?" Will asked. He didn't much like being injected with unknown substances.

"A paralyzing agent; we don't want you moving around too much," she replied. "But you'll still *feel* everything."

Just like the first woman he met, Dr. Smith, Will detected an underlying loathing in Dr. Johnson's countenance—something he might not have noticed, if it hadn't tinged her voice as well.

Poliakov's needle must have struck a vein, as he taped the device to Will's thigh and then proceeded to push a button on his cart.

A moment later a motor hummed, and Will felt a pain—like a collapsing cavity—reach as high as his stomach. He watched his blood move through the clear tube toward the apparatus. When it reached the machine's input, lights flickered on the display monitor, and Poliakov turned a knob on the needle end of the tube, stopping the flow. He then removed the device from Will's leg.

"That's it," Poliakov said, rolling the cart away.

Will had lost track of what Dr. Noh was doing on his other side, and when he turned to look he saw more than a pint of his blood in a clear container—he'd never seen so much of his own blood. He felt light-headed, and *colder*.

Dr. Johnson walked in from a back room—Will hadn't even noticed that she'd left. She carried a large syringe with a thick needle on one end—four or five inches long. A long, flexible wire with a plastic ring on the end stuck out the backside of the device, and a trigger protruded from the underside.

"Time for deep tissue samples for genetic tests," she said. "Let's see how that paralyzing agent is working." She grabbed Will's right arm with two hands and lifted.

Will felt her latex-covered fingers grip his forearm and biceps, then lift, but he could produce no muscular response. She dropped his arm from a height of about six inches, and it thudded lifelessly on the table. Will tried to speak, but was only able to muster a hissing gurgle. He was paralyzed. A sense of panic began to overtake him, but this did not register in his features; his eyes and facial expression seemingly dull and lifeless.

"We'll start with the muscle samples, but we'll have to get marrow, lung, and bone samples, too. At the end, we'll take some spinal fluid," Johnson directed to the other doctors, but looked at Will as she spoke. Her red lipstick accented a smile she no longer felt obligated to hide. "Time for the straps."

Will heard Poliakov open a drawer at the bottom of the table, but he couldn't see what they were doing until the first nylon strap was wrapped across his shoulders, followed by identical bands placed across his chest, hips, and knees. Next were Velcro cuffs—a pair for each wrist and ankle—which Noh threaded through steel eyelets on the table.

After everything was tightened up, Johnson said to Poliakov, "Let's get the quadriceps samples first."

Poliakov nodded, placed one hand above and the other below Will's right knee, and firmly secured his leg. Johnson then plunged the needle a full two inches into his upper thigh. The muscle twitched involuntarily, despite the induced paralysis, and the pain intensified.

As Johnson pulled the trigger on the syringe, Will felt something bite him deep inside. She pulled the wire out slowly, causing a sinewy tear that Will thought he actually *heard*. A second later the wire was fully extracted, and she examined the bloody lump dangling from the end of it, twisting it as if she were observing the oil level on a dipstick. She released the meaty nugget into a plastic sample tube, sealing it up. "Now, the other quadriceps," she ordered as she grabbed a new extractor from the cart, walking over to the other side of the table.

Will hadn't even noticed Dr. Noh had removed the needle from his arm until he saw the little man rolling a different cart over to his side. This one had an assortment of "extractors" on it, each resembling the one just used to get the deep tissue. Will felt sick.

Johnson plunged the steel shaft into his left thigh, and Will heard her yelling orders as he felt his vision dimming: "Get a damp cloth on his face—he's passing out," she said.

Poliakov squeezed a wet washcloth over Will's chest and lower abdomen, and then placed it on his forehead. It was enough to keep him conscious, but now he was very cold—the blood loss certainly didn't help matters. He felt Johnson's probe nip out another piece of his flesh, which she then retrieved and stored. Nausea crept up in him—from what he was currently experiencing, and from the anticipation of what was coming next.

The team of doctors continued methodically with the program. Each extraction had its own unique pain characteristics—and Will lost all concept of time. He'd learned quickly that it only took *seconds* to exact the worst pain he'd ever felt in his life—and it was a *violating* pain. If he recalled correctly from the orientation meeting with Dr. Smith, the "medical exams" were scheduled for two hours. *Two hours would be an eternity.*

The lung tissue extraction felt like a ton of weight crushing his chest; the pain dull and deep. The bone and marrow extractions were screamers—*grown man screamers*—though screaming was impossible under the paralytic. Finally, there was the spinal fluid extraction: shots of white-hot electricity shot down Will's legs like super-sciatica, and with such horrible head-pain he thought they were sucking his brain out through his spinal cord.

At the end, the effect of the paralyzing agent had waned, and he vomited and dry-heaved for five straight minutes. It felt like a combination of motion sickness and a migraine headache. The symptoms diminished slowly, and by the time he had gone in for the MRI and X-ray scans they were mostly gone. Will shuddered at the thought of what else might happen to him before the end of the day, and couldn't bear the thought of what might happen when the sun came up on the next. He wondered whether he'd ever *see* the sun again.

Although he'd only read a fraction of the Thompson files, Jonathan was already frustrated—he hadn't found anything to help him devise a strategy of attack. He turned to Denise, who was sitting at the large table in his office, and asked, "Find anything strange in the evidence log?"

"Not yet," she replied, "there's a lot to read—but so far it's all irrelevant: many character references—seems like quite a few friends of the fiancee were interviewed by the prosecution, and many of the defendant's friends and colleagues by the defense. Two lengthy, contradicting psychologist reviews, but no physical evidence."

"That's because there *was no physical evidence*—none that made it to trial anyway."

"It's shameful," Denise added. "Misplacing the DNA from the rape-kit—how could the lab possibly allow that to happen?"

Jonathan stood up from the large table, and slowly paced. The files would take a long time to read, and time was not on their side. He needed a shortcut, and thought of Thompson's fiancee. "Time to find Pam Sorrensen," he said, walking over to a computer in a small nook, surrounded by bookshelves. Denise followed.

Jonathan sat down and typed in the web address for Loyola University. "I have adjunct professor status there—I can get into their student directory. We'll get her home address—then you'll go meet her and request that she come speak with us."

"Just show up unannounced?" Denise asked.

"Sure," Jonathan replied. "Too easy for people to turn you down over the phone or through email." Jonathan typed in his Loyola ID and password, then searched for *Pam Sorrensen*. In a few seconds a link to her directory information appeared and Jonathan clicked on it. Her information and a picture popped up.

"Wow, she's pretty," Denise said.

Jonathan agreed. The woman's bright green eyes seemed the perfect match for her short, blonde hair, which framed the delicate features of her face beautifully.

Denise wrote down all of the woman's information, then opened her own laptop and searched for directions. "She's walking distance from Loyola."

"Good, you can take the red-line," Jonathan suggested. He knew it was a safe neighborhood to take the subway.

"Ask her to come tonight, and tell her we can compensate her for the interview."

"That should sweeten the deal for a starving student," Denise replied with a smile.

She slung her heavy backpack over one shoulder, and was out the door. Denise was tenacious, and Jonathan had little doubt she'd convince Sorrensen to cooperate. He just hoped Thompson's ex-fiancee wouldn't reveal something that killed the case.

After the doctors completed all of the medical tests, they measured every length of Will's body—*every* dimension.

"Why do you need all of that?" Will asked.

"It's for the *Engineering Department*," Poliakov replied. "They need it for the settings on some equipment."

Will recalled not being satisfied with Dr. Smith's description of the "equipment," and saw the opportunity to get more information. "What type of equipment?" Will asked.

"I don't know," Poliakov answered and walked away.

Will didn't believe him.

Dr. Noh arrived with an injection gun, and an array of syringes on a platter. He gave one word descriptions for each shot, for which Will was grateful. In the end, he'd received numerous booster shots, including tetanus, and was immunized for a number of other things, including the hepatitis series. Finally, a nurse came in and shaved his head—first with a clippers, and then with a razor and shaving cream.

"Why such a close shave?" Will asked.

The woman's eyes opened wide, and she shook her head as if to say: *you don't want to know.*

He closed his eyes, but kept his head still as the woman did her job.

A torrent of thoughts raged inside Will's mind: he'd fallen victim to the flawed judicial system, an incompetent defense attorney, and a jury of suggestible morons. And the negligence of the testing lab that lost the DNA evidence, evidence that *would* have exonerated him, was indefensible.

He admitted the circumstantial evidence had looked bad. He recalled the testimony of the school cop: "Less than ten minutes after the defendant left the trees, and the scene altogether, the girl came stumbling out of the pines, naked from the waist down. She had a serious head wound and was visibly disoriented."

"And what did she do when she got under the lights, in full view?" the prosecutor had asked.

"She cried out, fell down and tried to cover herself," the cop had replied. "She was slurring, but managed to communicate that she'd been raped before losing consciousness."

Will didn't *see* any of that, but he could imagine the scene—and what it must have looked like with the timing. Even more unfortunate than the lost DNA was that the girl's brain had swelled as a result of the head trauma, and she lapsed into a coma. He prayed she would come out of it before the end of the trial, but that hadn't happened. Now it didn't look good for either of them.

Will still had trouble believing all that had occurred—the circumstances were just too bizarre. Even more so, it was Pam's betrayal *at the most crucial moment* that had sealed his fate. He could never have predicted that. He told her he didn't do it, she didn't believe him, and things were over between them in an instant. He could never forgive her: she had called him a liar, and in light of the accusations, something *much worse*.

He *had* to survive the year, if only to clear his name.

Finally, Dr. Johnson informed him the session was over, and the orderlies were called.

Denise took the subway to Loyola University, and walked in the cold wind another fifteen minutes until she reached the front door of a small house. She was in a cozy residential neighborhood where the houses were packed so closely together there was barely room to walk between them. It was bright out despite being an overcast morning, and she squinted as she took off her sunglasses to knock on the door.

The floors creaked behind the entrance as someone approached. She heard the locks turn, the door opening to reveal a short, heavyset woman with brown hair and gold-rimmed glasses.

"Yes?" the woman said.

"Is Ms. Sorrensen in? I need to speak with her."

"One minute," the woman replied, closing the door.

A few moments later a woman that Denise recognized from the directory photo stuck her head out of the door.

"Ms. Sorrensen?"

"Yes, how can I help you?"

"I'm Denise Walker, I work for the DNA Foundation. I was hoping to spe—"

"The DNA Foundation?" Pam cut her off.

"We're a group of lawyers and law students who investigate cases in which DNA evidence might exonerate persons who have been wrongfully convicted."

"What's this about?"

Denise could tell from the woman's eyes she knew *exactly* what this was about. It would have been better to ease into the conversation, but now Denise figured she had no choice but to plow ahead. "We're investigating the conviction of William Thompson." She noticed an immediate reaction from Pam, who looked back as if to check that no one in the house was listening.

"I'm not interested," Pam replied, and backed into the doorway.

"I understand, Ms. Sorrensen, but it will only take an hour—and we'll compensate you for your time." To this Denise saw a more positive reaction; desperation was a feeling she knew all too well.

"I have a new life now. I'd like to keep this private," Pam said in a low voice. "What do you want to know?"

"We just have some questions regarding the case and trial—my boss would like to meet you... I think it would be best if you came in to his office." Pam seemed agreeable to this.

"How about tonight around 9:00 p.m.? I know it's New Years Eve, but it will only be an hour."

"Fine," Pam replied. "*Compensated* means cash?"

"I don't know how much, but yes," Denise said, handing her a slip of paper with Jonathan's office address and her own phone number. Pam took it and closed the door, and Denise began her walk back to the subway. It would be a working night.

Jonathan flipped on the lights in his office to account for the waning winter daylight as Denise sipped coffee and filled him in about her encounter with Pam Sorrensen.

"So what's our next move?" Denise asked.

"Thompson starts treatment tomorrow," Jonathan replied, "so the clock is ticking." He got up, retrieved the carafe of coffee, and topped off their cups. "Providing our interview with Ms. Sorrensen doesn't kill the case, I have a specific job for you."

"Yes?"

"I want you to go to the testing lab in southern Illinois to look for the lost DNA samples… It's a long shot, but it may be our best chance at reopening the case." Jonathan saw a hint of a grin on Denise's face. "What?"

Her grin turned to a smile, and she laughed. "Nothing … I'm just looking forward to doing some work that doesn't involve the law library."

"Yes, I suppose it's about time." Jonathan chuckled and continued, "You'll rent a car for the trip and stay in a hotel for a night or two. Make some reservations right away, and plan to leave tomorrow." He opened a desk drawer, pulled out a leather credit card holder, and handed it to Denise. "You can charge everything on this—it's a Foundation card."

"Thanks," Denise said and put the card in her backpack, together with her notes and some of the case files.

"How exactly should I proceed?"

"I'll call ahead and arrange for an appointment at the lab," Jonathan explained. "You'll go there and request all of the DNA samples—for the girl, Thompson, and the rape-kit samples taken from the girl after the crime… You'll request permission to *search* for them—or help *them* search."

"If they refuse?"

"I have connections that can put pressure on them."

Denise nodded and smiled. "Okay."

"A few more things," Jonathan continued, his face more serious now. "You'll need to conceal your identity. Make some fake business cards, get a pre-paid mobile phone—and pay for everything with the Foundation card. Also, create a dummy email address." Jonathan's face became even more serious, nearly frowning. "And *be careful*. If you sense any danger at all, get out of there immediately."

"What could be so dangerous?" Denise asked.

Jonathan now feared she might be too inexperienced for a solo assignment. It *should* be a relatively safe task, but she needed to develop smart habits: he had personally seen very dangerous situations emerge from seemingly benign activities. "We know very little about the Compressed Punishment system… We might be poking one hell of a hornet's nest here," Jonathan replied. "You have to keep your eyes open at all times."

He saw her smile and nod. It reminded him of his daughter's typical reaction after he'd lectured her; an expression of naiveté. He knew Denise was not a teenager—neither was his daughter anymore—but it worried him. "One last thing," he said as he pulled something out of a drawer in his desk; an object rolled up in a khaki cloth.

Jonathan watched Denise's smile fade away as he handed her the gun.

The orderlies brought Will to a door, upon which there was a sign that read: *B-Level: Rm. 2 Dental.* He knew it was coming—it was mentioned by the woman in his first meeting—but the words on the door frightened him. There was nothing wrong with his teeth, but he knew it didn't matter—there hadn't been anything wrong with his body when he'd entered the medical room, either.

The large orderly ushered Will into the room, and closed the door as he left.

Will stood near the entrance and peered around the room. Shards of light glinted into his eyes from an assortment of dental instruments arrayed on a cart beneath a bright, adjustable light. The dentist chair was more elaborate than any other he had seen.

Suspended from the ceiling, directly above the chair, was a metal grid, riddled with tubes, nozzles, and gas tanks, and illuminated panels of electronic instrumentation twinkled from a large rack against the far wall.

Will felt his muscles tense when he saw the subtly-placed, steel eyelets on the chair—a less-than-subtle hint he was not there for a routine checkup. The room smelled of antiseptic, and it was either too warm, or he was already developing a nervous sweat.

Will detected motion in his peripheral vision, and he turned to see a woman dressed in red scrubs walk out from a back room, stopping a few feet in front of him, near the foot of the chair. She was just a few inches shorter than Will, probably in her mid to late twenties, and very attractive. A mop of blonde hair mushroomed inside her hairnet, making it look like she was wearing a giant beret. She pointed to the chair and said, "Have a seat. The doctor and I will be back in a few minutes. The door is locked, so don't get any funny ideas." She disappeared again into the back room.

Will climbed into the chair, which was in the upright position and seemed comfortable—if only because he was exhausted.

Just as he was calming to the point of closing his eyes, Will heard the scuffing of faraway footsteps. His heartbeat picked up a pace as a small man walked in from the back. The dentist was skinny, to the point of being frail, and wore round, wire-framed glasses.

He put on a pair of latex gloves and faced Will. "Hello Number 524. I'm Dr. Colby—like the cheese. Everyone remembers me if I tell them that." The man chuckled as he pushed a button, and a motor lowered the chair into a nearly horizontal position.

Will was certain that no one who sat in his chair ever forgot this man—just as he knew he'd never forget Dr. Johnson, with her bright-red lipstick. Colby's smile gave away his age; the wrinkles around his eyes were deep, and his teeth had often bathed in coffee. Will guessed he was in his fifty's, even though he had a good hairline, and not much grey had mixed in with the yellow-blonde.

"They're referring to me as *523*," Will responded, forcing the words out of his tired body.

"Ahh … let's see …" Colby said and looked at the file. He sighed in disgust and dropped the file onto a desk, shooting a look of annoyance at his assistant who had just entered the room. "Please get me the *today's* file, Ms. Hatley—*523*."

The woman nodded, and walked at a hurried clip into the back room.

Colby turned back to Will, "Wouldn't do anyone any good if I had the wrong records now, would it?" he asked and then laughed. "Please put your arms up on the bars so we can secure you."

Will flinched.

Colby tilted his head raising an eyebrow. "There is no point in resisting," he warned. "I'll just call the orderlies to forcibly strap you in."

The man's smile persisted, and Will noticed a subtle German accent in his voice—*shtrop you in*. He nodded and tried to relax as the dentist proceeded to secure him.

"I'm sure you're wondering about what we're going to do here," Colby said as he assembled the restraints; it was a more elaborate restraining arrangement than that in the medical room. "First, we'll have a look at your general dental health. You see, we'll fix as much as we can while you're here—that's one benefit for you: free dental care. Well, not exactly *free, per se*." His face became more serious and his voice lowered. "The other things we'll do won't be very pleasant. We're going to assess your *pain thresholds*. If this isn't done carefully, and we acquire an inaccurate calibration curve for the control instruments you'll be hooked up to later, you could go into cardiac arrest, and possibly die during your treatment. And that isn't good for us or for you. So you don't want to fake anything—like passing out, etcetera—because that could be bad for you later. Get it?"

"Yes," Will said. His nerves tingled, and he felt a rash-like sweat break out on his back and neck. Now he anticipated the worst—but he had no way of knowing what that meant.

Colby secured the straps tightly, and walked around the chair, testing each one with a strong pull and shake. "Any questions before we begin?"

Will could hardly speak, but summoned the nerve to ask, "What do you mean by pain *thresholds*?"

"Ahh ..." The dentist's eyes lit up. "Interesting topic. You see, there are many different *types* of pain, as you may have noticed from your medical exam. Different nerve bundles deliver different types of signals—and the teeth and jaw possess *so many kinds*. They come from the gums, surfaces and roots of the teeth, bones, sinuses, and so on. Each type is processed differently by the brain, and we need to test *all* of them to get a good estimate of your limits. Dental pain is the king of all pains."

The dentist's response only made things worse, and the irritating itch on Will's back and neck made him squirm against the restraints.

Colby pushed Will's head firmly into the headrest of the chair folding up hinged wings on each side, near his ears. Next, the dentist wrapped a multi-strapped harness across his forehead and around the back of his head, feeding the open ends of the straps through winches mounted on the wings. He reached beneath the chair and moved a handle up and down, making a clicking sound with each iteration. The "strap-hat" pressed Will's head tighter and tighter against the headrest with each click of the ratchet. The pain built up quickly, and he soon felt his skull start to flex under the pressure.

"That too tight?" Colby asked.

"Yessss ..." Will gasped, wincing. A moment later he heard another click, and felt a quantum of pressure release on his skull. Colby grabbed the sides of Will's head and tried to wiggle it back and forth, then released the harness two more clicks. The pressure was instantaneously more bearable.

"That sucker could crush your head," Colby said, smiling constantly. "That should be better now."

Ms. Hatley returned with a different file, and Colby pulled some x-ray images out of the folder, placing them on a backlit viewer. He examined the images for a few minutes, then turned towards Will and said, "Looks like we have some work ahead of us—wisdom teeth, root canal— at least one—and some filling replacements."

Will couldn't move his head one millimeter in *any* direction, but looked around the best he could with his peripheral vision. Colby opened a cabinet and retrieved a rubber-coated device that looked a like a miniature car jack, or a spreader bar with curved ends.

"Open wide."

Will opened his mouth and Colby placed the curved up end of the device behind his top front teeth and the curved down side behind his front lowers. He turned a knob on the device with his unusually small hands, and the two ends of the jack pushed apart, forcing Will's mouth open. Will felt his jaw muscles involuntarily try to close, and he had to fight his gag reflex. Colby then produced a hex key from his shirt pocket and inserted it into a corresponding depression in the knob. He cranked the key and forced Will's jaws open even further—against his tightened muscles. The pain made him groan.

"Ms. Hatley, attach the sensors while I get the other tool cart," Colby instructed, and walked out of the room.

Hatley turned to Will and looked at him haughtily. She attached a monitor to each of his index fingers, left upper arm, chest, and forehead. She then opened his hospital robe and strapped something near his groin. She hesitated, took a closer look, and giggled. "I see a little uh ... asymmetry ... here," she said. "Maybe we should just castrate you, so you don't rape any more children, huh?"

The "huh" coincided with a stiff squeeze of his balls, making him yelp like a dog. It also made him try to close his jaw—and it felt as if he nearly dislocated it.

Hatley then moved closer to his face and smiled. "I'm so glad I get to be a part of today's little exercise. You see, Dr. Colby lets me do a few of the simple procedures as part of my training." She then got so close to his face that he could smell her minty breath. "And when I get to do the routines *myself*, I won't be as nice as the old man." She then gathered up some saliva and spit directly into Will's mouth, the glob landing in the back of his throat.

Will gagged hard, but managed to recover after a few seconds. His jaws tensed again and it caused enough pain to make him forget about the spit. Now he tried to ignore the *taste* of mint.

He saw Colby push a cart of shiny instruments into the room. He initially felt some relief that he was no longer alone with the woman, but this subsided as he recognized some of the pieces on the cart, including a high-speed drill and a large assortment of bits.

Hatley moved to Will's left, near an instrument panel that controlled the monitors. Colby rolled a stool to Will's right, selected an instrument, and sat down.

"Well *523*, you have an interesting nerve arrangement in your lower jaw. I think we'll need to explore that thoroughly. But first, just a routine dental exam—so we can plan specific procedures for later this year. Here we go …"

Will closed his eyes and prayed in his mind.

Denise's tiny office was conveniently located just two doors down from Jonathan's, but it gave her enough privacy to work without too many distractions.

She found the name of the DNA test center in the case files; it was located just a few miles west of the city of West Frankfort, in southern Illinois. She arranged for a rental car, and made reservations at a hotel just off of highway I-57, in the town of Marion, a larger town further south. She downloaded directions, and designed and printed some business cards under an alias. As she was cutting them out, she heard a knock at her door.

Jonathan stepped in and leaned against the door frame. "Are you ready for tomorrow?"

"On paper, yes. I'll have to prepare myself mentally, though."

"You'll be fine. Have you used this alias somewhere before?"

"A long time ago—to get into bars as an undergrad. I have a matching ID—good thing I don't look too different."

"Should do the trick. They shouldn't scrutinize you too much if I call ahead."

Denise nodded. "What do you think the chances are that we find the samples?"

"No idea," Jonathan answered. "But even the slimmest chance is better than none."

"I don't understand why we need Thompson's case so badly; can't we just demand information about the Red Box—invoke the Freedom of Information Act, or something?"

"It doesn't work that way with classified projects."

"It's classified? But *citizens* are serving sentences there," Denise argued.

"They've all *volunteered*," Jonathan explained, "and they, and the employees, have all signed non-disclosure forms regarding the program under penalty of treason."

"I'd think someone would leak information, eventually."

"That may be, but we don't have time to wait—those prisoners don't have time to wait."

"We've only been through about fifty case files—shouldn't there be hundreds to examine?" Denise asked.

"We can't even find the *names* of most of the people in the CP program," Jonathan explained. "The cases are low profile: rape, drugs, or murder II, and the defendants are given the option at the very last minute. They're gone before they can talk to anyone, and even the lawyers are left in the dark. Of course the *judges* know—but they're forced to sign National Security Nondisclosure agreements, as well."

"Stinks to high heaven."

"Undoubtedly," Jonathan said. He stretched his arms over his head and yawned. "I better get back to reading the transcript of Ms. Sorrensen's testimony. I'll have some tough questions for her tonight."

Jonathan walked out, leaving Denise to her preparations and her thoughts. A lot was going to happen in the next few days, but she didn't know what to expect. For the first time in her life, she had a gun in her possession.

Will tasted the latex gloves on Colby's hands as the man poked and scratched every crevice of every tooth in his jaw with a sharp wire-like instrument. Colby blurted out various numbers and letters; presumably codes for various things—cavity in this molar, filling replacement here, root canal there, and so on. When he'd finished, he grabbed the chart from Hatley and spoke to Will, "We have two new cavities to fill, five filling replacements, one—maybe two—root canals, and wisdom teeth removal—all four. By the end of the year, you'll have had a fine dental makeover."

Colby put the chart down on the cart and selected the same instrument he used for the "checkup." He nodded to his assistant, and she pushed a button on the instrument panel. Will saw the word 'recording' flash on a screen displaying heart rate, blood pressure, and body temperature.

Colby put the instrument in his mouth, and Will felt him exact extreme pressure on a back-right-bottom molar. The dentist strained, putting his weight into it. Pain built up in the center of the tooth and then, all at once, the sharp, stiff wire broke through a weak part and plunged in deep, through the soft dentin and into the root. Will's vision went a blinding white, a high pitched tone ringing in his ears, before everything went black.

When he came to, Colby was pressing a larger instrument on the area, and Will tasted a strong mint flavor. The dentist must have repaired the tooth while he was passed out.

"Your pain threshold is average, at best," Colby explained. "We plugged the hole we made in that tooth with a temporary filling—which should take hold well since that was a healthy, pristine tooth. We'll replace the temp when we do the real work later in the year. Now let's have a look under one of your fillings. That should give us an idea of what to expect regarding decay, and nerve sensitivity."

Will's jaw ached deeply, and his throat was already raw from screaming. This time they tied his tongue over to the side of his mouth—like they do with race horses.

Colby selected the high-speed drill and tested it: the high-pitched whine made Will recoil. Colby reached in with the drill, and Will felt him slowly grind away the filling of an upper-left molar. Hatley held a suction tube near the area to suck up the refuse, but the pieces she missed lodged under his tongue and in the back of his throat. The unsettling smell of burnt tooth and filling came to his olfactory system in the reverse direction—from the back of his throat through his nose, as he breathed out. The taste of it seemed to coat everything. His tooth became progressively more sensitive as Colby worked.

After a few minutes, Colby swapped the drill for the wire tool. "Filling's gone. Let's see what we have here."

Will felt him probe the edges of the newly exposed hole, and then dig his way up until he poked deep into one of the roots. The pain shot directly into Will's brain—but it was different than that of the lower tooth. He heard his voice crackle into falsetto as he screamed, and salty sweat trickled into his eyes. When the torment finally ceased, he noticed sweat on Colby's face as well.

"Seems your threshold is quite a bit higher on the uppers—that works against you though," Colby said. "Now, let's take a look at that special nerve bundle in your lower jaw."

He turned to Hatley. "I think we'll go through the outside gums for this one."

Will felt himself begin to slip away again. He felt his eyes roll back, but a stiff slap on his chest brought him back.

"Hey—you don't want to do that," Colby warned. "We'll have to give you a drug to keep you conscious—and that throws off our assessments. You *definitely* don't want that." He then grabbed another wire tool, similar to the first, except this one seemed thinner and was ground to a needle-sharp point. He grasped Will's right cheek between his thumb and forefinger, and pulling it aside to have a close look. He sighed, released his cheek, and walked over to the x-ray image on the display.

The dentist studied the image for a minute, then Will heard him say, "ahhh ... okay," under his breath as he walked back to Will's side.

"Come here, Ms. Hatley," Colby said.

She nodded and walked over to his side.

"Pull this aside like this," he instructed as he demonstrated pulling Will's cheek. "That way I can get in with my left hand. And stay out of the light."

Will felt Hatley's fingers as she pulled his cheek aside, and then Colby inserted the instrument. He felt the cold steel gently probing his lower gums on the outside, near his right cheek.

Colby turned to Hatley, "If we plunge in deep, right here ..."— Will felt a sharp poke on his gums between the first and second molars from the back—"... we'll hit the center of that spider-like bundle. It passes below the main nerve junction. But we need to be careful not to damage it."

Will felt the cold wire penetrate his lower gum, and he whined pitifully with his mouth propped open like the hood of a car. Colby explained the procedure to Hatley as he worked, but Will couldn't hear all the words over his own sounds. The wire scraped over teeth, roots, and bone indiscriminately. At one point it felt as if the probe was *beneath* a tooth, and was about to poke through the gum, out the other side.

After some digging around, Colby finally located the nerve bundle, causing a white-hot pain to shoot through Will's skull. It felt like someone was drilling into the roots of all of his lower teeth simultaneously. His bowels released uncontrollably, and a moment later he smelled a stench rise from his body like he'd never known before. Colby seemed to ignore it, as if it were a common occurrence; Hatley covered her face with her sleeve.

Colby then pointed at one of the meters with his right hand and turned his head slightly to Hatley. "Here the pain levels are at two. And here ..." He put a little pressure on the instrument.

Will gasped, his eyes fluttering.

Colby continued, "up to seven ... a little more pressure ... seven point five ... more pressure ... eight point two ..."

That was the last thing Will remembered—he passed out for the second time, only to wake up to Colby saying, "Now you give it a try, Ms. Hatley."

Kelly Hatley eagerly accepted the instrument and awaited the dentist's instruction.

"Enter the insertion point I made—it's about three quarters of an inch deep and angled towards the back. You should feel a small pebble-like mass. Exert some pressure, but be careful not to damage it; we don't want to paralyze the nerve. No pain in that now, is there?"

"Nope," she responded and started the insertion.

Will's head felt like it was going to burst. The bitter taste of the blood draining into his throat made him nauseous, and every muscle on his skull ached.

Hatley dug and twisted until Will felt her getting close to the sweet spot.

"I think I found it," she said with excitement. She looked to the monitor and then exacted some pressure.

Will squealed loudly.

"Whoa … you're at level eight already," Colby warned. "Slow down or he's liable to pass out again."

"Sorry, doctor. How's this?—down to seven …" she said, and looked into Will's eyes.

He was screaming inside, but now there wasn't much sound coming out. Blocking Colby's view of her face, she grinned at Will. He'd never forget that grin.

"Okay, that's enough for now," Colby said, instructing her to extract the instrument. "We'll locate the wisdom teeth next. I want *you* to do it, but first I need to set up the camera to see what you're doing in there. Have a look at the x-rays while I get the camera and monitor set up… And clean up his mouth."

Colby walked into the back room, and Will heard the sounds of cabinet doors opening and closing. Hatley connected some tubes to a panel behind his head, sat down on the stool, and looked at him with a smirk. "So … was it as good for you as it was for me? No, don't answer that." He couldn't, of course. "And it's not over yet. In fact, it hasn't even really begun. The real fun starts tomorrow. After today, you won't see *us* for a while, but don't worry, we'll be making numerous house calls this year."

She stuck two nozzles in his mouth—one sprayed water, the other sucked it away. He winced as the cold water hit the newly worked areas, and even the air flow from the suction caused pain.

"You're lucky I'm not running this show," she said. "Your whole disgusting case makes me think about my little sister—she's sixteen. Makes me happy you're *here*, and I get to do *this*."

She stuffed some gauze in his mouth; it was soft and comforting. It was his first bit of relief, although he knew it would be short-lived.

Colby rolled in a cart with the camera and monitor. He set up lights and focused the camera on the back of Will's mouth. Hatley finished studying the x-ray images, and then sat down on the stool to Will's right.

"See if you can locate the top-left wisdom tooth," Colby instructed, looking at the monitor. "Go in with the long explorer."

Hatley poked the flesh behind Will's last upper-left molar with the sharp wire instrument Colby had suggested.

"Go back a little further, angle the probe a little towards the front … yes, right there."

Hatley then plunged the wire deep into Will's flesh. A dull pain radiated through his head, then through his entire upper body. His stomach was giving way and he couldn't hold it down. Vomit sprayed all over Hatley's hand and lab coat. She squealed and pulled away in disgust, with the instrument still jammed in Will's upper jaw. Blood and bile leaked back down his throat, and he choked violently.

Colby reached in quickly and removed the instrument, as Will worked to recover from his gagging fit.

"Ms. Hatley! *Never* pull away like that, and never leave an instrument in a patient's mouth—he could choke to death," Colby scolded her in an instructive, rather than disciplinary tone.

"Sorry doctor, I …"

"Just go change your gloves and coat while I clean up his mouth. You can try again."

Five minutes later Will's mouth was clean, and Hatley had returned wearing a clean coat and gloves. She sat down, went to the same spot with the probe, and plunged it in deep. The pain overtook him again, dizziness turned to nausea, and he felt another bout of sickness coming on. His stomach wrenched, but there was nothing left to vomit up.

"I think you're too deep," Colby said.

Indeed she was. Will felt the tip of the probe penetrate his jaw bone, and heard the pain meter blare right before he blacked out for a third time. He awoke to Hatley locating the targeted wisdom tooth and pressing on it.

"I think this one is floating," she said, as she wiggled and pushed the probe.

Will felt the spongy flexing of the buried tooth as she moved it.

"Okay, that's it. We're done here," Colby said with a tone of finality. "The lower two are definitely impacted, and the other upper one is even more separated from the jaw bone than the first one."

"But shouldn't we check the other upper?" Hatley asked, her voice revealing eagerness.

"No, we're running late. We need to finish the repairs—we'll grind those temporary fillings down and finish the job in a professional manner. We need to get a mold of his full dental structure, and then do a full disinfection treatment."

The finishing process was the most relaxing fifteen minutes of Will's life. Endorphins flooded his bloodstream, and a few pokes here and there only amplified the effect. Finally, Colby released the jaw-jack, and untied the body straps.

Will sat up in a daze. The orderlies were already in the room—he hadn't noticed they'd arrived.

"Time for your final appointment," Colby said. "However, your orderlies better take you to the shower first." He pointed to a door.

Colby and Hatley left the room as the orderlies helped Will out of the chair and his soiled garments. They led him to the door, and guided him into a small shower room. "You have fifteen minutes," the smaller one said.

Will was barely able to nod as the men left him.

He turned on the shower, and sobbed.

Will had always done a lot of thinking in the shower. The warm water always had the feel of a safe zone, but not now. Now he only had deep feelings of despair, interrupted by attacks of fear and panic.

His thoughts shifted to his disgraced and embarrassed family, and to his traitorous ex-fiancée whom he knew would tell her friends, and *his*, that she had almost married a rapist. He was incensed that she might get away with such a betrayal.

Three loud knocks on the door startled Will from his thoughts. Shower time was over. He turned off the water and cracked open the door. The large orderly handed him a towel. Will dried off, and put on a clean hospital gown and slippers in front of the two men.

They walked out of the shower to the dental exam room, which was vacated. Will hesitated a moment before looking at the chair.

"Look at that fucking mess," the larger orderly said, and pointed to the soiled chair and garments on the floor next to it. His face was distorted in an expression of disgust. "We have to clean that shit up."

It was too much. Will could hardly contain his anger. "That's just too fucking bad," he snapped. "Maybe you idiots should get different jobs."

Will felt the men tighten their grips on his arms, but that was all—it wasn't going to escalate. They walked in silence, went up a level, and arrived at a new door: *C-Level: Rm. 50 Engineering.*

Will felt the larger orderly release his arm, and watched as he flashed a plastic card at a white pad near the door handle. He heard a beep, the lock clicked, and a green light illuminated on a nearby panel. The smaller orderly pushed the door open, and the three men passed into a white room as large as a basketball gymnasium. The ceiling was at least forty feet high, from which two overhead cranes were suspended on steel guide tracks. Metal machining stations lined the wall on the left. Metal parts that looked like robot appendages—legs, arms, spines—hung from hooks on the walls.

Sounds of milling machines and grinders echoed throughout the large room, and welding light flashed sporadically off the walls like blue-white lightning. Will counted about thirty people—mostly men—in red lab coats, moving busily about. They were all concentrating on their work through safety glasses.

From about fifty feet away, Will saw a man look at them, tap the shoulder of a second, and point in the direction of Will and the orderlies. The second man looked at his watch and nodded, then walked over to them, pulling the safety glasses off of his face and over his head. "All of your system components are finished, 523," the man said, itching his scalp through his short, gray hair. Will noticed a hint of sweat on the man's brow. "I'm Aubry Coates, the fitting engineer. I know it's been a long day already, but this is going to take a while. The Exoskeleton is complex and takes some time to assemble. We should be finished in about four or five hours—if everything goes well."

"*Exoskeleton?*" Will asked. He remembered them referring to some *equipment*, but it hadn't been given a name.

Coates took a firm hold of Will's upper arm and addressed the orderlies, "Okay guys, we'll take it from here."

As the orderlies headed for the exit, Coates directed Will to a chair in the center of the floor. "Yes, *Exoskeleton*. This is the assembly platform," he explained. "We have all of your parts roughly assembled—per the medical exam measurements—but we'll have to make some fine adjustments. All of the sensor data and medical imaging has been loaded into the computer program. We'll start with the mechanical stuff—feet first—and work our way up. Once that system is tested, we'll install the electrical, medical monitoring, and medical servicing systems. Understand?"

"No, I do *not* understand," Will said, shaking his head.

"You were informed of this during your orientation—during your first meeting."

"No, I wasn't. I was told about some biomechanical interface—nothing about an *Exoskeleton*." Will recalled that that first meeting had been called short. Dr. Smith had only given him the dime tour.

"The Exoskeleton *is* the biomechanical interface." Coates seemed to look for some recognition in Will's face, but Will was still confused. Coates continued, "Doesn't matter, you'll see as we go along." Coates let go of his arm. "Now, remove your clothes and slippers, and have a seat so we can get started."

Will's thoughts flashed back to that first meeting with Dr. Smith; how she'd treated him. He became even more tense as he thought of those who had followed her—Dr. Johnson, then Ms Hatley... But he kept his anger to himself, disrobed and sat in the chair.

Coates pulled out a blaze-orange walkie-talkie the size of a small cell phone, and spoke into it, "Lowers people—you're up. Mid-section—you're on deck."

A minute later four men drove up in a small electric cart. On its carpeted flatbed were a pair of robot-like legs, similar to those hanging on the walls, only dissected into feet, shins, knees, thighs, and hips. One of the men picked up a shoe-like piece, walked over to Will, and slipped it over his left foot. It felt heavy and cold. The device was extremely complicated—each toe was jointed—and there were many moving parts. The whole thing seemed to have more "bones" than the biological foot, but Will could still see a lot of his skin though the intricate structure.

The technician made a few adjustments with a wrench, making the foot curl into a tippy-toe position. Holding it in the fully-flexed state, another man inserted a large Allen key into a receptacle on the "foot" and turned, forcing it to curl even further. Will squirmed and tried to get out of his chair, but two other men held him steady. A moment later the stress was released, the men let him loose, and they went for the other foot. The process was repeated.

Next were the shins—not much pain there. The shins were then connected to the knee joints, and in less than an hour they had worked all the way up to the hips.

A second group rolled in with torso parts. The mid-section was a work of technological art. It looked like a human spine on the backside, the ribbed sides interconnected with shiny springs and tubing, and the chest-piece was made of interleaved titanium rods and plates. Everything but the head-cage was assembled in about three hours, according to a large analog clock, high on the wall above the entrance.

The Exoskeleton wasn't uncomfortable: the parts that touched his skin had a coating that was smooth and lubricating. It made Will wonder how often he'd be inside the machine.

The head assembly was delivered next. The technicians assembled a titanium frame around his neck and head, and connected the "spine" to the frame near the back of his skull. It seemed to Will that the bulk of the assembly was complete, and it was a lot more open than he'd originally imagined: he could see through it to his skin in many places—except his abdomen, where the plates and rods covered most of the area. It really resembled a skeleton framed around his body, but riddled with motors, hydraulics, and other components encased in the structure.

Coates barked into his walkie-talkie, "We need electrical here, stat. Pneumatics is on deck. Medical is in the hole," he said and walked over to Will. "How are things feeling in there—feel any pinching or obvious discomfort?"

"None right now," Will replied. "How long am I going to be in this thing?"

"What?" Coates replied. His expression was that of confusion.

Will repeated his question.

Coates shook his head. "They really didn't tell you anything? What the hell ..." He put his radio in his pocket and looked Will straight in the eyes. "You are in there for the entire three-hundred and sixty-five days."

Will couldn't respond, and just stared ahead blankly.

After an awkward few seconds, Coates said, "We'll do a full test in about an hour. You can have water now, if you want."

Will shook out of his bewildered, despondent trance, and replied, "Please." Suddenly he found himself desperately thirsty.

Coates nodded to another man who retrieved a water bottle. The red-coated technician stuck the nozzle of the squeeze bottle through the head frame and into Will's mouth. He was so thirsty that the water tasted sweet. He drank down half the bottle, and nodded that it was enough.

"Your file says you're a physicist," Coates inquired.

"Yes," Will replied. *Was a physicist.*

"Then you might appreciate the Exoskeleton—or just *Exo*, as we call it. It's amazing technology," Coates explained. "The frame is constructed of titanium and high-strength aircraft aluminum, with a few stainless steel pieces here and there, and some spring-steel. The joints are Teflon coated, and the bio-surfaces are a biocompatible, self-lubricating polymer that's resistant to all sorts of chemicals and environments. The "bones"—including the spine—double as electrical and biomedical conduits."

"Yes, it's impressive," Will said. He didn't care about the technology in the slightest. "But what am I supposed to *do* with this thing?"

Coates' expression revealed confusion and frustration, once again, but he seemed to ignore the question, and continued. "To control the motion, there are many different types of actuators; some are high-torque stepper motors, which run on electrical power. Others are controlled through hydraulics, and some are pneumatic—controlled by compressed air. There are heaters, cooling lines, complex biosensors, built-in program chips, fiber-optics, and even laser navigation for guidance into ports. And, most crucially, all computer control and power is linked to *one* external port, located on your lower back near the center of gravity. It's one of the most amazing systems I have ever seen, and I've been in bioengineering research for over twenty years."

Will was an experimental physicist; he understood well the engineering of motion control, and had colleagues who studied bio-interfacing. As far as he knew, no comprehensive biomechanical-interfaced system existed. Even prosthetics, though they had come a long way, had very limited functionality.

By the looks of the system they were assembling around him, Will surmised the development of the Exoskeleton must have taken decades. To integrate the biosensors, fiber-optic nerves, motion sensing, and the feedback to a central processor required the integration of many different areas of research.

How they had kept it secret was more interesting to him than the technology. Now, he thought, they must be in the test phase. Then it hit him: *maybe he was the test dummy for this new technology—that's what this was all about.* It made complete sense—*this* was the hazardous duty.

"Who developed it?" Will asked.

"Not sure, but *Syncorp, Inc.*, is stamped on all the major parts," Coates replied. "My guess is that it had many developers—probably government contractors of all kinds."

A cart pulled up, and the next phase of assembly was about to begin.

Stadler

Heinrich Bergman hung up the phone and put his head in his hands. Evidently, word had leaked about the missing project files, and one of the project's contributors had just backed out. He was hopeful that the contributors weren't in communication with one another. But, if they were, they might *all* back out; they were a skittish group, and rightly so—they could all end up in prison, or worse.

It was all getting very convoluted: now someone had leaked the leak. Bergman wondered if he had moved too slowly on Frank Weiss... He had every intention of enacting protocol for Weiss' selling of the technical plans, but he admitted it should have been done sooner.

Now he had to move. He picked up the phone and punched in a number. "Lenny, I have a job for you before you head to Illinois ..."

Will listened to the chatter of a group of technicians as they ran tubes, wires, and fiber-optic cables through the conduits of the Exo. They ran tests as they proceeded, and Will heard one man yell commands from behind him, out of his view. He heard the same tech hooking up wires at the control port located in the small of his back, and clicking on a keypad.

"Right-side hydraulics," the tech yelled.

"Right-side hydraulics actuated," a voice responded, and Will felt a subtle stiffening of everything, even the ribs, on his right side.

"Check," the port tech barked back.

They proceeded to test the left side, and numerous other systems, and finished thirty minutes later.

Coates came back. "Everything look okay?" he asked the port technician.

"It all looks good for electrical, hydraulics, and pneumatics," Will heard from behind him.

"Okay, medical," Coates yelled. "Let's get this thing loaded." He took the walkie-talkie out of his pocket and put it to his mouth, "Test group, you're on deck." He turned to Will, "The medical crew will install the hypodermic cartridges and biosensors, and then we'll give this thing a test drive."

"What are they for?" Will asked.

"They didn't explain anything to you, did they?" Coates shook his head. "The Exo is what conducts the *entire treatment*. *You* are not controlling *it*. *It* is controlling *you*. And, to answer your question, some treatments call for injections."

Will was even more confused, and starting to feel an itching anxiety; he was trapped, and at the mercy of the people around him. And now feelings of claustrophobia were starting to creep in to his mind. *The Exoskeleton conducts the treatments?*

Two technicians arrived and assembled a system of wires, tubes, and actuators on the underarm, neck, and inner thigh sections of the Exoskeleton. Afterwards, they snapped in cartridges and sensors, hooked up a computer to the main control port, and started the tests.

"Sensor readings are on-line," a tech announced. "Heart rate, blood pressure, breathing rate, body temperature—all six sensor-point locations are working. Muscle tension—all twenty-four points, electrical conductivity—twelve points, and blood oxygen sensors are operational."

"Test the blood sampling system," Coates ordered.

"Here we go." The tech at the computer clicked a button and Will heard a whirring noise, then a click near his right bicep. He saw one of the cartridges shift and a small hatch slide open. Without delay, a small hypodermic needle plunged into his upper arm. Will yelped—more from being startled than from the pain, and he squirmed as the needle, guided by a small actuator, searched for a vein.

"Take it easy in there—this part shouldn't be too bad," the technician said, clicking another button, activating another needle cartridge. The process was repeated for both of his inner thighs and each side of his neck. It wasn't pleasant, Will thought, but at least it wasn't the sadistic Ms. Hatley driving a sharp steel wire through his soul. A moment later, all of the needles retracted simultaneously and the cartridges were ejected to the floor, where they clanged around on the cement like bullet shells.

"Blood sugar is low, as expected. All systems check out—all bio-parameters in normal range," the tech said as he unplugged the cables and closed his laptop. Another man picked up the used hypodermic cartridges with gloved hands, and put them in a plastic bucket labeled *BIOHAZZARD*.

Will heard the sound of a large electric motor, but couldn't place its origin until he noticed motion above him. The two overhead cranes were moving; they were heavy-duty winches that moved independently on a steel I-beam. When they had stopped, cables with hooks lowered from each winch, and the techs snapped them into place on the Exo: one near the back of Will's neck, and the other near his tailbone. The winch motors again whirred, and Will and the Exo were lifted into the air. The cables were then adjusted so that Will was horizontal, facing the floor.

"Okay, bring in the docking truck," Coates yelled.

Within a minute, a large, battery-powered vehicle with a hydraulic arm rolled into the room. It resembled a giant, mechanical scorpion on wheels: a large appendage hung high over the front of the vehicle, riddled with hydraulic cables and tubes. There were at least three large joints on the "scorpion's" tail, almost like those of a finger, only universal in their movement.

At the tip of the appendage was a black, metallic cylinder, about a foot long, and at least eight inches in diameter at its thickest point. The cylindrical grooves that ran its length made it resemble the cylinder of a giant revolver, and it tapered to a smaller diameter at the tip.

Coates barked again, "Insert the control drive."

The vehicle's hydraulics hissed and sighed as it rolled closer. Will saw the appendage extend towards him, and heard the connector lock into the port on his back, causing the Exo to jostle. Immediately, the entire Exoskeleton stiffened—the steppers, servos, and pneumatics energized. *It had come to life.* Fear began to eclipse Will's curiosity as he now realized he was just along for the ride.

"Slack the crane cables," Coates commanded.

The winch motors hummed for a few seconds, and the techs disconnected the support cables. He was now suspended from the control arm much like a cockroach stuck on the end of a knife. The appendage elevated him to about fifteen feet above the floor, and turned his body so he was vertical. From this vantage point he could see the entire assembly facility—it was enormous. He saw four other rooms, separated by movable walls, each at least as large as the one he was currently in. Some smaller rooms that housed desks and computers were sectioned off near the perimeters of the larger ones.

"We need a mechanical systems check," Coates yelled. Nothing happened. After about ten seconds, he cursed and barked the order again.

"Oh ... sorry, that's me," a tech yelled as he emerged from a small cubical. He trotted over to the cart, plugged in a laptop computer, and typed. A minute later it was set. "We're ready to test."

"Arms," Coates bellowed.

Will heard a few clicks on the tech's computer and the Exoskeleton went into motion: The arms moved out to the sides until they were level with the shoulders. Then they rotated back and forth, and lowered again to the sides

"Now, the legs," Coates ordered.

The legs ran in the air, then moved to the sides, pointed the feet, and then finally moved back to the standing position.

"Torso and back."

Will was immediately bent forward, then backward, and then twisted back and forth.

"Everything checks out," the tech reported.

"Fine. Let's move to the next phase," Coates instructed.

Will was exhausted and hungry. Whatever else they were going to do, he wished they'd just get it done.

After a late dinner, Denise walked against the frigid wind to the Law School, arriving at Jonathan's office at ten minutes to nine. She saw Pam Sorrensen standing at the door, seemingly trying to decide whether or not to knock. Denise approached her and said hello, then led her through the half-open door.

Jonathan was leaning against his desk and gazing at the ceiling, deep in thought. Denise made some noise as she took off her backpack, and when Jonathan noticed they'd arrived he greeted them and led them to the polished wooden table in the center of the room.

"Coffee, Ms. Sorrensen?"

"Please," Pam replied.

He brought three cups, sugar and cream, and an insulated carafe, all on a wooden tray.

"So, let's get started," Jonathan suggested as he poured the coffee. "I want to explain the way we approach these cases." He directed his words to Pam. "Unlike the trial, we assume the defendant is *innocent*."

Denise held back a laugh. She was fond of the old professor—he was charming, and always a gentleman, but his sarcasm could be cutting. Such statements were usually punctuated with the elevation of one of his gray, bushy eyebrows—but not this time. She knew Jonathan's statement was meant to be taken seriously: she knew he'd concluded that the jurors had made up their minds well before examining all of the evidence, what little there was.

"And, since the man is *innocent*," Jonathan continued, "we have to reveal the mistakes that were made by the prosecution and the defense. I've read through most of the case files, and something just seems to be a little *off*. That's why we're interested."

"Why do you need to talk to *me*?" Pam asked.

Denise answered, "We need to know if we're wasting our time here."

Jonathan took out a pipe. "Do you ladies mind if I puff a little?" Neither woman objected.

"There were two crucial pieces of evidence," Jonathan continued. "The first was that Thompson could be placed at the scene. This was never refuted, so it's not important to us. The second was the DNA evidence—it went missing at the lab. Do you have any insight into that, Ms. Sorrensen?"

"I heard that it happened, that's all," Pam replied.

"Did anyone make a big deal out of it?"

"Not really. It seemed that the prosecution was confident that they'd win without it."

"Was the rest of the evidence really that overwhelming?—I'm just not convinced," Jonathan said. "Tell me if we're missing something."

"It was the timing of everything, and the testimonies of the witnesses," Pam explained. "If I'd been a juror, I would have had a hard time acquitting him."

"Another thing confuses me," Jonathan said. "What kind of idiot would do that at a public event with over a thousand people present? This guy—Thompson—was no idiot. On top of that, he denied it all—even after the prosecution had offered a plea bargain that would've halved his sentence."

"He was always stubborn," Pam said.

"Stubborn maybe, stupid no," Denise said.

Jonathan's pipe went out and he relit it while puffing in a slow rhythm. "So my question for you, Ms. Sorrensen, is the following: disregarding the abundance of circumstantial evidence, how did *you* know that William Thompson raped that girl?"

"I didn't *know*," she replied.

Pam's voice sounded defensive, and Denise saw it definitively in her face.

"I read your testimony in the transcript—it's in the case file," Jonathan said, and pointed to the cardboard shipping box on his desk. "You sounded pretty persuasive—in print anyway. I don't know how you actually sounded during the trial."

"I only answered their questions."

"I'm sure that's true," he replied, "but it's easy to tell the difference in your demeanor—even through the written transcript—between your interactions with the prosecutor and the defense lawyer. You were obviously a witness for the prosecution, and if I were the defense attorney, I would've objected to much of your testimony." He tapped out his pipe, which had gone out again. He sighed and put it in an ash tray.

"Like I said, I just answered the questions—the most embarrassing questions …"

Denise saw Pam's lip quiver almost imperceptibly.

"I just can't understand how he was convicted," Jonathan said. "The evidence was all circumstantial, and there was no input from the victim obviously."

He poured more coffee into his cup, and then Denise's.

"The community was frightened by a string of rapes that had occurred in the months leading up to his arrest," Pam explained. "When he was arrested, the local news even reported that the 'serial rapist' had finally been caught."

"That's why Thompson's attorney should have requested a *change of venue*. This is a classic case of inept defense," Jonathan said. He opened a notebook and read for a few seconds, then looked to Pam. "I don't really understand the relevance of your testimony."

Pam shifted in her seat and responded, "My understanding is that it was meant to compare some of the defendant's behaviors with specific attributes of rapist profiles."

"The *defendant?*" Jonathan replied. "*Really?*"

Denise could tell the conversation wasn't going to go well from this point forward.

"The man was your *fiancé*, and you refer to him as *defendant?*" Jonathan reiterated with a look of irritation. "I have to say, Ms. Sorrensen, I don't understand *at all* what happened there. To answer the questions posed by the prosecutor was necessary, but many of your answers were speculative, and the defense attorney should have objected." Jonathan glanced at his notes, sighed, and continued, "You testified that you two were having problems; please explain."

Pam seemed to process his words for a few seconds before she responded. "We'd been having problems for months—mostly arguing about our plans for the future. Things became much worse once he was arrested, and I pretty much lost any feelings I had for him once the evidence came out."

"Excuse my bluntness, but you jumped ship pretty quickly," Jonathan retorted. "And I don't really care why, but I need to know if there was some special circumstance. Did he abuse you? Did you know of someone else that he'd assaulted? We need to know—are we wasting our time here?"

"He never abused *me*," Pam replied. "I only testified regarding our relationship and our sex life, which was nonexistent near the end." She looked as if she was about to cry, and her lips quivered more now. "As far as I know, he never assaulted anyone until that night... The media accused him of those other rapes at first, but he was never charged with them... They were brought up during the trial, but it was supposed to be stricken from the record."

"My lord. So the jurors *heard* it—although, it's likely they had already heard it in the news anyway." Jonathan shook his head in disapproval. "This man needs a new trial. This is very disturbing." He opened a file folder and said to Pam, "According to your testimony, you two weren't sexually active for many weeks before William's arrest?"

"We hadn't had sex in over two months, and I was out of town for the two weeks before he was arrested. I was still in Wisconsin with my parents when I got a call from a friend about Will's arrest. I testified that he might have been sexually frustrated at the time of the assault."

"What were the specifics of the problems between you two?" Denise asked.

"The future," Pam replied immediately. "I didn't want to live in a shitty little college town, and not have a career." Her eyes became glassy, and her voice cracked. "If he wasn't willing to risk his career, and try to move to city where I could find a job, I wanted to get out of the relationship altogether."

"Then why didn't you just *leave him*?" Jonathan asked.

Pam glared back at him. "I *couldn't* leave him. My mother was pressuring me to *marry* him—have her grandchildren, all that crap," Pam almost yelled, but seemed to catch herself and toned it down.

"Have you spoken with him since the conviction?" Denise asked.

"I haven't communicated with him since I testified," Pam replied. "I'm sure he sees it as a betrayal, but I don't... I doubt I could have done anything to stop the conviction."

Denise tried to see it from the man's point of view: he was hanging off the edge of a cliff, and the woman he loved was basically *indifferent* to his predicament. She didn't peel his fingers from the edge or anything, but she maybe kicked a little sand in his face to help him along.

"Do you even know where William is?" Denise asked.

"Yes, I do," Pam snapped. "Some experimental treatment—he's going to be out in a year. I heard he's getting off easy."

Denise saw Jonathan shake his head in disgust, and his face redden to the point of bursting. "Nobody knows exactly what that so-called *treatment* entails, so let's not refer to it as 'getting off easy' just yet," Jonathan hissed. He walked over to his desk, retrieved something from a drawer, and returned to the table. "We have a lot of work to do." He tossed an envelope onto the table in front of Pam. "Here's something for your time. Thanks for coming." He grabbed his coat from a chair next to his desk. "Denise, please lock up when you leave," he said as he walked out.

Denise knew they would now undoubtedly proceed with the case.

Stadler

Will waited for the next phase of the assembly with some anxiety. After ten minutes of nervous stewing, he finally heard Coates get things started.

"Time to finish the head frame—call in the med group," Coates spoke into the walkie-talkie.

"Roger that," came back, and Coates put the radio back in his pocket. "We have one more minor procedure, and then you'll be ready to be inserted into the system."

"What's the *minor* procedure?" Will asked nervously.

"The frame needs to be rigidly fastened to your head," Coates explained. "Some of the procedures that you'll go through later require precise positioning. The Exo uses a modified version of stabilization technology that's employed in brain surgery and radiation oncology. It keeps the head perfectly stationary—and precisely positioned."

A cart approached, chirped to a halt, then backed in towards Will's feet. Two men got out and opened a container on the flatbed, revealing a stainless steel hand-drill, and the remaining parts of the head frame.

Coates pushed a button on a remote control, and the Exoskeleton tilted backward until Will was facing the ceiling and suspended three feet from the floor, as if he were lying on a table. A tech started working immediately, fastening rods and brackets, and plugging in wires around his head. After a few minutes he said, "Time for the straps."

Will didn't like the word "straps" anymore. He knew something bad was coming.

Another man retrieved the nylon straps, and together the two techs weaved them through the frame and around his head. Will then heard a familiar ratcheting sound, the straps tightening around his skull until it was painful. When they were finished, his head was completely immobilized.

One tech walked to the cart and returned with a roll of gauze and a scalpel, while the other assembled the drill. Will thought he knew where this was headed, and tried to prepare himself. Sweat trickled into his eye.

The man with the scalpel rubbed ink around the edge of the metal rod and fed it through a hole on the head frame until it touched Will's forehead. Will saw his reflection in the tech's safety goggles: the cold, metal rod left a circular, blue mark on the upper-right part of his forehead, about an inch below where his hairline had been. The tech then made two incisions, forming a bleeding cross pattern centered on the blue mark, and then soaked up the blood around the incisions with the gauze. He then tore open one of the four pie sections of the cross pattern with a needle-nosed pliers, revealing white skull for a split second, after which the void filled with blood.

Will hissed in pain as he felt the skin being ripped away. His eyes watered, blurring his vision, but he felt the man tear open the remaining three flaps. Next, the other tech came in with the drill. He fed the drill bit through the same hole through which the marking rod was fed, and began drilling. It was slow and painful, and seemed to make his entire skull vibrate. Will now understood why the nurse had shaved his head so closely after the medical exam.

When the drill was removed, the tech inserted an object into the hole, and slowly twisted it back and forth. About a minute later, he removed the object and said, "It's tapped. Get the cement and anchor, and let's get this one set in."

In the distorted reflection from the goggles, Will saw them fill the hole in his skull with a white paste, thread in an anchor, and then feed a threaded, blue-metallic rod through the head frame and into the anchor. They finished by tightening two lock-nuts to secure the rod to the frame.

Although he couldn't see their work, Will *felt* the process being repeated three more times, for a total of four holes and four threaded support rods, all rigidly mounted to the frame.

Coates walked over. "That epoxy will be fully cured in an hour, and we'll release the straps at that point to make some final adjustments," he explained. "Then we'll put you into the insertion room for the night.

Tomorrow morning you'll start treatment. We're on time, thankfully."
Coates seemed relieved.

"Yes, thankfully," Will repeated quietly.

"Good work everyone. You all can leave—except for you guys,"
Coates said and pointed at a group of technicians. Coates now spoke into
his radio, "Let's get him something to eat for after that epoxy hardens." He
turned to Will, "We'll get you a burger; it's our only choice—New Year's
Eve."

A young tech jogged around the corner and stopped next to
Coates.

"Get the man a burger and some fries, and get me the same,"
Coates said.

The tech dug into his pants pocket and pulled out his car keys. A
few others placed their orders and gave him cash before he left.

"That'll take about forty-five minutes," Coates said. "We'll have
to *feed* you through that thing. It'll be a little messy, but don't worry—
you'll get a shower before you're put into rotation for the night."

"Rotation?" Will asked.

"You'll have to experience it for yourself."

The place was full of secrets, Will thought. The little information
he'd been able to acquire along the way was incomplete, and didn't help
him any. "I sure didn't know what I was getting into," Will said. "I
thought this was going to be a hard labor facility, or something to do with
hazardous duty ..."

"It's quite a bit more than that," Coates cut in. "We had a guy
come through last year who said he wasn't going to give them the pleasure
of hearing him scream. What a jack-ass... *Everybody* screams."

"*Scream*? Why did he scream? What happened to him?" Will
asked, even though he wasn't surprised—based on what he'd already
experienced in the medical and dental exams.

"You still don't get it," Coates said, shaking his head. "Why do
you think they were testing your pain thresholds?"

"Because the treatments will be painful," Will responded.

"They're *designed* to be painful."

The words made Will's blood run cold.

Coates spoke into his radio, and they lowered the Exo into a seated
position with its feet almost touching the floor. Coates then walked into

another room, leaving Will to himself for a few minutes until the food arrived.

Will was thoroughly frightened, but just sat there in an exhausted, unthinking daze. Before he knew it, the young technician had returned with the food, and was feeding him bite-sized pieces through his head gear.

Richard was enjoying the calming glow of his fireplace when his cell phone rang. He set his wine glass on the coffee table, sat forward on the couch, and looked at the caller ID on his work phone. The pit of his stomach always tightened when heard that ring-tone, but it was fully yanked into a knot whenever he saw Bergman's name. *It was 10 p.m., why was Bergman calling him at home so late?* He answered the phone.

"Richard, I wanted to see where you're at on that presentation," Bergman said.

Richard thought Bergman's words were slightly slurred. *Had the man been drinking?* "I just got the data from the Long Island facility this morning—they're always late—but it's ready to go. I'll get it to you tomorrow morning."

"This is an important one," Bergman said. "You know it's not just about the funding anymore."

"I know."

"It's about the *people*—the *subjects*," Bergman explained. "If our suppliers abandon the project, we're screwed—it won't matter how much money we have."

"I know," Richard replied. This was *not* news: *of course* Richard knew that the supply of human subjects was the most crucial aspect of the project. Bergman had successfully tapped every military, foreign, and penal resource available, and had generously compensated the respective suppliers. However, the more time that passed without results, the more nervous the suppliers became. And they *should* be nervous, Richard thought. One day, they'd all be hunted down like Nazi war criminals.

Bergman continued after an awkward pause. "There's something else I needed to talk to you about, but we can do that after the presentation."

"Something important?" The knot in Richard's stomach tightened even further.

"Of some importance, yes. Not to talk about over the phone," Bergman replied. "Having a nice New Year's with the wife?"

Richard felt it was an awkward change of topic. "We're just taking it easy tonight. And you?"

"And how are the girls—in bed already?"

"Hours ago."

"Sounds good… Have a happy New Year, Richard."

"You too," Richard replied and then hung up. He stared blankly at the fire. *Why was Bergman asking about the kids? And why had he been drinking?* He'd never known Bergman to drink.

"Something wrong?" his wife asked, interrupting his thoughts. She'd just walked into the living room with a newly-opened bottle of wine.

"No, just work stuff." He smiled the best he could, but knew his wife saw through it. He hated keeping things from her. But he'd done it for years now. He *had* to. It only added to the guilt.

Will watched Coates sign some paperwork and hand it off to one of his minions.

"Make the transfer—send him to the showers."

Will heard what sounded like claps and sighs of relief from the onlookers as the scorpion-vehicle transported him towards two giant, white doors. They extended all the way from the floor to the high ceiling, and had a large, red emblem in their center. The emblem looked like a tic-tac-toe board, but with a few extra line segments on the outer edges. He'd never seen such a symbol before, but it had a foreboding familiarity to it; something he couldn't put his finger on. The emblem split at its center as the two doors slid apart, to the left and right. The truck took him through the opening and into another room, where another Exo support arm, identical to the one on the vehicle, hung from a flat, chain-like track in the ceiling. Two winches lowered cables with hooks to aid in the switchover.

The techs made the switch, performed another quick systems check, and then left. The doors closed behind them with a loud, metallic latching sound, and Will assumed he was finally "fully inserted" into the system.

After about a minute of tense silence, Will saw and heard small hatches open on every surface of the room—the walls, ceiling, and floor. Nozzles poked out, and all at once warm water and soap sprayed from them with great force.

The Exoskeleton twisted and leaned, and even turned completely upside down at one point. After a few minutes, the soap and water mixture turned to pure water, then to some type of disinfectant—which made Will's eyes burn—then back to water again. After a final rinse, the nozzles retracted.

For a few seconds, all was quiet except for the sound of dripping and draining water. The calming sound was then interrupted by the rumble of two massive doors opening—one to Will's right, the other to his left. The Exo turned to face one of the newly exposed openings, leaned forward, and spread its arms and legs as if it had jumped out of an airplane.

Then began the whine of what sounded like an accelerating turbine. Hot air, rushed though the large doors, through the Exo frame, and over and around Will's wet body.

Everything was dry in less than a minute, and the doors began to close as the turbine slowed. Before the doors were fully closed, another—opposite the one he initially came through— descended into the floor. The track above rumbled and clicked as it moved the Exo through the opening. It stopped in the geometric center of a large, cubic room, as the door closed up behind, and the Exoskeleton repositioned itself horizontally, so that Will faced the ceiling.

The room was illuminated by a deep, blue light, the source of which Will could not locate—it seemed to be coming from all directions. A minute later, the light dimmed to near darkness, leaving a purple-haze afterglow in his mind, and a computer-generated female voice said, "Sleep time." The Exoskeleton then began to rotate slowly about an imaginary horizontal axis. Will estimated that it went through one revolution per minute, like the second hand of a clock. He now understood what Coates meant by 'putting him into *rotation.* '

The longest and worst day of his life was finally over. The longest and worst *so far*, he corrected himself.

CHAPTER III
Day One

Will awakened. It took him a few seconds to realize where he was, and he had no idea how long he'd been sleeping. He was still and faced the ceiling in a horizontal position—he was no longer rotating—and the room was now dimly bathed in a deep red light. As if it sensed he was awake, the Exoskeleton repositioned him upright, and turned him to face a door that was beginning to recede into the floor. Once the door had fully retracted into the threshold, Will was transported into a new room, which was identical to the one he'd just left. The door closed behind with a metallic clank, leaving him to stew in his thoughts.

After about ten minutes, the quiet was violated by the blast of a booming male voice. It resounded off the walls, and there was no way of determining its origin.

"Affirm that you are William Thompson by lifting your right arm and saying, *I am,*" the voice commanded.

Will instinctively moved his arm without thinking of his confinement to the Exoskeleton. As he raised it, he heard the high-pitched spinning of servo-motors and the hiss of pneumatics, and realized the machine was *assisting* his motion. "I am," Will replied.

The voice continued, "You have been convicted of rape and attempted murder, and were sentenced to twenty-five years in prison. You have opted instead for a three hundred and sixty-five day treatment in the compressed punishment system. You have made this choice without threat or coercion. With your right arm raised, say *I agree.*"

With his arm still raised, Will repeated, "I agree."

"Your treatment will start in twenty minutes, and will not stop until the program is complete, or you expire. You will not be released for any reason. Say *I understand.*"

"I understand."

His attention was then drawn to a humming sound coming from below him. He looked down to see a small hatch open in the floor, and watched as an object rose up through it. It stopped in front him, at chest-level; it was a metal post with a glass ball on the top.

The voice boomed again, "All patients are given the option of *self-deliverance.* The glass case on the device in front of you will retract to reveal a button. Pressing that button will release a poisonous gas into the room, and you will die in less than three minutes. It is painless. You now have seventeen minutes to make your decision. If time expires and you have not actuated the system, your treatment will begin. You will not be given this option again. Your right arm is mobilized so that you may actuate the device."

The glass case retracted to reveal a large, red button. A small projector lowered from a slot in the ceiling and projected the *time remaining* on the wall across from him: it read 16:43, and was ticking down.

Will was stunned. *Suicide?* Although he'd considered this on his own, he was astonished to be offered the opportunity so directly. He didn't know how to react, his emotions were all mixing together—but eventually it was anger that won out. He finally yelled, "Fuck you! I'm not giving up—*you'll* have to kill me!"

Will waited and listened, but there was no response. He stared in disbelief at the countdown clock: 11:43. His heart pounded and he released a scream of rage—no words, his mind reeling. Die painlessly, or go through a year of what? *Torture?* He'd probably be driven insane within the year anyway—especially being confined to the Exoskeleton.

The time ticked down to under two minutes, and Will shivered from the cold sweat that coated his body. His thoughts ricocheted back and forth between life and death. He argued both options to their respective ends a dozen times. Should he fight and try to start life over in a year? What did he have to look forward to in this world anyway—what was the rest of his life really *worth*? The decision became firm with a minute still left on the clock: his choice was not for life, but against death.

When the clock hit nineteen seconds, Will's right arm—the *Exoskeleton's* right arm—*moved.* Initially confused about what it was doing, he suddenly realized it was heading for the button. He resisted it with all his strength, but couldn't counter its motion even slightly. "You bastards!" he yelled, and continued to fight desperately against the arm.

The right index finger of the Exo made contact with the button and pressed it. Will felt his ears pop, and a sweet-smelling gas filled his nose and lungs. He had to close his stinging eyes, and everything went black.

It was so dark that Will couldn't tell whether his eyes were open or closed, and he could not sense his physical orientation. He felt like he was suspended in space with zero gravity, or in some sort of limbo. He squeezed his hand, couldn't make a fist, and concluded that he must still be in the Exo. His head throbbed with a hangover-like headache and he felt nauseous. "Where am I?" he yelled. The only answer was the immediate echo of his voice.

After waiting for an amount of time he couldn't quantify, the space around him gradually illuminated in dim, red light. A few minutes later, brighter red light poured in from above him. He realized he was oriented vertically, and saw parts of the Exo head frame in his field of view. The light came from a balcony above him, and the silhouette of a man came into view.

"Welcome to Hell, Mr. Thompson," the stranger said. His voice was loud and deep. "Did you really think you could escape punishment for your sins?"

Will was confused and couldn't respond.

"Now you can add *suicide* to your list."

Will recounted the events, despite the clouding headache. "I remember what happened. You can't trick me. I'm not dead."

"*Dead* is difficult to define, isn't it?" the man responded. "I'm sure even *you*, an arrogant scientist in your former life, suspected there could be life beyond death. Alive, dead—it is difficult to know. All that really matters is that you are *here now*."

"I'm alive. I'm still inside this fucking machine you put me in."

"Couldn't that machine be a part of your Hell?" the man asked and chuckled. "It would be logical to think that experiences from your former life might influence such things. No matter, you will come to your own conclusion in time."

"Who are you?" Will asked.

"I am in control. That is all you need to know."

The light in the booth brightened, and the figure that formed the silhouette was revealed: the man was tall and broad. Will couldn't tell if his face was red, or if it was just the red light with which it was illuminated. His hair was dark, and slicked back.

"Introductions are over... From now on you will be interacting with my ... employees ... who will conduct your torment. Good luck, *523*," he said, then turned and walked out of view. The balcony went black.

Will's eyes readjusted to the dim conditions, and he looked around impatiently. He could tell there was glass up high on the wall, to the left of the balcony and about fifteen feet up—a one-way window, he figured.

A male voice crackled from speakers on the wall, above the window. "We start each day with announcements," the voice said. "There are none today, except that it's New Year's Day."

The room suddenly lit up in white fluorescent light, forcing Will to squint his eyes tightly. The Exo hummed and vibrated, and he couldn't tell what it was doing until he felt a pull on his lower back; it was *stretching*. In a span of thirty seconds, every vertebra in his back had cracked, which felt good *initially*. But it kept going ... and going ... and the pain quickly became unbearable. Cold sweat rolled into Will's eyes.

"This is pain level six," the voice said.

The Exo hummed again, and Will's only reaction was an involuntary hiss that quickly built into a scream. He still heard the voice from the speakers over his own.

"This is PL 8.2," the voice said. "It will stay above eight most of the time."

After what seemed like an eternity, the pain decreased, and his screams faded. But he was unaware of any relaxation of the Exo. It hummed again, and this time it bent him slowly to the right, at the hip. Being already stretched near his maximum vertically, the strain on his side was immense. The muscles between his ribs stretched to the point of tearing, and it felt like one of his ribs might snap and poke through the skin. It held him in this state.

"That should give you a taste of what is planned for today," the voice said. "Since you continue to maintain your innocence, you will regularly be given the opportunity to confess your crimes. If you do, your treatment will be suspended for the remainder of the day. However, you'll be moved to the next treatment unit the following day, and your program will resume."

The Exo contracted and straightened, and the pain ceased. Will exhaled a breath of relief.

"Do you understand?" the voice asked.

"Yes." There was no way he was going to confess.

Thirty seconds passed and the voice boomed through the room again. "Did you rape Cynthia Worthington?" After a minute of silence, the question was repeated.

"Fuck off," Will finally replied.

"Very well." The message ended with an electrical click.

Will was more frightened than he had ever been in his life. If there had been any ambiguity as to the function of the Exoskeleton, it was gone now.

The Exo hummed again, only this time it lifted his arms to the sides, ending in an "iron cross" configuration. A second later the arms stretched slowly outward. It was like having a horse tied to each wrist, pulling in opposite directions. But rather than ripping him apart, it seemed the Exo would stop right at the tearing point. It twisted and bent— whatever it took to keep the pain level above eight. Will wished for death.

Richard watched as Bergman waited for the phone call; the man seemed to be under great stress. When the phone finally rang, Bergman leaned forward at his desk and hit a button activating the speaker-phone.

"What happened?"

"He didn't confess," a man replied. Richard recognized the voice as that of the Red Box Warden, Jack Halbreath.

"Damn," Bergman said and sighed in disappointment. "Did he push the suicide button?"

"No. He was quite defiant, actually."

Richard knew about ten percent of the subjects pushed the suicide button, although it wouldn't really *kill* them—it just knocked them out with some nonlethal gas... Although he had learned to hate every aspect of the CP program, he understood the significance of this initial event. It served two purposes. First, it was a *test*. If the subject pushed the suicide button, they would know he was susceptible to certain things—and the treatment would be adjusted accordingly. The second purpose was to instill fear and confusion in the subject; a few *really thought* they had died and gone into the afterlife. Incidentally, those were also the ones that seemed to end up in high-security, mental health facilities following their release. The illusion was more difficult to impose when the Exo had to force a subject to push the button, but it usually served its purpose: it set the tone for the psychological torment that would come later.

"The confession is not always an indicator," Richard said. He knew what Bergman was hoping for: confessions came early from those who were truly guilty. Bergman was looking for some reassurance, but it didn't come.

"A confession would have been nice to hear," Bergman replied. "We'll have to clean this up another way."

To Richard, Bergman's words had the darkest of connotations.

Will's throat and sinuses burned from hours of screaming. His muscles and tendons were inflamed, and his head felt like it was pressurized. He'd never imagined the pain one could feel from having their hands stretched to the brink of bursting apart. He figured his legs must be next—they hadn't done much with them yet.

A voice announced that it was "feeding time." He wondered *how* and *what* he would be fed, even though he hardly felt like eating. His questions were answered when a panel slid open in the ceiling, through which two tubes lowered and stopped directly in front of his face. The Exo adjusted its position, and tilted his head back, so that one of the tubes touched his mouth.

"Open your mouth and consume," a computer-generated voice ordered.

"What is it?" Will yelled.

A horrible shock jolted Will's body. "What the fuck?" he yelled. It hurt like hell.

"Open your mouth and consume," the voice repeated, coldly.

"Okay, okay," Will yelled, and opened his mouth. The tube went in, the "food" oozing out of it in spurts. Its texture was like that of oatmeal, but it had the smell of ground up multivitamins. The taste was awful—bitter—and he had to swallow without chewing, his stomach filling quickly. The first tube was removed, and the second moved in to deliver a fluid that tasted like an electrolyte drink. Finally, the tubes retracted and it was over. He felt like a caged, force-fed animal.

Will was already exhausted, but he knew the day was far from over. He hoped they would hold the treatment while the food settled in his stomach. While he waited, the *only* thing he could really do was to think, and his thoughts floated on a sea of fear.

He wondered why the Exo pushed the suicide button. *What did that mean? Could I really be dead?* He believed he wasn't, but how could he know what being *dead* was really like? And what was the *purpose* of the treatment—just to *torture* him? That didn't make sense: why would they need such an elaborate piece of machinery just to torture him?.

Will's thoughts were disrupted by the stiffening of the Exo's joints: stepper motors hummed, pneumatics sighed, and hydraulics hissed. It was time for the legs.

Denise was out of the city and onto the southbound highway before noon. The roads were clear of ice once she got south of Urban-Champaign, and the traffic on Interstate 57 was sparse. It was a perfect time to think.

She'd never considered that working for the Foundation might be *dangerous*: Jonathan had given her a *gun*, and the thought of it had been in the back of her mind ever since. She knew how to use a firearm—Jonathan knew that—but she never thought she'd be *carrying* one. And it was *illegal* in Illinois—at least it was for *her*, as she didn't have a license.

Jonathan had explained that, as far as he could tell, the CP program was run by elements of the Federal Government; *not* the Bureau of Corrections like most other prisons. The problem was that it wasn't clear *which elements* of the government were actually involved.

Two hours into the trip, Jonathan called to let Denise know he'd arranged an appointment at the DNA test center, and gave her the name of the contact. A few hours later, the GPS system warned her that the exit to West Frankfort was coming up on the right in one mile. She pushed a button on the display to zoom in on the target destination, and took a sip of coffee. Just a couple more miles to the DNA test center. She was starting to get nervous.

A minute later, she exited the highway and pulled into a gas station. She needed fuel, but she really stopped to gather her thoughts before the impending meeting, and possible confrontation. What *authorization* did she really have to be there? The case hadn't been reopened, she wasn't law enforcement, and she wasn't *legally* involved in any manner. The DNA Foundation was a *private* organization; what authority could they have?

She finished pumping the gas and used the bathroom, then pulled her Jeep Cherokee back out to the road and drove west, into the late afternoon sun. A few minutes later, she approached a plain white building on her right. It seemed to be of relatively recent construction, and of modern design, but it looked out of place with the surrounding scenery— especially with respect to the broken-down convenience store across the street, with its oil-stained gravel parking lot. The DNA facility had large, tinted windows in the front, and a brick sign on the brown lawn that read *StanTech Solutions, LLC.*

Denise pulled into visitors' parking, retrieved her briefcase from the back seat, and walked into the building. The front door led to a lobby with a few chairs and an unattended reception desk. Her eyes were drawn across the room to a metal door with an illuminated sign above it that read *Restricted Access.* There was a card slot with a flashing red light on the wall next to the door handle.

Her hands were sweaty, and she slowly paced and gathered her thoughts one last time. When she was ready, she knocked on the restricted access door. A moment later, a tall, pale woman in her late forties opened it and stuck her head out. She was wearing a white lab coat and latex gloves.

"Can I help you?" the woman asked.

"I'm Carmen Davis. I have an appointment with Kristine Camden," Denise replied, using her alias.

"She's in the lab. I'll tell her you're here," the woman said, and then disappeared behind the door.

Denise walked over to the unattended reception desk and noticed a sign-in ledger. Curious, she paged through it. At that moment, the restricted access door opened.

A small woman wearing light-blue scrubs and holding a pair of plastic goggles walked into the reception area. She itched the side of her head through her short brown hair, where the bands of her safety goggles must have been just minutes before. "Ms. Davis?" the woman asked.

"Yes."

"I'm Kristine Camden, nice to meet you," she greeted Denise and shook her hand.

"Thanks for meeting with me on such short notice. I'm surprised you're open on New Year's Day."

"We work every day except Christmas and Thanksgiving. Who are you with again?" Kristine asked.

"The DNA Foundation."

"Oh, right. Why don't you sign in," she said and nodded towards the ledger, "and I'll need to make a copy of your ID."

"Sure," Denise replied as she handed the woman her fake license.

Kristine made a copy, and handed the ID back to Denise. "Now, how can I help you?" Kristine asked as she crossed her arms and sat on the corner of the reception desk.

"We're interested in the William Thompson case," Denise explained as she put the ID back into her wallet. "Are you familiar with it?"

Kristine nodded and replied, "Of course, we were supposed to handle the testing for it. But that was a rape case; I thought you only took capital cases." Her facial expression changed from friendly to wary.

"We're also interested in cases where the sentences involve Compressed Punishment facilities."

"Compressed punishment?" Kristine seemed surprised.

Denise nodded.

"He just went into the Red Box two days ago—Detroit."

"So ... I can guess what you are looking for *here*."

"The DNA sample taken off the victim's body."

Kristine was silent. After a few seconds, she got up and walked over to a small office. She invited Denise to come in and sit down, and then closed the door. "I'll try to help you," she said as she sat down behind a small desk. "But I'll have to get a formal request to do it officially."

"I'll arrange it as quickly as possible," Denise replied.

"I can tell you few things—off the record—okay?" She was almost whispering.

Denise nodded and leaned in closer.

"The entire case, at least as far as StanTech was involved, was a complete disaster," Kristine explained. "A new technician, a novice, was responsible for those tests, a young woman—maybe twenty-two years old. She misplaced the samples."

"How many samples were there?"

"Five—two for the victim, blood and hair, the same for the suspect, and one from the rape kit, sampled from the girl's body immediately after the crime," Kristine explained.

"The most important one is the rape-kit sample—it can't be replaced."

Kristine closed her eyes and nodded. "Of course. They're *all* missing—either mislabeled or disposed of."

"I suppose you looked pretty hard for them," Denise said. It was a question.

"*I* didn't look for anything—the girl who lost them did. It wasn't my case," Kristine said. "But she was fired not long after that; completely incompetent."

"Do you think we could have another look?"

"You mean *you* want to go into the facility and search for those samples?" Kristine asked. Her eyes expressed doubt.

"Yes, but not *alone*, of course," Denise replied. "It's a long shot... But a man's life is at stake."

"Of course," Kristine said and nodded. "I'll have to ask my supervisor, but I can't guarantee anything... If it were up to me, we'd go in there right now, but—"

"Don't worry," Denise cut in, "clear it with him first. If he gives you trouble, tell him to call this man," Denise said, pulling out one of her alias business cards. She wrote down Jonathan's name and number on the back, then turned it over and showed Kristine her information on the front. It had the number of the pre-paid mobile phone she'd purchased the day before, and a dummy email address she'd set up to forward everything to her real Foundation email.

"Do you think you could give me a call, or send me an email, when you know something? I'll be here for a few more days."

"I will. In the mean time, I'll see if I can dig up those samples myself," Kristine said, and handed Denise her own business card. "I wouldn't get my hopes up if I were you, but I suppose it couldn't hurt to look again."

Denise thanked her and said goodbye. She got into her car and headed for the city of Marion, a half hour further south.

Even though the medical and dental tests of the day before had been horrific, Will thought the first day of real treatment was far worse due to the *duration*; the torture lasted the *entire day*. During the afternoon session, they had to insert a rubber mouthpiece because he'd bitten his lip several times, and continually ground his teeth together. He struggled so hard that his head bolts had bled, the blood trickling down his face in streams.

By the end of the treatment they had methodically addressed every body part, of which the feet were by far the worst. The arch and heal were particularly sensitive, and they finished the day by pulverizing the soles of his feet. The rod was pneumatically actuated, like a kill gun in a slaughter house, and it pounded away like a pool cue. The pain persisted after the treatment had stopped, his feet throbbing as they swelled and pressed against the surrounding metal of the Exo.

There were times during the day he pleaded to go back to conventional prison—he would've taken *life* imprisonment just to make the pain stop. At those points they'd again given him the opportunity to confess his crimes in exchange for relief; but he'd refused. They'd taken his name, his freedom, his life—he would not forfeit his innocence.

Will figured that they would take him to that point every day—the breaking point. Then again, he thought, the term *breaking point* had no real meaning; they would not stop just because he had a nervous breakdown. The program would keep running with complete indifference as to who it was contained within the Exoskeleton, or what they were *feeling*.

It was almost 11 p.m. when Jonathan's pipe went out for the last time, and he decided it was time to pack up and go home. There seemed to be no one else in the law building, and he was startled when the phone rang—the office landline. He answered, to find it was his wife, Julia. She wanted to know when he was coming home, and he told her he'd be leaving right away. He hung up, and sorted a few files he hoped to read in bed, if he could find the energy.

He twitched as the phone rang a second time. It was probably Julia again, he thought—she forgot something. He answered.

"Jonathan McDougal?" a gruff voice asked on the other end.

Startled, Jonathan replied, "Yes, who is this?"

He didn't recognize the voice.

"Drop the Thompson case immediately—or there will be consequences. This is your only warning."

The line went dead.

Jonathan checked the phone display, which read *Blocked ID*. Evidently, someone was aware that he was investigating the case—someone who perceived the action as a threat.

His thoughts moved to Denise, and he felt his stomach tighten—he'd call her as soon as he got home. Was she in danger now? Was the phone call in response to her probing the DNA lab? It made him nervous, but he concluded that they should proceed as planned—Denise would just have to work quickly.

Jonathan sighed, grabbed his coat and briefcase, and started the long walk home in the bitter cold.

The feeding process was messy, and Will estimated that nearly a third of what they'd forced on him had fallen to the floor. Nonetheless, he'd felt his stomach fill very quickly, and it was close to full capacity when the feeding had stopped. He was told that he had to make up for calories lost from vomiting during the day. Following a cleanup/sterilization process, the Exo lowered him into a low, horizontal position. A door opened, and four men in red overalls walked in, each carrying a tool kit. They didn't speak a word as they made some small mechanical adjustments, and changed out an electronics module. They were in and out in less than five minutes.

The Exo then moved Will to the middle of the room, and into a position about ten feet above the floor, facing the ceiling. All was silent; he only heard the white noise static of his own eardrums. The dim, blue light had appeared, and the uniformity of the room made the corners between the walls and the ceiling blend together. It gave him the impression of a vast, empty space with no boundaries.

Will was exhausted, but couldn't sleep. The anxiety of what might happen the next day kept his brain whirring. His thoughts finally converged on his parents, as they often had in the past year. He thought about all the sacrifices they had made for him, and now: all the wasted *time*. Having kids was a gamble: regardless of the effort, one could raise a serial killer—or a *rapist*. Or they could be lost to fluke circumstances—a car accident, or some other horrible thing.

Will had been ruined by fluke circumstances—*wrong place, wrong time*. And he wasn't only being robbed of his future, but also his *past*; all of his hard work, the respect of his family, his fiancee, career, and friends…

Will's thoughts were interrupted by a burst of loud clicking sounds. It startled him, but he quickly dismissed it as electrical discharge through the speakers in the room—there must have been a power surge. He felt the hair on his legs and arms raise, and he suddenly felt extremely cold—even seeing wisps of his own breath. Then something happened that sent a deeper chill through him: he thought he heard a *voice*—a whisper—maybe over the speaker system. It lasted just a few seconds, ended with another burst of clicks, and everything went back to normal, warm and quiet.

Will listened intently for a full minute, but heard nothing. He decided it was probably all in his head. The Exo began its slow rotation, and the faint blue light went deeper, leading him down into sleep.

Denise checked into the Marion Ramada Inn, then drove around town in search of a place to eat. It was getting late, but she found a fast food restaurant and took some food back to the hotel. She watched the local news while she ate, and saw that the top story was about William Thompson. His mug shot appeared behind the anchor man.

"Late yesterday evening," the anchorman explained, "Dr. William Thompson, a former local university professor, was taken by helicopter to St. Louis, and then transported to a private, maximum security prison in Colorado. Though details are limited, we understand he is to participate in a new correctional program for sex offenders." The footage showed Thompson, dressed in an orange prison jumpsuit and escorted by prison guards, boarding a helicopter. "Thompson was convicted of the rape and attempted murder of a local minor. Now, off to commercial ..."

Denise was startled by the ring of her cell phone. It was Jonathan.

"How are things are progressing?" he asked.

"Things went smoothly at the lab—did you get my voice message?"

"Yes, we faxed the formal request for the samples just a few minutes ago. Should be all set... I assume you'll head back to the lab in the morning?"

"Still waiting to hear from Kristine Camden, but it should be soon," Denise replied. "I'll let you know when we get started."

"Should you find the samples, I want you to come back immediately—even if you have to leave in the late evening. Understand?"

"Okay," she replied. The seriousness in Jonathan's voice frightened her a little. "Is something wrong?"

He hesitated. "No... Just better to get back as soon as you can."

Denise agreed and they hung up. Her level of anxiety ratcheted up a notch.

She sat back on the bed and took out a file folder. It was the background information that the prosecution had dug up on Thompson during the trial. The picture clipped to the first page struck her: it was recent, and he looked boyish. His eyes were friendly and intelligent, and they were of the darkest blue she had ever seen. She flipped through and found more pictures that ranged from his college days to his prison mug shot.

Thompson's appearance hadn't changed much since college. He was five foot ten, two hundred and fifteen pounds, with an athletic build and short brown hair. He was an All-American football player in college, and team Captain his senior year. He'd earned a doctoral degree in Physics from Louisiana State University, and then worked for the Department of Defense briefly before accepting a teaching position in Illinois. He did charity work in his community, received a teaching award from the university, and won a prestigious research grant from the National Science Foundation... Denise could see why Sorrensen's mother wanted her to marry him: *on paper* he seemed perfect.

But that was all irrelevant. The only thing that mattered now was finding the DNA evidence—and from what Jonathan had told her about the CP system's survival rate, even that might not be enough to save Thompson.

CHAPTER IV
Numbers and Voices

Six electric shavers simultaneously weaved their way through the Exoskeleton, over every accessible part of Will's body; something he would have to get used to as part of the morning maintenance routine. His joints ached from the treatment he'd been subjected to the day before, and although he could not see them very well, he knew his feet were particularly bruised and swollen from the abuse they had endured.

He waited in extreme anxiety, haunted by the thought of what this day might bring. After about twenty minutes, a door slid down in front of him, and the Exo was transported to a new room. The chamber was identical to the one in which he had suffered the day before—except for the odor of vomit and feces, partially masked by disinfectant. It was a combination he was sure he'd smell often, but knew he'd never get used to.

The transport appendage positioned him vertically in the geometric center of the room, and paused. Cold sweat trickled down Will's back.

Then it started: the Exo rocked from side to side, and up and down, like a boat on rough seas. He felt okay for about twenty seconds, but the motion quickly became more complex; random combinations of tilts and bobs. Violent twists were added— then sudden free-falls. The motion then became progressively more dramatic, with accelerations and decelerations that seemed to mimic collisions. It was not long before Will felt like his brain was sloshing around in his head. The nausea followed shortly thereafter, and he vomited a horrible acidic fluid—his partially digested breakfast. The kinetic torture went on for over an hour until the Exo slowed and came to a stop. Will was anxiously awaiting the next subroutine when the Exo turned him upside down, and the lights cut out.

Stadler

132

Richard Greene was relieved the presentation was over, but he knew from experience the real show had yet to begin. He peered out at the small audience, about a dozen people scattered about a conference room that seated fifty. The civilians wore dark suits, the military men donned respective uniforms, and not a soul spoke. Richard felt terribly awkward; at thirty-seven years old he was by far the youngest person in the room, and some of these men had been involved with the project before he was even born.

An ancient military man finally broke the silence.

"So let me get this straight: we've spent twenty-three percent of DARPA's total budget on this project, and we have *nothing* to show for it?"

"Admiral Sparkes," Richard replied. "Despite our lack of progress, it's too early to draw any definitive conclusions. The data we've collected—"

"Data? *What* fucking data? Tell me, why should we keep pumping *billions* of dollars into this sinkhole of a project? The risk is off scale."

A man in the back of the room spoke from the darkness.

"Admiral," Bergman said, "we'll keep funding this project because its success would be epic and transformative. The impact on our military supremacy would be similar to that of the Manhattan Project... It took the Germans *three years* of constant testing—at a rate that more than doubled ours—to get just *four* positive results. If *they* could do it, so can we; just like they *started* developing the A-bomb, and *we* finished it. This research is a low-yield process—like finding diamonds. Remember, the current objective is to *refine* the search process—and then to optimize the yield. It might mean just one success out of thousands of attempts. And, as you know, the quality of the starting material might slow things in our case."

"Bergman," the Admiral replied, "so far the total *yield* is *zero*. We've been in the testing phase for two years now—*more* than two years—and there's nothing reported that even resembles the predictions. *Not one event.* And even if we *do* have a successful conversion, what the hell are we going to do with it?"

"We'll study it. We'll determine what we did right, and try to develop it," Bergman replied, and looked out to the rest of the audience. "You all know that the plug could be pulled on this project at any time. Between the press, private organizations, even the new President, things are starting to get a little hot. Some people are already campaigning to shut down the facilities. If that happens, we'll *never get a chance to do this again. Never.*"

Bergman walked to the front of the room. "As you know," he said as he turned on the lights, "DARPA funds high-risk, high-potential research. This project constitutes both— both the risk and the potential gain being ... well ... *unlimited.* As the leader of this project, I've decided to keep the facilities running as they are for at least another year. We have the funds to do that, but all of you must renew your agreements for the supply of human subjects... As the risk is increasing for everyone, your compensation packages will be increased by fifteen percent for this renewal."

The crowd mumbled in a tone that Richard perceived as appoving. Money could buy a lot of things—even souls, it seemed.

"According to the projections, how much longer should we expect to wait for a positive event?" asked an aged woman near the front.

Bergman nodded for Richard to field the question.

Richard selected a slide on the computer presentation, and spoke as he guided a laser pointer over some numbers. "Figures from numerous studies, assuming we process over seven hundred subjects per year, indicate that it should take two years to produce a positive event. But this is only a statistical projection."

"Won't your processing rate go up when the new facility goes on line?" a navy man asked.

"Yes," Richard replied. "The Baton Rouge facility should speed things up dramatically. But it won't be operational for another twenty-four months."

Richard fielded a few more technical questions before Bergman adjourned the meeting.

"Thank you all for coming. We'll meet again in six months."

He placed some files in a metallic briefcase, then pushed a button on a remote, rolling the projector screen into the ceiling. He turned to Richard and said in a low voice, "Don't run off just yet, I need to speak with you."

Richard nodded and packed up his things. His stomach fluttered; maybe he'd finally hear what Bergman wanted to talk to him about on New Year's Eve.

Will felt a twitch and knew his inverted wait in the darkness was over. The Exo came to life again, beginning to orbit the room as rows of lights—hundreds of them—ignited on the walls. The lights scrolled by him faster and faster, changing color from bright white to red as he accelerated around the room. His stomach churned, and after about fifteen minutes he heaved. What little came out sprayed through the head frame of the Exo and onto the walls. Will's head pounded and he faded out of consciousness momentarily.

When he came to he was still orbiting, but at a reduced speed. Eventually he felt the machine come to a gradual halt, yet the room continued to spin. At first Will was confused, but then something dawned on him; it was the *lights*—they were programmed to maintain the illusion of motion. He closed his eyes but this did little to steady him, and he began to dry heave. It was the worst case of motion sickness he'd ever experienced, and the treatment had only just begun.

Stadler

Richard nearly had to jog to keep up with Bergman as he followed him to his office on the seventh floor. They entered and sat down at a small conference table.

"I think that went fairly well," Bergman said, referring to the meeting.

"I suppose we'll know in a few days when they renew their commitments... If they renew their commitments."

"Yes," Bergman replied, clearing his throat before he continued. "You know as well as I do that this project carries huge risk—"

Richard nodded. He sensed something bad was coming.

"And it's not just because of the amount of funds involved," Bergman explained. "The biggest risk is what history is going to say about *us*, Richard, and our country—when the cat is out of the bag... If that happens before we get any results, I worry what they're going to *do to us*."

Richard nodded. It was a legitimate concern. They could be tried for everything up to and including mass murder.

"We have a problem," Bergman said as he leaned back in his chair.

"Yes?"

"Have you heard of Jonathan McDougal?"

The name sounded familiar but Richard shook his head.

"He's a popular activist lawyer—been on TV here and there," Bergman explained. "He gets his nose into all sorts of things; he was involved in the death penalty moratorium in Illinois, and he's the current director of the DNA Foundation."

"What of him?"

Bergman took a deep breath and said, "*He's* the one pursuing the Thompson case. And it turns out there's a chance he could get it reopened."

"And you think he wants to expose the program?"

"That's *precisely* what he intends," Bergman replied. "Pulling an innocent man out of the program is a nightmare scenario. Investigative journalists would hone in like sharks. We'd have to shut down and scrap things in a big hurry."

"What do you want *me* to do?"

"We're going to monitor McDougal's communications, and I want you to head it up," Bergman answered.

"Why me? Security isn't my area."

"I need someone I can *trust* on this one."

The delivery of the statement, and the man's expression as he said it, made Richard uneasy. *Was Richard next in the interrogation chair?* He knew his imagination was getting the best of him: Bergman had no reason to think he was the source of the leak. If anything, it should be just the opposite: he would go down just as hard if the program were to be exposed. He had *designed* many of the system components. Just like the Israelis tracked down the designers of the death camps, the authorities would get to him, too.

"That reminds me," Bergman continued, "any news on the missing files?"

The words made Richard itch. "No. But I saw on the news this morning that they pulled Frank Weiss' body from the Potomac last night."

Bergman nodded. "Yes, it's unfortunate."

"Suicide?"

"Of course not," Bergman replied without hesitation. "The consequences of disloyalty are quite clear."

Richard couldn't believe Bergman had just admitted to killing the man, or *having* him killed. He knew such things occurred, but this was the first time he'd ever been so close to it. "I guess he rolled the dice, and lost."

"Sure did," Bergman replied.

Richard left Bergman's office and headed for his own. The situation was getting pretty heavy now, but it seemed an ending was in sight. He just didn't know what that ending *was*. He could feel a plan forming in the back of his mind—all of the pieces were there. Soon it would be *his* turn to roll the dice.

They'd given Will an unusually long lunch break—probably so his body had a chance to absorb the nutrients before he vomited the food out again. But his insides felt progressively worse as time went on.

He remembered the form he'd signed giving consent for the insertion of a *feeding tube*. If he couldn't hold down his food, they'd probably do just that. He had no idea how it worked—but he was sure he didn't want to find out. Presently, he had new problems brewing that required his attention. The Exo twitched: it was time to commence the treatment.

The Exo started by spinning Will around the room, legs-out now, and he felt the blood drain from his head. He grayed out continuously, just barely holding on to consciousness, and the pain in his lower abdomen progressed. Finally, the pressure buildup in his bowels was just too great—and he let it go, the contents dousing his back and legs. The stench was immediate and strong, causing him to gag. The Exo continued to spin and twist, and with the help of the horrible smell in the air, Will dry-heaved on and off for the remainder of the treatment.

After what seemed like an eternity, the Exo decelerated and returned to the center of the room. Will felt utterly humiliated—he was coated in his own excrement, dizzy-drunk and completely exhausted. Maybe, he desperately hoped, it was over for the day.

A male voice came over the loud speaker, "Give us the number."

"What?" Will yelled, utterly confused. After a few seconds of silence, a horrible shock jolted his body. "What the hell?!"

"Tell us the number," the voice repeated, more forcefully.

Will searched desperately for a number—the walls, the Exo, the ceiling. There was no number anywhere.

Another shock tore through him. "Tell us the number."

"Okay, okay." He gave them the first random number he could conjure. "Twelve." He waited in anticipation. No shock, no response.

Denise opened her email and found over twenty unread messages. Weeding out the junk mail, she found four or five legitimate messages: one from Jonathan, a few from personal friends, and one from "KCamden@StanTech.net," with the subject line reading: *Your Visit.* The email was addressed to her alias, and read:

> *Ms. Davis:*
> *We received the DNA Foundation's fax formally requesting the release of the DNA samples (if we find them). My supervisor said you are welcome to help us search after hours -- which means after 8:00 p.m tonight. —Kristine*

Denise had nothing to do until 8:00 p.m. In the mean time, she'd read case files and wait.

Will thought his head would never stop spinning. The feeling persisted through his feeding, and he fought to steady his queasy stomach, still fearing the possibility of a feeding tube. It was only during the cleaning routine that he began to recover.

It felt like a year since he'd been inserted into this earthly version of Hell, but it had only been two days, three if he counted the first day of medical and dental tests. Will already felt as if he'd been fundamentally changed. He recalled what the psychiatrist—Dr. Cole—had said about the treatment involving 'spiritual aspects.' It seemed he was starting to understand what that meant. If spirituality had anything to do with *hope*, his so-called spiritual outlook had most certainly shifted towards the negative.

Will examined the blue-white metal of the Exoskeleton. There was a certain beauty in its complexity—but it was still his captor and tormentor, and he felt hatred for it. He was its soft, organic inhabitant, like a snail in a shell: only his shell served a very different purpose.

The lights dimmed, and the Exo began its slow rotation in the sleep cycle.

Will knew a new day would arrive all too soon.

As she headed north on the interstate toward StanTech, Denise wondered about the orange glow in the sky to the northwest. Her nerves tingled, and though she wasn't sure how, she knew something was wrong. She exited the highway, but kept up her speed. As the jeep rounded the final bend, she felt the heat from the blazing inferno just a hundred feet ahead. The flames illuminated a dozen scurrying firefighters, as well as the emergency vehicles, their flashing lights almost invisible against the fiery backdrop.

Denise's first thought was of the evidence; *even if it had been there, it was gone.* She drove closer, watching numbly as the firefighters sprayed down the ruined building. Flames licked high into the night sky, and hot gasses hissed sporadically. Suddenly her mind flashed to Jonathan's warnings of potential danger, and she had to fight the urge to flee. She pulled into the gravel parking lot of the convenience store across the way, then stepped out and approached a fireman.

"How did this happen?"

"Ma'am, I can't answer any questions unless you're law enforcement, in which case I need to see a badge," he replied as he rolled out a hose.

"Was anyone hurt?"

"Like I said, if you're not law enforcement you need to move along. Go on now."

Denise was about to say something to the man, but suddenly felt sick to her stomach and ran back to her car. She got inside and pulled out her temp phone to call Kristine Camden. The call went straight to voicemail, and gooseflesh perked up all over her body. She locked the car doors, and frantically searched her purse for something. Taking out the

Glock 40, she inserted the clip and clutched the weapon in her trembling hands. A few seconds later, she sighed, removed the clip, and put the gun back in her purse. She was just being paranoid.

Denise turned the Jeep around and saw that the firemen had put up a road block to stop traffic from coming in from the west. One car had already turned around to head back when a dark SUV approached the barrier from that direction, and stopped. A large man, the driver, got out and spoke to the firemen. A second man emerged from the passenger side, and stared at Denise's car as the driver argued with the fireman; she could see he was trying to talk his way through the barrier.

The hair on her neck bristled. She panicked and gunned the Jeep, causing the tires to spin and spit gravel until they chirped on the pavement of the road. In her rear view mirror she could see the driver was now yelling at the firemen. She sped away. She had no idea why she was fleeing in such a panic, gut instinct was directing her actions.

Denise sped the two miles back to the gas station she'd stopped at the day before, and parked the car in the lube-service lot on the east side of the building. It was dark there, and she backed in between two cars so she could see the oncoming traffic from the west. She dialed Jonathan's number, but there was no answer. Once more she removed the handgun from her purse, cradling it in her lap. A few seconds later, she saw the headlights of the dark SUV speeding in from the west. Her heart pounded, and she slouched down as far as she could without obscuring her view of the road. The SUV slowed to a crawl as it passed the station, and she saw the face of the driver scanning the lot through an open window. She was right—they were looking for *her*.

To her relief, the driver gunned it towards the interstate. *They'd missed her*. She could see the northbound on-ramp of I-57 out her side window, and watched the SUV speed down it and onto the highway. She'd survived their initial pass, but they would most likely double back at the next exit.

Denise didn't want to be caught on any back roads—there might be others looking for her as well. Instead, she thought of a way to get past them on the highway. The timing of her departure was critical—she'd want to be about a mile behind them when they hit the first exit to turn around. That way she could catch them as they crossed the overpass. She turned on the GPS and found the next exit to the north—it was six miles up. She started the Jeep, and headed for the interstate.

She drove down the ramp, and was on the highway for a mile before she turned on her lights. There were a few cars ahead of her, none of them the SUV, and a semi-truck was approaching from behind. There was little oncoming traffic from the north, and she passed the exit she thought her pursuers might use to turn around—it was dark.

Then something happened about a mile ahead that made her heart skip a beat: she saw brake lights, and a vehicle bouncing across the grassy median—the SUV turning around. *It was foolish to think they would use an exit.*

The approaching semi was now a few hundred feet behind her. Denise slowed from seventy to sixty, and prayed for the truck to pass her. To her relief, she saw the bright yellow turn signal in her side mirror, and the truck switched to the left lane. As it started to pass, she sped up slightly to keep up, shielding herself from the view of oncoming traffic. She watched her rear view mirror and saw the tail lights of the now southbound SUV. She bumped up her speed up to 80 mph—she had to get back to Jonathan.

It was 8:20 p.m, and the GPS calculated her ETA to be 1:35 a.m.

The situation had gone over the deep end; who were her pursuers, and how did they know who she was? She reached for a bottle of water on the passenger seat and felt her hand tremble. As Jonathan had warned, this was much bigger than a *rape case.*

Denise's mind raced with her all the way back to Chicago.

Stadler

Will was awakened by the sudden halt of the rotating Exo. The night had been just a flash, and morning had dawned on Day Three. He flexed and stretched—the best he could in his confinement—and the lingering pain from the activities of the previous day pulsed through his body. The pressure behind his eyes was immense; it couldn't be too healthy having one's brain sloshing around for hours.

The feeding apparatus came down to fill him with his morning mush. The paste he was force-fed changed flavors for breakfast, lunch, and dinner—or meals *one*, *two*, and *three*. He felt it was better to give the meals a number—like his personal name—rather than associate them with anything from the civilized world.

After *meal one*, he went through the usual maintenance and sterilization routine, and the Exo transported Will to the next room, where he noticed the faint scent of chlorine. There were no announcements, and he was given the opportunity to confess his crimes in exchange for a "day of rest." He told them to "fuck off." This, he'd decided, would be his usual response.

"Very well," the voice boomed.

The Exo lowered to the floor and positioned Will on his back. He heard valves squeak open and water rushing onto the floor—they were flooding the room. He felt the cold water slowly inch up his body through the Exo. The process was the epitome of a claustrophobic nightmare.

Soon the water level rose above Will's mouth so that he had to breathe through his nose. His ears fully submerged, he could hear the burble of running water superimposed on white noise. The water finally engulfed his nostrils. After a half minute his lungs were on fire, and he badly needed a breath. He was on the verge of panic—soon he'd inhale uncontrollably, and his lungs would fill with water.

At the precise moment his breath would no longer hold, the Exo rose several inches, pushing Will's nose and mouth about one inch above the surface. He gasped hard, coughing violently. Snot ran out of his nose, and he tasted the salty mucous on his lips. He caught his breath and shouted, "Fuck you, assholes." His anger momentarily surmounted his fear.

The water inched upwards.

It was 7:30 a.m. when Denise knocked on Jonathan's office door. She needed rest, but she needed his company even more. She'd made it home before 2:00 a.m. that morning, but was unable to sleep due to the residual adrenaline of her encounter, and the thought that Kristine Camden might have burned to death in the lab. She heard Jonathan's voice through the door.

"Come in."

She walked in and quickly sat down as her vision blurred from the tears welling in her eyes.

"My God—What's wrong?" Jonathan asked, moving to console her.

"I tried to call you last night... I was just trying to keep my head on... I had to think—"

"Denise, take it slowly—tell me what happened." He took a seat across from her.

She wiped her face and took a deep breath, steadying herself.

"The DNA test facility burned to the ground last night. When I arrived, they were trying to put out the fire, but the place was already wiped out—completely... My contact, Kristine Camden... I think she might be dead..."

"My god," Jonathan said as he stood up and retrieved a remote control from his desk. He opened a large cabinet between two massive book shelves to reveal a large TV, and turned it on. "I don't know if the local news will cover the southern part of the state, but we'll see. It comes on at eight o'clock. If not, we'll check CNN or something—maybe it made national news." He took a seat across from Denise and poured her a cup of coffee.

Denise took the cup, and another tear rolled down her cheek. "I know it has something to do with our case... When I got to the lab I was chased by two men in a black SUV... Oh God, maybe if I'd been more careful—"

"This is not your fault," Jonathan said, cutting her off. "You can't think like that, because it just isn't true."

Denise nodded. She understood, but still felt guilt.

"We've been nosing around on this case, and others, for months—requesting files, and so on," Jonathan explained. "Our adversaries, whoever they are, aren't stupid. They're *watching* us; they know what we're doing... I got a phone call—"

He was distracted by the television and grabbed the remote to turn up the volume.

"... Now let's turn it over to Gillian Stevens, reporting from West Frankfort, Illinois," the news anchor said.
"Thanks Todd," a young, female reporter continued. "The bodies of two female employees were found in the burnt wreckage of the StanTech Solutions building, a DNA testing facility here in southern Illinois. The women have been identified as Kristine Camden, a resident of West Frankfort, and Lynn Crebbs of Benton, Illinois. Initial reports indicate foul play: both women were shot, doused with accelerant, and burned along with the building... Police have no suspects as of yet..."

"I knew it," Denise cried as she stared at the women's pictures. She recognized Kristine's face, but not that of the other woman.

Jonathan shook his head slowly and grasped one of Denise's hands across the table. "We're in pretty deep now."

"I know," she replied. She had a dark feeling, like falling into a well. But she had to let it go—she had to press on. "You were saying something about a phone call?"

Jonathan let go of her hand and sat back. "Yes— a man called and threatened me about investigating the Thompson case."

Jonathan turned off the TV and turned to Denise, looking her directly in the eyes.

"I'm going to ask you a very important question now… Knowing the stakes, considering the fact that two people are now dead, do you want to continue with this?"

"*Of course I'm going to continue*," she shot back, almost yelling. "Of all things—I'm not a quitter... I'm seeing this through, Jonathan."

"Okay, okay …" he cut her off and seemed to smile in relief. "I had to ask. You're my intern, my student, I'm *responsible* for you."

"*You* don't want to quit, do you?"

Jonathan answered with a loud laugh.

"So what's the plan?" Denise asked.

"Without the DNA, we're in trouble—the Thompson case is probably dead for us," Jonathan admitted. "We need to reevaluate our plan of attack. But right now I'm more concerned about the men who came after you… How did they know you? How did they find you?"

With her mind on the chase, and the demise of Kristine Camden, Denise hadn't fully realized the implications of the previous night. *What kind of people were they dealing with?*

The submersion process repeated until the room filled to a depth of about ten feet—halfway to the ceiling. That's when the lights went out. In the pitch darkness, the Exo took Will on a hellish ride during which he was slammed on the surface of the water, and repeatedly dunked at varying speeds and intervals. His perception of his orientation was so skewed he couldn't predict when he was approaching the water, or when he was about to surface. When out of the water, he gasped desperately to fill his lungs—so that he might survive the next excursion into the dark depths.

Stadler

Bergman answered his phone, "I saw on CNN you took care of that business in Illinois." He was not pleased it made national news.

"We had to move quickly—one of the women hit an alarm," Lenny explained.

"So we're clear then?"

"Yes and no," Lenny replied. "If the DNA was still in the building, it's destroyed... But we know there was someone poking around the place the day before... One of McDougal's... They may have been at the lab that night as well."

Bergman perked up. "Who?"

"A woman, *Carmen Davis*. We got a copy of her driver's license and a business card off one of the lab techs. The license is fake, but the card says she's an employee of the DNA Foundation."

"And what about the contact information?" Bergman asked.

"McDougal's info was handwritten. Her phone number is unlisted," Lenny replied. "It's a pre-paid phone. But we might get something from her email."

"Have security hack it," Bergman instructed. "We'll discuss our next move once you're back."

He hung up the phone and sat down at his desk. It was always going to be like this, he thought, always plugging little holes in the dike. If they could just get one positive event, he'd be able to justify quitting. He'd revel in glory as they refined the program, and found new ways to utilize new human weapons. He'd be famous, within certain circles anyway, and *free...* But there was still so much to be done.

Will consumed meal two and afterwards was suspended horizontally, facing the water, for forty-five minutes. There was usually about an hour of down time during lunch, and a fifteen minute break in the afternoon. He knew that there had to be people behind the glass, controlling and observing the treatments. He figured the down times were probably for their lunch and breaks.

Will wondered about the degree of human control in the treatments, as their nature allowed little room for error. He thought it might be better for him if they did screw up—he'd be spared the remaining torment.

His thoughts were interrupted by a female voice over the intercom, it said, "Tell us the number."

Wanting to avoid a shock, Will immediately shouted the number seventeen. There was no response, and he wondered what the point of this exercise was. Were they playing games—was this part of the psychological torture? He admitted it did cause some added anxiety.

They started the afternoon session, and the remainder of the day involved similar, but more violent water play than that of the morning. At one point he woke up with a tube down his throat and blood coming out of his nose. He'd *accidentally* taken a breath at the wrong time, and they'd had to revive him. He could easily have died right then and there, but the program wouldn't let him off that easy.

When the treatment was over, Will was forced to consume a double dose of food at meal three to make up for all he'd vomited during the day.

After the feeding, the Exo positioned him horizontally for the brief period before the sleep cycle began. Suddenly, out of nowhere, Will thought he heard a voice. Somehow close, but distant at the same time.

He felt a chill, and his skin puckered into goose-pimples. For the next full minute he barely breathed, listening intently—but all he heard was the pounding of his heart. After a few more minutes he concluded that it must have been his imagination. The lights dimmed to cold blue, and then to black as the sleep cycle started.

CHAPTER V
Genesis

On Day Ten, Will got his first announcement: "Your house, and its contents, have been sold at auction," the voice on the intercom informed him. "The balance of what you owe will be covered by a federal loan in your name, with interest to be accrued retroactively to the day of your insertion."

He figured the balance was a large number; but *he didn't care*. "Good luck collecting," he scoffed. Will was angered by the thought of his possessions being auctioned—he had a vintage classical guitar, given to him by an old, now deceased, friend. The item had great sentimental value to him... But he currently had more pressing things on his mind— like what unknown horrors were planned for him on this new day.

The controller gave Will the standard opportunity to confess, he gave them his usual response, and then it started. The Exo stretched out his left arm as though he were reaching for a door knob, and spread out his fingers. Two appendages lowered from a port in the ceiling and passed a few feet from his face: they were complex, robotic *hands*, a left and a right. They were sleek in design, and had a flat-black finish. One of them positioned itself near Will's outstretched hand, and a glistening, curved blade popped out of one of its fingertips—the thumb. It moved in slowly, and all Will could do was watch as it approached.

He felt cold metal touch his skin, and the blue-metallic blade slowly sliced its way under his left thumbnail, vibrating as it moved. It dug in about half way to the cuticle, and stopped. His thumb throbbed and burned at the same time, and the pressure mounted even though the blade remained still. After about five minutes, it continued on its path to the nail bed, and paused. His legs and arms twitched uncontrollably, but the blade remained stationary.

A few minutes later, another blade popped out from the mechanical hand, and slowly carved a path under his left index fingernail. It took another five, long minutes to reach the nail bed.

Will screamed sporadically, his voice diminishing to a raspy whisper, as the procedure was repeated for each of his fingers.

After about two hours, the machine had finished inserting blades into the ten nail beds, and the program paused as the pressure in his fingertips increased. The fluid that oozed from under his nails had gone from blood to a clear liquid, and he heard it drip on the floor.

Just as Will's nerves were beginning to settle, the bladed, mechanical fingers started to *tap*. *Tap tap tap* … the machine played a tune of pain. Every muscle in his body convulsed with each minute percussion of the blades.

After what seemed like an eternity, the program reached a final phase: the twisting of the blades. Will whimpered pitifully, continually on the verge of passing out.

The blades finally retracted, and his bleeding fingertips were dipped in an antiseptic fluid. While his fingers stung horribly in the chemical solution, the controller asked Will for a number, and he gave him one. As usual, there was no response, and it was time for meal two.

On the morning of January twelfth, Richard heard Lenny mention something about *StanTech,* and the "Illinois facility" to Bergman. That afternoon he ran a quick internet search on StanTech and was mortified by what he found; evidently they were now killing civilians.

Richard knew he'd had enough. First, he decided, he would have to come clean with his wife: he'd tell her everything about the project. It was the only way to convince her to leave, and even if she divorced him, at least she and the girls would be safe. Second, it was time to set his plan in motion: Bergman had supplied him with the perfect contact: Jonathan McDougal. It was time to roll the dice.

The morning of day fifteen was no different to Will than other days—but the announcement he was given caused him more pain than he'd ever known.

The voice over the speakers said, "Two days ago, both of your parents were killed in a car accident. It was a head-on collision, and both were pronounced dead at the scene. The other driver is in stable condition. Reports indicate that your father was legally drunk at the time of the crash. The funeral is this afternoon." An electrostatic click ended the announcement with a dead sense of finality.

When Will was finally able to process the information, he screamed at the top of his lungs. No words, just guttural, agonized screaming. A sense of profound emptiness engulfed him. He didn't believe it—he couldn't believe it. His father didn't drink—at least not before he had been arrested.

Will's sadness turned to shear rage, and he tried to shake himself free of the Exo. The effort was violent but futile; his struggling only made his head bolts bleed, and the tantrum was put to an abrupt end by a harsh and prolonged shock that nearly knocked him out.

A minute later the Exo hummed and positioned Will to face the glass. The voice on the intercom asked, "Did you rape the girl?"

Will didn't reply; his anger had paralyzed him.

The voice continued, "Did you rape Cynthia Worthington?"

Will spoke calmly and deliberately. "Fuck you. When I get out of here, I'm going to find you. *All* of you."

After a short delay with no response, the Exo hummed, and Will felt something adjust on his left leg. The Exo had an *extra* joint—at the midpoint above his knee and below his hip—right in the *wrong* place. He understood immediately what he was in for. The "thigh joint" on the Exo flexed and Will felt his femur begin to bend in small increments. The machine hummed, then stopped. Hummed, stopped. After the fourth iteration, his quad muscles quivered uncontrollably, and the pain deepened. He noticed other Exo joints now; in the middle of his shins, arms, and forearms.

The technician flinched when Warden Halbreath slammed his fist on the control room table.

"Damn! This one usually breaks them."

The tech never had the Warden come into his control room so early in the morning. And he'd certainly never seen him look *worried*.

Halbreath addressed the tech, and the medic sitting next to him. "I want you to keep the pain level as close to nine as you can. Offer him the afternoon off *again* in exchange for a full confession—and double check that the recorders are on. We need to break this guy."

The tech and medic nodded in unison.

"We can't have patients getting this far without confessing. Do you understand?"

"Yessir," the tech responded.

Halbreath looked at the medic, "Give me an update after you make the offer."

The medic nodded.

Halbreath whirled to leave, his jacket blowing a Styrofoam cup off the technician's desk as he nearly *ran* out of the room.

"What the hell?" the medic said under his breath. "Ever have that happen?"

"Nope," the tech replied, shaking his head. "But I haven't seen a patient make it this far without breaking, either."

"We're at PL-seven," the medic informed. "Let's inch it up." He stepped up to the control panel and turned down the volume for the treatment room microphone—the screaming was getting to be a bit much for so early in the morning.

Richard tried to calm himself as he watched for his wife through the café window. He and Claire met for lunch on occasion, despite their busy schedules. Claire's was more unpredictable than Richard's; as a pediatrician, she was called in often, and at strange hours. But today she was supposed to be completely free.

He watched Claire pull her Volvo into the parking lot, and navigate ice patches on her way into the Café. He waved to her as she came in, and she walked over, kissed him on the cheek, and sat down across from him.

They both ate light, and when they were finished Richard said, "Would you like a refill: I have something I want to talk to you about."

Claire responded with a look of mild alarm, and handed him her cup. A few minutes later, he returned with the fresh coffees, and took his seat.

"This is very important," Richard began, "and you have to promise you won't overreact."

"Richard, are you cheating on me?"

"What?" Richard was confused for a moment. "No." He almost wished it had been something like that. "No, it's about work." He looked at her face and realized he'd missed a joke. She was trying to lighten the mood, but it didn't make things any easier.

"Are you losing your job?"

"Please, Claire, let me talk," Richard said in a serious, yet shamed tone. "What I do for a living isn't exactly what you *think* I do—at least not anymore." He shook his head. "It's turned into something else entirely."

Claire's expression turned to confusion. "You're still a *bioengineer*, right?"

Richard nodded.

"You're still lead engineer on the DARPA project?"

"Yes," Richard replied, and nodded again. "But the *project* has gotten out of hand, along with the people who run it."

"Aren't you still developing the Exoskeleton?"

Richard motioned with his hand for her to keep her voice down. "Yes, we are. But not for the reasons you think."

"You mean it's not for helping accident victims?"

"It *started* that way—at least I *thought* it did—when I was at Syncorp," Richard explained. He remembered being recruited by Syncorp right out of grad school under the premise he'd be working on a new bio-interface system, for medical purposes. It was designed for rehabilitation: spinal injuries, nerve damage, muscular atrophe, etc. The Exoskeleton could keep bones set, supply spinal traction, administer medications, monitor bio-data, and so many other things. From the very beginning, he knew that Syncorp was a government subcontractor; which had made the position even more attractive. He knew the funding would be plentiful, and he'd have the opportunity to develop a state-of-the-art system that would actually help people. When he was offered a position with DARPA, he jumped at the opportunity—he had no idea where the work would eventually lead.

"What is the Exoskeleton used for now?" Claire asked.

"Can I see your phone?"

"What? Why?" she asked as she handed it over.

Richard quickly took out the battery and the SIM chip, then did the same to his phone. He knew there were ways to monitor conversations through cellular devices. He didn't want to take any chances.

"What the hell's going on, Richard?"

He could tell Claire was frightened, and found himself thinking it might be a good thing. She needed to understand the gravity of the situation, and the consequences of what he was going to do. He proceeded to tell her everything, even about the murders.

While trying to get the taste of meal two out of his mouth, Will thought he wasn't going to survive the afternoon. In the morning treatment, the Exo had methodically worked over his left femur, shin, upper arm, and forearm. Each had been extremely painful, but the femur had been the worst by far. On occasion he thought he actually *heard* the cracking of his bones. He was sure the stress must have produced a multitude of hairline fractures.

Even through the physical pain, his thoughts were of his parents. Will realized that, in a single year, his existence had been reduced to a periodic toggling between physical misery and acute mental anguish; one pain always on the verge of eclipsing the other.

The Exo stiffened and his thinking time was over.

The intercom voice boomed, "Admit that you raped the girl and you will be spared the afternoon treatment."

"How many different ways can I tell you bastards to fuck off?" Will shouted.

"This will be the worst treatment so far. Are you sure you won't reconsider?"

"I said, *fuck off.*"

Seconds later, the Exo sprang to work. It started with his right forearm, then switched to his shin, upper arm, and femur—which is when his bladder let go. The program then repeated the sequence, only bending the limbs in a different direction.

Two hours later they returned to the femur. Will's vision was going dark and he felt he was on the verge of losing consciousness. But then something unexpected happened …

It was the *pain* … it was *gone.*

Stadler

The medic came back into the control room, closed the door, and took his seat behind a computer. "The warden was pretty pissed," he said, shaking his head. "Said to make sure we 'rode him on nine' for the rest of the afternoon."

"Why is this guy getting so much attention?"

"Don't know…He's a pedophile—raped a teenager…"

"Oops—sounds like he went out again," the tech interrupted.

The medic checked the sensors, first on the computer monitor and then on the control board. The computer displayed the most basic sensor readings, but the control board had everything—over a hundred readouts.

"Not according to my sources. He's still conscious."

"But he's not making any noise… The pain level is at 8.9," the tech said, and clicked a button to increase the strain. Still no sound. "What the hell's going on?" He stood up, looked through the window to the experimental floor and shrugged.

"Maybe the PL monitors aren't working," the medic suggested. Again he examined the panel of readouts. "They all seem fine. They're multiple-redundant systems, anyway—they don't *all* fail at once. Better call engineering."

The pain was gone, but for a reason Will didn't understand. He was even more confused about his current state of mind, or *perspective*. He was now observing his own straining face *from above*.

The pain was still present *somewhere*—he could *sense* it—but he was not *feeling* it. He was somehow on the *outside*. He looked at the Exoskeleton, then *touched* the hydraulic piston that was exerting pressure on his femur. It was warm and vibrating. He felt his right thigh muscle twitching—only from the *outside*. And then, without warning, the pain was back …

Stadler

"... oh ... never mind—it's okay," the tech said to the engineer over the phone. He turned down the volume of the floor microphone. "We're back in business," he added as he hung up.

"Never saw anything like *that* before—a man not screaming at PL 8," said the medic, shaking his head.

"Me either," the tech replied. "Well, whatever it was, we should write it up... and we better get the final program loaded—I want to get out of here on time."

He set up the program and initiated it.

Stadler

The pressure on Will's femur was released, and he hoped it would be the end of the treatment for the day. But it seemed too early.

After a five minute lull, he heard a humming near his ears, and his hopes were dashed. The *head-cage* contracted slowly, and he felt an immense pressure on his skull. In just a few seconds, it felt like his head was being run over by a truck. The pressure persisted for about ten minutes, during which the head-cage made slight radial and lateral adjustments. It then contracted slightly again, the pain intensifying and producing nausea. Somehow Will held down the contents of his stomach; he was getting better at that.

When the head-cage finally expanded back to the neutral position, a rush of headache pain surged in his skull, and his eyes felt like they were going to pop.

After a short lull of inactivity, the head-cage hummed again, even though Will hadn't fully recovered from the head rush. This time it *expanded*—pulling outward on the four head bolts. It felt like his head was bursting apart, and this time his eyesight blurred, faltering. He still heard and felt the Exo making fine adjustments for what seemed like twenty minutes, after which the pressure decreased slowly, and his vision gradually returned.

Was it over? After a five-minute, anxiety-ridden wait, he heard the servos whine again: this time they *all* moved—from those at his feet, all the way to his head. It was the *grand finale.* They were bending everything at once—both femurs, both shins, both arms, and the head-cage was expanding again. The pain was tremendous, growing exponentially worse—but then, for a second time, *it was gone.*

… No pain at all …

Again Will saw everything from the *outside*. It felt like a dream, but far more lucid. From his overhead view, he saw all of the moving Exo joints. He heard the hydraulics, pneumatics, and stepper motors. Yet he *felt* nothing.

"Okay, what the *fuck* is going on here?" the technician exclaimed. "Why is he not unconscious, or screaming? We're giving him everything and he's not even *reacting*."

"The sensors all seem okay," the medic informed him. He reached over to the control panel and pushed a button to mute an alarm. "The pain level is at 9.3—the max. That's cardiac arrest territory." He grabbed the phone. "I'll get the engineers up here."

In less than three minutes, an engineer came into the control room. "What's the problem?" he asked, seemingly annoyed.

"Hear that?" the tech asked in response.

The engineer tilted his head and closed his eyes. "I don't hear *anything*."

"Exactly. He should be screaming like a little girl."

At that moment Will's screaming resumed.

"Seems okay now." The engineer shrugged and walked out of the room, shaking his head.

The tech cursed and sat down. "I've never seen anything like this. Either something's wrong with the system, or something's wrong with that guy—or both."

"I agree," the medic responded. "We better write this one up carefully."

Will's bones ached horribly, his head throbbed, his stomach churned. When the nighttime prep was over, the Exo placed him in the horizontal sleeping position. He knew he had about a half hour before the rotation would start. He thought about his parents and wept softly for a few minutes. He wondered if it was this great sadness, coupled with the physical pain, which had caused his hallucinations. Otherwise, he thought he might be going insane.

Will was starting to doze when a noise startled him back to consciousness. It reminded him of how, in his life before this current nightmare, he would sometimes dream that someone had knocked on the door. It would startle him awake, but no one would ever be there.

A few seconds later, out of the silence, he heard the sound again; a voice.

"William," it said.

It was a man's voice. It wasn't loud, like the voice over the speakers, but it wasn't quiet either. Will was sure it originated from inside the room, but he couldn't tell from which direction it came.

"What ... who is that? Who the hell's in here?" he asked. He strained his eyes, but couldn't see anyone in the dim light.

"Be calm," the voice said, its tone deep and soothing: the voice of an older man.

"Who are you?" Will kept straining to see.

"I just want to talk," the voice replied.

Will was suspicious. This could be one of their games.

"What do you want?"

"I just want you to know that you are no longer alone."

"What do you mean, I'm *not alone?*'" Will asked, but there was no reply. "Hello?"

He listened carefully, but heard nothing more. He was frightened—not only by the possible presence of someone else in the room, but by the idea that he might be losing his mind. If he survived the year, he might be taken out of the Exoskeleton and put directly into a padded room.

On January seventeenth, Richard Greene rented a van and drove to a storage facility with some old furniture. A miserable wintery mix had started in the late afternoon, and the roads were treacherous by 7 p.m. By eight o'clock he'd swapped the furniture for the crate of files, and was on his way to his brother-in-law's house, an hour west of DC. He wanted to get the files out of the city, but needed to keep the storage space filled in case someone was to check.

Richard thought Claire handled the news fairly well. She even suggested that he keep the files in her brother's barn until he could transport them. As soon as he could, he'd personally deliver the crate to Chicago. He didn't want to further involve anyone else—Claire, family, friends. And he wasn't going to ship it; the files were too valuable. He had no choice but to drive the twelve hours, maybe more, depending on the weather.

His next step was to make up an excuse to request a few days off. Bergman never had a problem with that, and would likely be amenable to the request.

Claire and the kids would go to Iowa to stay with her sister for a few weeks while everything went down. They would leave after the files were in McDougal's hands. Richard dreaded that future drive back to DC, to say what might be his final goodbye to his family. Even if he wasn't dead after everything played out, he'd probably end up in jail.

Many people had died because of the program—patients killed by the treatments, others terminated because they were security risks—and many more would die if the program actually accomplished its goal. Richard hoped he could stop it in time.

Room nineteen was a hypobaric chamber.

That day Will's ears popped, his eyes bulged, and at times his sinuses felt like they were on the verge of exploding. He experienced high altitude sickness, and got the bends. It was a day he'd never forget, same as the first eighteen.

There were no hallucinations during the day's treatment, but he wished there had been; they brought release from the pain. By the end of the day, his body ached more than he ever thought possible. Nineteen days gone, three hundred and forty-six to go.

Will was just beginning to drift to sleep when he heard the voice again. His heart sank: it had taken great effort to convince himself the first occurrence was a hallucination. In some ways, the prospect of mental illness was more frightening than that of physical pain. He could heal, presumably, from the physical abuse, but he questioned whether he could recover psychologically.

"William?" the voice queried from somewhere in the dim blue.

Will was startled but silent, as he again tried to determine if he'd *really* heard the voice. Finally he responded, "Who are you?"

"You are not going insane," the voice replied.

Will remained silent.

"Why do you think you are here?"

"Damn," Will huffed, "still trying to get me to confess? Well you can just f—"

"—No," the voice interrupted. "Why would I ask you to confess to something you are not responsible for?"

Will was dumbfounded. "What the hell does *that* mean? Why am I *here* then—why are *you* here talking to me about it? How do *you* know I am not responsible for ..."

"Slow down."

Will stopped.

"May *I* ask a few questions?" the voice asked.

Will remained silent, hoping the voice would go away.

"Are you afraid to die?"

He was not expecting this question. "Why should I answer any of your questions?"

"You don't have to," the voice replied. "Maybe I will leave you to sleep ..."

"No ... no, please," Will said, suddenly panicked. Conversation was a luxury he'd forgotten, even if it was some elaborate mind-game.

"I'll try to answer your question. But first, tell me your name."

"You may call me Landau."

"Okay, *Landau*," Will said. The name sounded familiar to him, but he couldn't place it. "I can't see you. Maybe you could step out of the shadows."

"I'm afraid we'll have to go on like this, William. Now, please, my question ..." Landau said.

"Dying? Yes ... I'm *afraid* to die... But I *want* to die at the same time; it sounds strange, I know ..."

"Not at all," Landau replied. "I think such a paradox exists in everyone. Some want to see what's on the *other side* of this life, but most are afraid to cross over, of course. They are afraid of the unknown."

"I don't blame anyone for being afraid of the unknown," Will responded.

"What do you think *happens* when you die?"

"I think I was pretty close to being dead already," Will said, referring to his near-drowning. "Based on that, I think our consciousness just fades out, and that's it—we cease to exist."

"Next question," Landau continued. "Can you tell me where you were on July nineteenth, 1952?"

Will stewed in confusion for a moment, and replied, "I think you must have the wrong file or something. That was way before I was born."

"I don't have any files," Landau said. "Please, answer the question."

"Okay; I wasn't born yet. *I didn't exist.*"

"So your fear of death is rooted in uncertainty—even though, according to your vague definition, you were dead before you were born?" Landau asked.

"Is *unborn* equivalent to being *dead*?" Will replied. "And there's also the pain involved with dying."

"I see. And you think that death might be more painful than what you've experienced so far?"

"I don't know if it will be *more* painful... I guess I don't really know *anything* at this point."

"But you believe you simply cease to exist when you die?" Landau asked. "The molecules that make up your body just disperse into the universe, and whatever it is that is *you* will be gone forever? You believe that *you* are just a property of your physical body—of your atoms?"

"I don't know *anything* for sure," Will replied.

"Think about what we have discussed until we speak again."

"*When* will that be?" After a few seconds with no response, Will said, "Hello?"

He waited for a reply until the Exo began the sleep cycle, after which his thoughts gave way to nightmares.

Heinrich Bergman took a swig of the clear liquid and swallowed hard. "This wasn't exactly what I had in mind," he said, coughing as he spoke. He walked to his office window and gazed over the nightscape of Washington, DC, while the burning in his throat slowly waned.

"Wodka calms the nerves, Heinrich," Lenny replied, and swallowed three fingers worth in a single gulp. He refilled his glass before he even took another breath. "So you've identified the woman from the lab?"

"How do you drink like that?" Bergman asked, astonished. He broke his stare from Lenny's glass and answered, "Yes, our techs broke into the email account from the card you recovered. Everything was forwarded to a *Denise Walker* at the DNA Foundation. She's McDougal's assistant."

"Do I need to pay her a visit?"

"That won't be necessary. According to her e-mails she was there that night to *begin* looking for the samples… So McDougal is no longer our immediate concern—and with any luck your business at the lab scared them off our case entirely."

"What about the files?" Lenny asked.

The words grated on Bergman's mind. ""I'm hoping Frank Weiss was our culprit… Perhaps he hid them away; someplace they won't be found."

Lenny nodded.

Bergman felt his gut tighten up a notch. He didn't believe Weiss took those files. He watched Lenny down another two fingers of vodka. He envied Lenny a little: if the project collapsed, he could just walk away—unless they could connect him to any of the terminations he'd carried out. But that was unlikely—Lenny was very good at his business. Bergman knew, on the other hand, that *he* would have to answer for everything.

On the morning of Day Twenty-one, the Exo brought Will *up* a floor. It was the second time since the beginning of his "treatment" that he'd moved up a level. There were no announcements, which came as a relief since they only conveyed bad news. The latest, which had come the previous morning, was that Will's inheritance from his parents' estate had been claimed by the government to *partially* fund his stay at the Red Box. His parents weren't rich, but he figured it must have been a fair sum of money—well over a hundred thousand dollars—with an equal amount going to his sister.

It only reminded him of what a waste the entire situation had been. There was nothing he could do about it now, but he worried what he might do later, if he ever got out of this place.. His thoughts frequently darkened to the point of frightening him. It seemed to happen almost every day now.

They didn't solicit a confession this morning, which Will thought was strange. Instead, the Exo positioned him in a reclined position near the floor. A few minutes later he heard a door open, and two people walked in. His heart sank.

The dentist and his assistant, Ms. Hatley, each rolled in a cart. Colby positioned his at Will's right side and actuated the cart's brake mechanism with his foot, producing a horrible screech. Hatley did the same with hers on the left.

Two harnesses of cables and hoses lowered from a port in the high ceiling, and were connected to receptacles on the carts. The cart on Will's right held tools, including a *drill*, and some hand instruments. The one on his left had an x-ray viewer board, a sink, sprayers, blowers, and other medical supplies.

Colby turned on a light and faced Will. "Nice to see you again, 523. I suppose you remember me—I'm Dr. Colby, like the cheese."

"How could I forget *you*?" Will replied sarcastically.

"And what about me? Do you remember me?" Hatley asked with the same degree of sarcasm, and a smirk.

"Have we met?" Will shot back, deadpan.

Hatley's lips dissolved into a thin line, revealing the pent up anger inside her. Will honestly wondered what was wrong with the woman— what had happened to her? Had she been abused, or was she just a natural sadist?

"Enough of the niceties," Colby said, grinning. "We have only today to get the basic procedures done—good thing we don't have to worry about anesthetics." He turned to Hatley and said, "We'll start with the root canals so we can have the caps made before the end of the day. Let's start with the lower right."

Colby retrieved the jaw-jack and adjusted it as he'd done over three weeks earlier. It stretched Will's jaw to the brink of tearing the muscles, but it seemed he'd developed a higher pain threshold since their last encounter.

"Ms. Hatley, the tongue-tie please, while I assemble the drill," Colby ordered.

"Yes, doctor," she replied as she retrieved the item, then reached inside the Exo's head-cage. Will was tempted to bite off the woman's fingers, but restrained himself. Hatley tied his tongue off to the left, which cleared a wide space on the right side for Colby to work.

Colby tested the drill, the high-pitched whine echoing throughout the room, and then plunged in without hesitation. Will's vision dimmed and went black. When he regained consciousness, he heard Colby saying, "Maybe that was a little too quick."

As the procedure resumed, Will heard voices over the speakers periodically giving updates on his bio status—pain level and heart rate.

When the drilling was completed, Will knew the *reaming* was about to start. The reamers, which looked like grooved wires, were inserted deep into the root canals in order to remove all of the material— including the nerves. He felt Colby press a reamer deep into his tooth, and the pain spiked as if the dentist were stabbing a red-hot needle into his

jawbone. The pain quickly increased beyond tolerance but then, suddenly
…

… It was gone.

Instantly Will was watching himself from *above*—viewing the
scene from about six feet overhead. He could see the tag on the back
collar of Hatley's lab coat, and the bald spot on the top of Colby's head.
He saw his own contorted face and the whites of his own eyes—he looked
like hell. And he could hear them speaking …

"Okay, he's out again, Ms. Hatley. Let's give it a moment,"
Colby instructed. He paced back and forth, and looked up to the glass.
After a short time, he called up, "Hey, are you guys paying attention up
there?"

A voice boomed down, "What's the problem? Everything's
reading normal. The pain level was fluctuating around nine, but falling.
Heart rate's 130."

"He's passed out," Colby yelled.

There was a brief pause before the reply. "Not according to our
sensors. He's just *not screaming*—the muscle sensors read high tension,
and all other indicators read normal."

"He should be screaming his head off—he has to be out. Look
…" Will saw Colby take a new reamer and clean out another root. A
minute later Colby turned back to the booth, "Nothing. Not even a twitch.
What do you say to that? That was a fresh nerve."

Again there was silence, this time for more than a minute, before
the reply. "Just keep working—we'll monitor the vitals. He seems okay—
he's just not screaming."

Colby turned to Will and yelled to him, "Thompson!"

Will heard Colby's scream from two places simultaneously: from
his position *above* the scene, and from his body. He then felt himself
being dragged back to consciousness—back to the Exoskeleton. He
awoke to horrific pain, his body convulsing wildly.

"He's awake now, but you better wait a few minutes—his heart
rate is through the roof," the voice said from above.

"Then what the hell was going on *before*?" Colby asked.

"Don't know, Doctor, but we'll have to write it up as an incident
when you're finished today."

"What?" He seemed confused and flustered. "Write what up?"

"Any strange incidents need to be documented—this qualifies," the voice replied.

"Fine," Colby yelled, and then turned to Hatley, "We have a lot of work to do today, let's get rolling."

Will suffered on as Colby performed two root canals that morning, and replaced five fillings in the afternoon. The newly fabricated porcelain caps were fitted and installed by the end of the day. Will had been on the verge of blacking out through most of the process, and had one more hallucination during the day. During this last hallucination, he observed that the room seemed to be *uniformly* illuminated—even the dark corners were fully visible, which wasn't the case when viewed from his body.

When it was all over, and his mouth was cleaned up, Colby pulled off his gloves and said, "We'll be seeing you next week for those wisdom teeth. Bet you'll be glad to get rid of those."

Will said nothing in return.

Will's mouth felt much better after his feeding. It still throbbed, but not nearly as bad as earlier in the day. The pain had nearly subsided, and he was on the border of sleep, when he was startled by the voice of Landau.

"You left your body again today," Landau stated.

"How do you know that?"

"It doesn't matter how I know. What do you think you were experiencing?"

"It *does* matter how you know, and I think it was a hallucination. Now, how do you know about it?" Will repeated.

"Our time is limited, and there are things you still need to resolve." Landau replied. "Do you think that what makes you *you* are just the atoms that make up your body?"

"What do you mean 'our time is limited?' Seems we have all the time in the world," Will said, ignoring the question.

"You need to answer my questions or our conversations are going to end."

Will sensed impatience in Landau's voice. He answered, "The whole is greater than the sum of the individual parts, and I think we don't understand this very well. But, yes, I think we are just atoms."

"Understanding physics as you do," Landau said "would you say that atoms of a given type—same atomic number and same isotope—are *indistinguishable*? Meaning, for example, that a gold atom here in Detroit is *exactly* the same as one on Mars, and no one could tell the two apart if they were next to each other?"

"Yes," Will replied. This, he knew, was accepted as *fact* in modern physics.

"And the same for Molecules?"

"Yes, of course," Will answered. "All water molecules are the same if made from atoms of identical isotopes. All glucose molecules are the same, etcetera … where is this going?"

"In principle then, I could make a brain and body that was, in all physical respects, absolutely identical to yours?"

"In *principle*, yes," Will replied.

"Suppose I do that, and put your new perfect copy next to you. Could anyone tell the two of you apart?"

"I suppose not."

"What about yourself?"

"Yes, of course, *I* could tell."

"How?"

"I would be looking out through my own eyes," Will replied. He wondered *why* Landau was leading their discussion in this direction—he knew where it was headed. He'd heard variations of this argument before, back in college.

"The thing to which you refer as 'I' in your response, is your *soul*. There is a clear distinction between what is matter—atoms—and what is your soul," Landau explained. "I want you to give this some thought. It's important."

"Why?"

"Because there are certain things you need to be convinced are *real*," Landau responded. "And you need to give some thought to where you were in 1952."

"Yes, you said July nineteenth, 1952. Is there some significance to that date?"

"None, except that it was before you were conceived."

"Then the answer would still be: *I didn't exist*," Will answered in a tone of finality.

"In that case, why do you exist *now*?" Landau asked.

"What the hell does *that* mean?" Will felt he'd had enough of the conversation, but it didn't matter: it was the last he heard from Landau for the night. Landau, Will tried to convince himself after some thinking, was an entity his mind had created to help him cope with the solitude and agony of this place; a subconscious defense mechanism. Since his current situation wasn't something he could explain well with science or common sense, his mind was forced to dig deeper. Maybe this was the onset of psychosis—or maybe he was already in the thick of it.

CHAPTER VI
Revelation

On January 23rd, Jonathan McDougal navigated the mid-morning Chicago traffic from the campus to his house. He pulled into the driveway and got out of the car, retrieving his briefcase from the back seat. He had a full schedule for the day, but had promised Julia he'd stop home for a quick brunch.

Julia met him on the front porch, and he kissed her loudly on the lips. "Hey, good lookin'," he said, kissing her again on the cheek.

"We have bagels. Are you home for the day?" she asked.

The look in her eyes made it clear she wanted him to stay—but he couldn't, there was work to be done. Since the Thompson case was hopeless, he had to reopen the search for new cases—CP sentences were not widely publicized, surely by design.

"I have to pick up some new case files, and I have a meeting this afternoon on campus, but I won't be home too late. For dinner, maybe we can make those steaks your brother gave us."

Julia smiled and shook her head. "Too late, I got the slow cooker all set up for a roast."

"Even better."

Jonathan had started on his way into the house when Julia said, "Oh, you should take a look at the package in the garage before you do anything else."

"What package?"

"You weren't expecting anything? It's a huge crate."

Jonathan shook his head. He noticed some alarm in her expression. "Is something wrong?"

"It's just a little strange, that's all," she replied. "The man who delivered it had to use a dolly to get it in."

Jonathan raised the garage door, and standing in the middle of the floor was a large cardboard box. It was cubic, four feet by four feet, and was strapped to a wooden pallet with high-tension plastic binders.

"Holy crap," he said, "What the hell *is* this?" He walked over to the box and examined it. "There's no name on it—to whom was it addressed?"

"The man who delivered it said it was for you," Julia replied.

"Did you have to sign for it?"

"No."

"Was it UPS or Federal Express?"

"It was just a man with a rental van."

"Did he say anything about it at all? Who it was from?"

"No dear, just what I told you." She laughed. "Why don't you quit asking me questions, and just open it?"

Jonathan walked around the crate and examined it more carefully. "There's nothing written on it at all." He retrieved a utility knife from a tool drawer and cut the plastic binder tapes. The box slumped slightly to one side due to the reduced support, and he strained to slide the box and pallet against the wall.

"Geez, this thing is heavy—must be over two hundred pounds."

With one side of the box propped against the wall, Jonathan sliced the tape that held the top two flaps together, and pulled them apart. He did the same to a second layer of flaps, revealing a tightly packed assortment of folders, binders, and envelopes. On top of the contents was a handwritten note:

> *This information should help you with your investigation. Your telephone has been bugged, and all of your email accounts have been compromised. If it gets out that you have these files, your very life (and those of your colleagues) will be in danger. Move quickly! --A Friend*

"Jesus," Jonathan whispered. He handed the note to Julia and she read it quickly.

"Our phones are bugged?" she asked, alarmed.

Distracted, he replied, "Yes, we'll have to deal with that." He pulled a random file from the box and opened it. The first thing he noticed was the *TOP SECRET* stamp. Next he examined the seal: DoD, which he knew stood for *Department of Defense.* He fanned through it and quickly realized that many of the pages had a common phrase in the heading or subject lines: *Punishment Compression Experiments.*

"Look at this." He showed Julia the seal and the file. He pulled out another one, also labeled "Top Secret," but this one had the DARPA seal on it, and a contact address: *DEFENSE ADVANCED RESEARCH PROJECTS AGENCY, 336 Overlook Ave. S.W., Mailstop 2304, Washington, DC 11415.*

"What is all of this?" Julia asked. Her face was pale.

"I'm not sure... Something to do with the CP program," Jonathan speculated as he pulled another file. He opened it and was stunned by what he saw, staring in bewilderment until his wife broke his trance.

"What is it, Jonathan?"

He slowly turned the folder so Julia could see the emblem on the front. When she saw it, her eyes widened and she put a hand over her mouth.

It was a *swastika.*

Stadler

Jonathan drove his car towards Schaumberg, just outside of Chicago, to pick up three newly discovered case files from a colleague. The crate of files and the note were on his mind the entire time. He'd closed up the box in his garage and decided to take some time to think carefully about how to proceed. He knew the consequences of reading classified documents without proper clearance, and had to decide whether or not to take the chance.

His thoughts quickly converged: *of course* he would take the chance. His objective was to crack the program wide open—whatever the risk. The laws he broke now were irrelevant; the end more than justified the means, even if he went to jail. Those files being sent to him, especially with the note, meant there was something very dark going on indeed, and he would be the one to expose it. Thankfully there was someone else, someone who was also taking a risk, who felt the same way.

Fifteen minutes later, Jonathan met with Brian Taggert, his longtime friend and fellow lawyer, at his house in Schaumburg. Even though he wanted to run out of there and speed home to explore the new information, Jonathan chatted with his old friend for an hour over coffee. He had to be on campus in the afternoon for a committee meeting anyway, so he thought it better to just be patient. He was anxious to dig into Taggert's new files as well, but knew his success depended on the contents of the crate in his garage.

Stadler

212

William Thompson was changed forever during Day minus one, and had continued to change in large quanta every day since. But it was the out-of-the-ordinary *lunchtime* announcement on Day 23 that made him realize he was completely alone in the world.

With its usual absence of emotion, the voice said, "Your sister, Andrea Marie Cramer, and your two nieces, Tabitha and Tia, were brutally murdered three days ago by your brother-in-law, Terrence Cramer. Mr. Cramer then took his own life. The incident was ruled a murder-suicide. Mr. Cramer's family indicated that the couple had recently been arguing about Mrs. Cramer's half of your parent's estate. As a consequence, the money has been willed to you, and has therefore become the property of the Federal Government, to be applied against your debt."

Will felt sick but remained quiet; no tears, no screaming. There was nothing left to cry about. Everything and everyone was gone.

The voice came back, "If you confess your crimes, you will be spared the day."

"Fuck off," Will said, more quietly than usual.

Today, he welcomed the distraction of pain.

Jonathan got home from his committee meeting around 5:45 p.m., and was tired and hungry. Julia served a large pot roast with onions, carrots, mashed potatoes and gravy—and it all would have been better had Jonathan's mind not been elsewhere.

He was raring to get at the files, but first he'd have to get them to a safe place. He'd already solved the phone bug problem: he'd instructed Denise to get a new temp phone, and he'd done the same. They would also need new, anonymous e-mail accounts.

"You're thinking about that crate in the garage, aren't you?" Julia asked.

"Yes, and many other things," Jonathan replied, forcing a smile.

"I've been thinking about it, too, and I'm curious: we could get into a bit of trouble for reading those files, couldn't we?"

"We could get into more than *a bit* of trouble for just *having* them," Jonathan replied.

"I thought so." A mischievous smile formed on her lips. "So when do we start?"

"I *knew* I married the right woman," Jonathan said and laughed. "We can have a look at them tonight, but we're going to move them to campus first—I've arranged a special place in the law building where they'll be safe."

"You're worried they'll be taken?"

"Not too much," Jonathan replied, "but better safe than sorry. I'll heed the warning on the note—people are watching us."

"What if they come after us?"

Jonathan shrugged. "We'll just have to be careful." He changed the subject. "It's going to take us *weeks* to get through that many files, and

I'm not even sure what we're looking for. But there's *something* in there, something that ties the whole thing together—and we're *going* to find it."

"What on earth were those documents with the *SS* symbols and swastikas?" Julia asked.

"No idea—but I'm sure we'll learn soon enough."

Ninety minutes later, they were out of breath and standing in the old law library, which was located in the same building as Jonathan's office. A dozen or so wooden tables ran down the center of the enormous room, illuminated by stained-glass lamps that hung from the twenty-foot, arched ceiling. Some of the lights were burned out, leaving patches of dark that blended into the rows of empty bookshelves down either side of the library. The wall on the far end, opposite the entrance, was entirely glass, framing what Jonathan thought was the most beautiful view of the campus.

Julia seemed skeptical. "They'll let us work in here?"

"For now; renovations start in the next couple of months—we'll have to be out by then," Jonathan replied. "Let's get started."

After a moment of hesitation and a small sigh, Jonathan opened the first of many small boxes he'd packed with files to make the transport more manageable. The files had been roughly organized by their respective sources, and he and Julia were careful to try to keep some order to their unpacking. They stacked them in piles, each about a foot high, on one of the large tables.

After about twenty minutes of careful unloading, they stopped and gazed at the files and binders. Jonathan examined the seals and labels that identified their various origins. There were many with the Nazi *SS* seal— from Auschwitz, Dachau, Treblinka, Ravensbrück, and more. Others were from DARPA, the US Department of Defense, the Israeli Defense Department, the CIA, and some from various American and foreign universities. He estimated there were over fifty thousand pages of material—it was going to take quite some time to get through them. They'd have to read day and night.

During the day Jonathan had pondered whether or not to drag Denise into reading the files. It was a dilemma for him: she was just starting in law, and getting caught up in something like this could very well ruin her career. In the end, he resolved to let her make her own decision. She'd probably elbow her way in even if he tried to stop her. He called to fill her in on the situation, and as he expected: she was most certainly in.

After he'd hung up with Denise, Jonathan noticed that Julia had picked up a file. He walked over to get a better look, peering over her shoulder. The page she was reading had the *SS* emblem and another strange swastika-like symbol as part of the letterhead. Each document had a corresponding English translation clipped to it, and some of the pages had notes scribbled on them. The title page read, in English, *Results of Absolute Threshold Experiments at Auschwitz Medical Laboratory.* The subsequent pages were cluttered with graphs, tables, and lists of data that related time of exposure, temperature, humidity conditions, age of subjects, and "time until death."

"This one describes experiments they did at Auschwitz. Hypothermia." She put the file back on the table. "I'm not sure I ..."

Jonathan saw Julia's eyes tear up, and he immediately understood why. At just eight years old, Julia's mother had witnessed her parents and two sisters die at the hands of the Nazis. If they'd managed to evade capture for just a few more weeks, they would have survived the war. Her mother had been rescued from Auschwitz, but wrestled with survivor's guilt for the rest of her life. This guilt had somehow been passed down to Julia, and Jonathan was sensitive to it.

He hugged her. "I'm sorry, darling... Don't look at any more of that... Are *you* okay?" he asked and kissed her head.

"I'll be fine," she replied. A tear rolled down her cheek. "But what could those old experiments have to do with the compressed punishment program? Are they doing tests like that here—in *America*?"

"I don't know, but the answer has got to be in here somewhere," he said as he looked over the pile.

"Denise is coming?" Julia's eyes looked hopeful.

Jonathan nodded. "Day after tomorrow—she's out of town for her mother's birthday. In the meantime, you and I should dig in."

Julia agreed, and they worked into the early hours of the morning.

Day Twenty-three was the day Will found out about the death of his sister and her family. It was also the day of extreme exposure treatment. At first it was strange to see snow indoors, and to feel the air blowing as hard as it was—but the novelty wore off quickly. It reminded him of the night he was delivered to the roof of the Red Box, only worse.

The treatment was horrible: it was dark and cold and he was occasionally sprayed with water. As awful as it was, there were times when Will had almost fallen asleep. He supposed that's what it was like to freeze to death; you'd feel pain for a little while, but then just slowly fade away. During the worst parts of the treatment, he again hallucinated that he was near the top of the room, looking down on his shivering body. He saw his pale skin and blue lips, and the frosted, caked blood around his head bolts.

It was difficult to eat meal two, and Will could hardly speak when they asked him for a number; he could hardly move his lips, and he shivered uncontrollably. There was never a response after he gave a number, and he was growing tired of the exercise.

When his torture was done for the day, they slowly warmed Will with moist air—which caused a deep, aching pain in hands, feet, and joints. He was fed once more—the food paste served warm, accentuating some of the more *unpleasant* flavors, and leaving him nauseated.

After meal three came the dead time before the start of sleep rotation, and as Will expected, he heard the voice of Landau.

"Been waiting for you," Will said.

"Is that so?"

"You seem to appear every time I hallucinate."

"So you still believe those to be hallucinations?"

"Yes, and I still believe you're a hallucination as well."

Landau changed the subject: "Have you given some thought to our last discussion—about making a replica of your body, atom by atom?"

Will *had* thought about it, but he wanted to know *why* Landau was asking that question, as well as the question of where Will was before he was born.

"Yes— as I said, I would know which body was mine because I was looking through my own eyes."

"Right, but what if you were somehow transferred to that other body—how would you know then?"

Will answered, "I guess I couldn't know—everything would be exactly the same."

"So, you could *move* from one body to the other, and you wouldn't know the difference?"

"I suppose so, yes. Why are you asking me these questions?" Will asked. "Are you trying to say that my consciousness is mobile, or *transportable*, or something?"

"Your *soul* can't stay in your body forever—the body is *temporary*," Landau replied. "Unless, of course, you *really do* believe you cease to exist after you die, and didn't exist before you were born."

"Suppose that *is* what I believe?"

"Then you'd be living a finite, hopeless existence," Landau answered, his voice revealing a hint of frustration. "But then the question would still remain as to why you are here *now*. And I am not referring to your *purpose*; I mean why do you *exist*? *Where did you come from?* You think the *atoms* that assembled to make your body in your mother's womb made your self-aware soul? Your body could function very well in this world just as it is—without *you* being in it—and no one would ever know the difference."

Will caught himself mouthing the last few words of Landau's rant as they were being spoken. It was strange: *had he been hallucinating again?* Had he been speaking to *himself*? "Landau?" he called out.

There was no answer. A few seconds later, the rotation started.

Denise climbed the stairs to the old law library at about 8:00 p.m. She hadn't been in the library in over a year, ever since the university had moved everything to the new building, and was immediately struck by how large the place looked with most of its contents removed. The familiar scent of coffee and cherry pipe tobacco permeated the air; the aroma of her usual work environment.

Julia greeted Denise with a hug and a kiss on the cheek, and led her deeper into the vacated library, where Jonathan was buried behind a mound of papers at the end of a large mahogany table.

He stood up. "Glad you're here, Denise. We need another set of eyes to get through all this."

"Why are you in *here*?" Denise asked.

"People might come looking for the files at some point, so I couldn't have them at the house or in my office," Jonathan replied. "And, as you can see, we needed some space."

Denise acknowledged with a nod. "You said there was a lot of material, but I didn't imagine this." She was astounded at the volume of files on the table. From the reflection in the large window, she saw even more stacked on the floor behind Jonathan's chair.

"Grab some coffee and let's get started," Jonathan said, pointing to a coffeepot on the table behind her.

"It's getting a little late for coffee, isn't it?"

"We've been up past three in the morning for the past two nights," Julia explained. "And we'll probably be at it for a while. Trust me, you won't have a problem staying interested."

"What do you have so far?" Denise asked.

Jonathan and Julia explained how the files were delivered, the implications of the seals on the file folders, and the note.

"We have a huge knowledge gap," Jonathan said, "and it's going to take us some time to fill it in. Whoever sent this to us may have saved our entire effort. Do you realize how long it would take us to replace the Thompson case?"

"We may never find another one," Denise acknowledged.

"The information here seems to be comprehensive," Julia explained. "We have files that date from the Nazis to present day."

"The *Nazis*? What are you talking about? ..." Denise was startled.

"This is much deeper than I had anticipated," Jonathan said. "DARPA, or the *Defense Advanced Research Projects Agency*, which funds high-risk projects, has been funding the so-called Compressed Punishment research since 1947. It funded research in bio-sensors, biomechanics, abnormal genetics, pain-management—including torture and, of all things, research on various religions and the paranormal—debunking ghost stories, in particular. The main accomplishment up to this point has been the development of an integrated bio-system, called an *Exoskeleton*."

"Sounds pleasant," Denise said and shuddered.

"Some of the DARPA documents refer to an American project called *Red Wraith*," Jonathan continued, "and they also make reference to certain *incidents* that have occurred throughout history. The Nazi's are mentioned the most, but so are the Russians under Lenin and Stalin, and there are even references to the Catholic Church, and to witch trials and burnings. All of these had one thing in common: *torture*. But there's still a lot of information missing—some major gaps: I haven't been able to find reports on any of the *incidents* mentioned—so I have no idea what they entail. Maybe we'll find something in the SS documents— that's where I'd like *you* to start, Denise. There are hundreds of them."

Denise took a cup from the table and filled it with coffee. She felt as if she were in a dream, or playing a part in a movie; the plot was becoming more and more convoluted, but also more exciting.

"Julia is tackling that pile of CIA files," Jonathan said. "And I'm up to my eyeballs in DARPA documents."

They filtered through the enormous collection of papers, and worked until they could no longer see straight. The chime of a large clock, located high above the entrance inside the grand library, rang out four bells before they called it a night.

Richard placed his empty travel mug on a filing cabinet and logged on to his computer. He sighed at the sight of the large envelope on his desk. Today was January 26th, and there should have been *two* such envelopes; the New York facility was late again. Nevertheless, it was time to write up the report summary. He turned his attention back to the computer and opened a template document. He had standard responses that he could cut and paste, always expressing the same undeniable point: NTR. Nothing to report.

He opened the envelope and pulled out a large binder: it was the Red Box report, as he had predicted. He went straight to the cover page for the summary, and his eye was quickly drawn to the number '2' for total *Number of Incidents*. Richard's heart skipped a beat. This number had been nonzero before, but they always turned out to be mistakes. In one case, the room medic who had written the report mistakenly thought that *sleep-talking* was considered an incident.

Next to the entry were the words "see page 24." Richard went to the page and was surprised to find the report for *Patient 523: William Thompson*. He read it carefully, and found himself somewhat relieved. If anything, the controllers had observed *precursors* to incidents: Thompson hadn't responded to pain stimuli. As a scientist, Richard should have been excited; as a human, he was downright frightened. He thought he could get away with summarizing the information as *NTR* in his report to Bergman, but the urgency of the situation had just leapt a few quanta. He had to get McDougal moving.

Will listened to the morning announcement: "Your ex-fiancée, Pamela Sorrensen, is to wed Matthew Donavan on April 21st of this year," the voice said.

It was strange news. Will knew Pam had always liked Matthew, but he was surprised that his old friend was going to marry her. Evidently Pam was carrying on with life as if nothing had happened. This angered him even more than the fact that she was marrying his former college roommate.

"If you confess that you raped Cynthia Worthington, you will be spared treatment for the day," the voice continued.

"I'm running out of ways to tell you people to *fuck off,*" Will replied.

"Very well," the voice said with finality. The intercom clicked off.

Will awaited the unknown horrors that lay before him.

Stadler

On the eve of Day 26, Will was not fed. His stomach churned from hunger, and he was worried: missing a meal always preceded something horrible. There was no breakfast on Day 27, and Will was not surprised to see Dr. Colby and Ms. Hatley walk through the door that morning.

"Today is the day of wisdom," Colby said, smiling broadly as he rolled in a cart. "Remember me? I'm Dr.—"

"—Yes, Colby," Will cut him off. "Like the cheese. I remember." He'd seen the man just days ago, although he had lost count.

"Right. See? It works," Colby responded, and had an expression of approval.

It was exactly the same setup as for the previous "dental appointment" for the root canals and filling replacements, only there was an additional panel of hand instruments. There were scalpels, flat blades, and an assortment of curved pliers—all made from polished stainless steel. The drill motor had a head on it that looked like a small, circular blade.

Hatley inserted the jaw jack and tongue tie while Colby hooked up cables. She gave Will her evil wink and whispered, "Boy, are we going to have some fun." She stopped talking just as Colby got within earshot, and a few minutes later they started the procedure. *No anesthetics meant no delays*.

They worked on the upper left wisdom tooth first. Will felt Colby slice into the thick fleshy gum behind the last molar, and wedge a flat-bladed instrument down under the tooth. He moaned in response to the deep, dull pain as it surged through his entire skull, and leached into his neck, shoulders, and upper back. The first tooth was out in ten minutes, and Colby showed it to Will. It was a solid, but deformed, piece of white-polished ivory; a human-made pearl.

"That's one," Colby said and dropped it into a steel pan with a clank. "Would you like to extract the other upper, Ms. Hatley? It should be straightforward—it's floating."

"Absolutely," she replied.

Will heard the excitement in her voice. Strangely, without even feeling pain, he felt himself begin to fade away, but he didn't fade out completely.

He felt Hatley make the first incision; it was much larger and deeper than the one Colby had made to extract the first tooth. She then selected the sharp, hardened-wire instrument and poked it deep into the incision. It missed the tooth entirely and penetrated deep into Will's jaw bone. He squealed in pain.

"Ms. Hatley, what are you doing?" Colby asked.

"Locating the tooth," she replied.

"You're too far back, and too deep," he said.

"Sorry doctor," she said as she pulled the instrument out of Will's mouth. "I think I see where it is now." She selected a flat blade and drove it in deep under the tooth—again, too far.

This time Will faded out entirely. The next instant, he was looking down upon the operation. He felt no pain, although he sensed it in the background of his consciousness. He saw Colby look up to the window and ask a question. While the doctor had his back turned, he saw Hatley drive the flat blade in as deep as she could.

An uncontrollable surge of rage overcame Will, and suddenly he swooped down, striking her bluntly on the side of her head. He didn't know exactly *how* he did that, but it was his *intention*—he just *did* it. He saw her fall to the floor, and a moment later he woke up again—back in his body. The pain was immense.

"Ms. Hatley," Colby yelled. He pulled the flat blade out of Will's mouth and hurried around the Exo to her side. "What happened? Are you all right?"

"I don't know, doctor—I must have gotten lightheaded or something."

"Did you bump your head?"

"I think maybe I hit it on the floor," she replied, feeling around her head with her hands.

Colby looked at her more closely. "But you fell to the left—there's a big bump forming above your right temple. Did you hit something on the way down?"

"I don't know …" she said as she touched both sides of her head again. She looked disoriented.

"Take a break. I'll handle the other upper. You can join me this afternoon for the lowers, okay?" Colby looked up to the glass. "Did you see what happened?"

"No, but it will be on the video," a voice said. "We'll have a look at it before we write the report."

Hatley staggered out, and Colby finished extracting the remaining upper wisdom tooth. The pain was substantial, but not enough to put Will out again. The dentist packed the holes with something that felt like gauze, but tasted and smelled like a mixture of cloves and mint. He concluded the operation by removing the tongue tie and the jaw-jack. Will saw Colby's Rolex before the man left for lunch: it was just past 11 a.m., and Will was left to enjoy the lingering and evolving pain for the rest of the morning.

After lunch, more than an hour and a half later, Colby returned with Hatley, and Will knew the real fun was about to start. He remembered Colby saying that the lower wisdom teeth were *impacted*— connected deep into the jaw and pressed forward, against his other molars.

Colby started by slicing the gums, while Hatley suctioned the blood away from the area with a vacuum nozzle.

"It's going to be hard to get any leverage with this head cage in the way. We'll need to fracture the tooth," Colby explained to Hatley. He then selected an instrument and reached in with what looked like a thick, curved bird's beak. Will felt him clamp down on the tooth and increase the pressure until it shattered. A blast of white-hot pain seared through his brain, and again he was at the ceiling looking down on the scene. There was no more pain. He sensed the misery in his body, but couldn't feel it.

Will looked around and found he could move with a little more ease now—if it could be called "moving" without a physical body. He made his way to the one-way window, and pushing on the glass, he felt his hand press through it with only the slightest amount of resistance— like passing through water. He pushed his head through and saw two people, a man and a woman, in a control room of some kind. They were talking, and one said, "… never seen anything like that before ..." The other one replied, "Yes, especially for dental pain ..."

Suddenly Will felt himself being drawn back to his body and the Exo.

As he opened his eyes, Colby was in the process of sewing up the freshly hollowed wisdom tooth socket.

"Are you awake in there, 523? ... We're never sure whether you have passed out or not—you are a strange one." Colby said and stepped aside, allowing Hatley to move in.

"My turn," she said with a giddy voice and a smile, her face slightly swollen on both sides.

Will's vision darkened and he felt himself slip away again—this time without an extreme stimulus. Instantly he was above the scene, watching Hatley select an instrument. She picked up a scalpel for the initial incision, and Will felt anger boil within him. Before she could even touch his mouth, he was after her.

Dr. Colby watched as his assistant approached the patient with a scalpel— and in what seemed like an instant, her head jerked to the side, her body falling limp to the floor. The motion defied physics—completely unnatural: one second she was nearly stationary, and the next moment she was flying. He ran to her side of the table. "Ms. Hatley! My God!"

"What happened?" she asked, her expression distant.

She shook her head, trying to regain her bearings. That was when Colby noticed the scalpel sticking out of her shoulder, and the blood seeping through her lab coat. Before she could notice, he gently pulled the instrument from her shoulder and placed it in a metal pan. He then soaked a piece of gauze in alcohol and applied it to her shoulder.

"Here, keep pressure on it and go see Dr. Noh right now. You may have had a seizure of some sort—you better get checked out right away."

Hatley walked a drunken path to the door, pressing the gauze with one hand and rubbing her head with the other.

Will returned to his body just in time to hear a female voice come over the intercom.

"Everything okay down there—is your assistant all right?"

"I sent her out to be examined," Colby replied.

"What the hell happened?"

"I have no idea." Colby shrugged.

"We'll have to write this up when you're finished. Come up here when you're done," the woman instructed.

Colby nodded and waved towards the booth, and then turned back to Will. "Well, 523, another write-up... I never had to write up *anyone* before—but this is the *second* time for you... Well, looks like it's just us guys for the rest of the afternoon." He then proceeded to take out the other tooth. Although the pain was intense, there was no intent on Colby's part to inflict more pain than what the procedure required.

Afterwards, he rinsed out Will's mouth, then took off the tongue-tie and jaw-jack. "That jaw is going to be painful for a few weeks—I had to take out some bone... An oral rinse will be provided automatically through the system, and you'll get an antibiotic injection tonight and tomorrow."

Colby collected his tools, disconnected the cable harnesses, and rolled his cart out of the room. A moment later he came back for the other cart, the one that would have been handled by Hatley. Before he exited, he turned and looked back at Will.

"What a strange day." He shook his head as he walked out the door.

Strange indeed, Will thought. He was just as confused as they were.

Bergman instructed Lenny to take a chair on the opposite side of the coffee table.

"We have a big problem."

Lenny maintained eye contact, and remained silent.

Bergman continued, "The girl has come out of her coma."

Lenny responded with a grave nod.

"She is not yet able to communicate, but she's alert, and her brain activity is steadily increasing. She'll be talking in a week, two at the latest."

"How do you want to handle it?"

"I need you to go to Detroit, and organize Thompson's termination for Warden Halbreath," Bergman instructed. "No subject has ever maintained innocence for this long... He's become too much of a liability."

"Sodium pentothal ?"

"Yes. And immediate cremation," Bergman responded. "Head out tomorrow; I want this done ASAP."

Lenny nodded and walked out of the office.

The Thompson problem would soon be resolved, but Bergman's relief was dampened by the thought of the missing project files. *The damn things could be anywhere.*

Everything Will did hurt his jaw. Sneezing was particularly awful, and his head felt like an inflated balloon due to the swelling. The paste for meal three was probably the best thing they could have fed him under the circumstances, but it still hurt going down. He was exhausted, but still patiently awaited Landau's voice.

"William?"

Will responded with muffled gibberish. He didn't know how Landau was able to comprehend what he was saying, but he did.

"You had the view from above again, only this time you acted—or, I should say, *reacted*."

In Will's mind he was aware of the conclusion he'd drawn more than once—that these conversations were hallucinations—but they still seemed so real.

"*How* do you know about that, and *who* are you working for?" Will demanded.

"I cannot answer those questions," Landau replied.

"What is your purpose?"

"To guide you."

"I don't understand. Guide me to *what*?"

"Please, William, let's move on," Landau said, changing the subject.

"Would you like to be free of this place? Free of that machine?"

Will was silent. Of course he wanted out.

"Are you trying to anger me?"

"Why don't you just leave?"

"What the hell are you saying?" Will asked in frustration.

"Your body is trapped inside of that cage of metal, electronics, and tubes, and you want to get it out of there—"

"Of course, damn it," Will spat. His emotions oscillated between anger and desperation.

"And since your soul is trapped in your body, and your body is being tortured—what do you think your *soul* wants to do?"

Will snapped, and no longer had control over his words.

"It wants to get the hell out! IT WANTS OUT! I WANT OUT! I WANT OUT!"

His shouting echoed throughout the room, and when he finally quieted, Landau was gone. The Exo began its nightly rotation, and Will trembled as he cried himself to sleep.

Denise walked out from her kitchen with a glass of wine, and sat down on the couch. Since Jonathan and Julia had to attend a law school event, she would be reading without them for the night. She didn't like being alone in the old library, despite how beautiful it was, so she took some files home with her.

Denise pulled a file out of her knapsack, tucked her feet beneath her, and began reading. This one had two seals on it: the Nazi *SS* symbol, and a large bird of prey, clutching a strange emblem in its talons. The emblem looked like a tic-tac-toe board, only with swastika-like tails on the outer edges.

She skimmed through the document, her expression gradually changing to one of excitement. After two straight days of reading, she had finally found one of the files they were seeking. It was a report from the Auschwitz medical lab, concerning the 'SS-4897 incident.'

DATE: 12 August 1943
LOCATION: Auschwitz Medical Facility
SUBJECT: Human Subject Experiments (The SS-4897
Incident)
      This is the full account of a classified incident that led
to the deaths (unknown cause) of nine German military
personnel, including four medical doctors, two armed
soldiers, a nurse, and two engineers.
      The human subject (SS-4897), Benjamin J. Horowitz,
was subjected to pain threshold experiments including
pressure chambers, extreme temperature conditions, burning,
scalding, beatings, and amputations. The subject endured

twelve days of extreme torture before the incident occurred. He was subsequently terminated.

The doctors recorded unusual events starting on day eight, just after the first amputation (right foot above the ankle) without anesthetic. The first incident was the mysterious stabbing of a doctor with a scissors. The scissors pierced the doctor's left shoulder blade, which required significant force—yet Horowitz was thoroughly restrained at the time.

Leading up to the massacre, numerous other incidents were observed in connection with the subject, including the tipping over of tables and chairs, the emptying of cabinets, and the spontaneous bending of iron window bars in the treatment room.

On 8 August 1943, at approximately 9:00 p.m., witnesses reported hearing a loud, high-pitched sound, along with the crashing of heavy objects, emanating from inside the room. Nine people rushed into the room, none of whom survived.

Limbs and heads were torn from some of the bodies; some were crushed beyond recognition, and some of the victims suffered extreme burns. Of special mention was the extreme force required to exact some of the damage: i.e., a 110 kg (240 lb) man had his leg completely torn off from the mid-thigh region. Witnesses reported that the event took less than five minutes from start to finish ...

Denise was shocked. What the hell had happened there? The Nazi bastards got what they deserved, but *what* had happened to them? She got a chill; not so much from the graphic detail of the file, but from the direction their investigation might be *heading*.

The document went on to report that the subject, Horowitz, was still alive when the incident was over. However, an SS officer executed him later that evening. The report went on for a dozen more pages, detailing each specific treatment the patient had undergone.

Denise didn't want to pull away from her reading, but she felt the need to call Jonathan. She had read many disturbing things over the past week, but there seemed to be an underlying theme that was forming. She called Jonathan's temp phone number and he answered after two rings.

"I think I found a file describing one of the *incidents* referenced in the DARPA and DoD reports," Denise explained. "This came from an SS report from Auschwitz: during a torture experiment on a prisoner, there was a massacre of nine camp personnel—doctors and soldiers alike. The killings were absolutely brutal—the bodies were dismembered, crushed, and even *burned*. But they were never able to determine what exactly happened."

Jonathan was silent for a few seconds before he spoke.

"Good. Now you have to find three more—so far, I've found a total of four incidents mentioned in reference to the Nazi files." He cleared his voice and continued, "I've made some interesting discoveries myself—but I don't want to talk about them over the phone."

"Is something wrong?" Denise asked, her voice tensing.

"It's just… very disturbing stuff… We'll talk about it tomorrow."

After they hung up, Denise's nerves tingled with anxiety and excitement. She took a sip of wine, pulled another file from her book bag and read.

When Will awoke, he realized he had lost track of the days, although he was sure it was still January. While he tried to count backwards, he was disturbed to find there were days of torture that he'd almost forgotten. He didn't want to forget *any* of them: each one had cost him so much.

After the usual morning maintenance, he was given two injections from the built-in hypodermic apparatus of the Exo—the antibiotics promised by the dentist, he assumed. As he was inserted into the next room, he got the usual offer in exchange for a confession. Will offered his usual response, and the treatment proceeded.

Will heard a faint hissing sound, and he followed the noise to the numerous nozzles that protruded from the walls and the ceiling. His ears popped, and he felt an oily film build up on his skin. A moment later, a burning itch started. It penetrated everything, but seemed to settle deeply into the most sensitive areas—armpits, neck, mucous membranes, and crotch. He began to sweat profusely.

The day was only beginning.

Richard would remember the sunny morning of January 28th, not because it was his first full day without his wife and daughters, but for the events described in the *Supplemental Incident Report* he'd received from the Red Box Facility. There were detailed accounts of incidents that had occurred the previous day, all pertaining to William Thompson. And these weren't benign reports of him not responding to pain; these were kinetic events.

Richard's heart sank: all of his efforts, and the risk—to both him and his family—might have been for naught. Thompson was showing signs—he still couldn't believe it; *signs.* It would be more than enough for the government to justify all the atrocities that had been committed in the name of the project. The program would not only go on, it would be revitalized. He had to stop it.

Richard had a few advantages that might give him some time. First, no one at the Red Box, including the Warden, really knew what was going on. They had all just been reporting what they observed, without any idea of the true goal. Second, all of the reports came to Richard for evaluation before being passed to anyone else. Other than weekly summaries, he only reported to Bergman when something out of the ordinary occurred, or if a patient had died.

Richard knew that Cynthia Worthington had come out of her coma, and he also knew hat Lenny was on his way to Detroit. He concluded that Bergman wanted things cleaned up before the girl could talk. It would look suspicious if Thompson happened to die *immediately after* the girl declared him innocent of the crime—if that were to happen. But what Bergman *didn't* know was that, by killing Thompson, he'd be putting a nail in his own coffin: he'd be extinguishing the only flicker of hope the project had ever produced.

Richard had to talk to McDougal face-to-face, and as soon as possible. He quickly came up with a plan. It was Thursday—he could go home "sick," take a long weekend. As soon as he got home, he'd start the eleven-hour drive to Chicago, to meet McDougal. It was a long drive, but it was the only way his whereabouts couldn't be traced. He'd use a prepaid phone, and pay for everything with cash. Being sick a couple of days was also the perfect excuse not to submit the incident report summary to Bergman.

He had to push McDougal and his colleagues to act *immediately*—to use the files, to try and shut down the program. In the mean time, Bergman would hopefully have Thompson killed. The program had to be stopped at all costs. The world wasn't ready for what it might have *already* produced.

Will had gained a large measure of control over his new ability throughout the day. He could now use the memory of pain to separate. He'd relive the feelings for an instant, but then he'd be free—free of his body, free of the Exo—the pain gone. He'd separated three times that afternoon, but each time he was eventually drawn back. It seemed his range was very limited; maybe thirty feet.

Not having much else to do, he examined his body closely, noting how much he'd changed in less than a month's time. Lumps had formed on his head around the head bolts they'd implanted—scar tissue was building up around them. His body was very muscular and lean, an unexpected benefit of his diet and the physical intensity of the treatments. But he was deathly pale, and his face was still swollen from the oral surgery.

When the final chemical exposure session was over, the residues were washed off. Afterwards, he was given another shot of antibiotics.

Not long after meal three, Will sensed Landau's presence, and spoke before he had the chance.

"Hello Landau."

"You are progressing."

Will was confused. "Towards what?"

"Let's try a little experiment," Landau said, seemingly ignoring Will's question.

"Today you used the *memory* of pain to remove yourself from your body. Do what you did today," Landau instructed.

"How do you know what I was *thinking*?" Will asked. These conversations always seemed to reveal that Landau knew something he couldn't possibly know.

"Wouldn't you like to have more control over your ability?"

Will thought about it for a moment. "Yes, of course I would." Anything to escape the torture—even if only for a short time.

"Then try."

Will did as Landau instructed, he thought mostly of Colby's root canals, and a moment later he was out. He could see his body, this time in no physical pain. He was drawn back in after just a few seconds. It seemed more difficult to separate when his body was comfortable.

"Excellent," Landau said. "It will be some time before you're able to hold it indefinitely, but you're doing well... Do you realize this is something quite extraordinary?"

"I think it's just my mind's way of protecting itself from pain," Will replied. He had no other explanation.

"You still believe it's only a state of mind? Could your mind have knocked Ms. Hatley to the ground—*twice*?" Landau asked.

"She slipped. My imagining I had something to do with it was just wishful thinking."

"You are wrong," Landau said. "You should try doing something you cannot explain... Why not separate during a treatment, and go through the glass to the control room. Note a few details about the people in there. When you return to your body, recite them aloud, and see what kind of a response you get."

Will tried to absorb what Landau was saying.

"What *is* all of this, Landau? And why are you so concerned about how I develop this ... ability?"

"Because there's something else at stake here. This goes beyond just you."

"I don't understand. I don't understand why I'm here. Sometimes I even wonder *if* I'm really here. Maybe I'll wake up from a coma or something, and find out this was all a dream."

"If that were true, your existence would be much less significant," Landau said.

"What do you mean?"

"You'll understand later—if you survive... Now, I must leave you."

Will closed his eyes and was quickly asleep.

During the morning maintenance routine, Will found his anxiety had decreased considerably. He decided to spend a good portion of the day exploring his new ability, and lose track of time—which seemed to have no meaning when he was separated.

The Exo positioned Will vertically in the center of the room, and a robotic arm descended from the ceiling. He immediately recognized the device on the end of the arm: it was a *jaw-jack*. Directly behind it was a complicated, denture-shaped mouthpiece, riddled with wires, white tubes, and metallic parts.

A voice instructed Will to open his mouth. When he hesitated, a horrible shock jolted his body until he complied. The jack went in and pressed just behind his front upper and lower teeth, forcing his mouth into a strained-open position. The oversized mouthpiece was then inserted, and the jaw-jack contracted and withdrew. Will's teeth settled easily into the custom fitted crevices of the device—a perfect fit.

A moment later, the mouthpiece vibrated slightly, then *expanded* to force his jaw into the full-open position once again. Will quickly forgot about the discomfort of his jaw when he felt two needles prick his gums. One was cheek-side and the other tongue-side, near the back molars on the lower right of his mouth. The two needles slowly penetrated into the root areas, and began to probe about. Will knew immediately what they were searching for; they were locating the special nerve bundle Colby had discovered. But he wondered why they were inserting *two* needles.

Will's thoughts were disrupted when one of the probes struck gold—the pain was awful, but the needle backed off almost immediately. It seemed to be waiting for its companion to find the mark.

It took the other probing needle a minute to hit its target, and then it backed off as well. Will was confused as he felt them both jockeying for position through very fine adjustments. He wondered if they planned to use them both at the same time—jabbing and prying from opposite sides of the bundle. He got his answer just a few seconds later: they *did* use them simultaneously, but the action wasn't mechanical; it was *electrical*. They were electrodes.

When the first blast of current surged through the nerve bundle, the pain went beyond anything he'd ever experienced. He didn't even have time to scream, before everything went black.

"Wow ... I better cut down the current a bit... Could've killed him," the tech said to the medic. "I'll reduce it by half."

"That was *too* close—his heart skipped a few beats," the medic replied as he examined the heart monitor on the control display. "And who knows what it did to his *brain*—the PL went off scale."

"Duly noted," the tech replied, and entered the new parameters.

Stadler

Will woke up confused: he didn't immediately recall what had happened, but it all came back to him when the electrical current again surged through his nerves. He screamed feverishly. This time he was able to exit before it got any worse.

He separated and began exploring, turning to see his suffering body. Due to the violent, shock-induced spasms, his head bolts were bleeding, and blood ran into the outer corners of his eyes and down the side of his face. He felt extreme anger, but didn't know what to do.

Will suddenly realized something; *maybe now it was possible to kill himself.* Maybe he could attack his own body, like he'd done with Hatley—only more violently. He quickly decided against this—he was now better equipped to survive the year than he had ever been... Still, the freedom to choose gave him a degree of comfort; the option of death was there if he needed it.

Will's thoughts were interrupted by a horrible screeching sound. He looked around but saw no sign of its source. It sounded *alive*, but not *human*. Even though he felt no *physical* response, the *emotion* of fear overtook him. The sound grew louder and more shrill as a white, cloudlike substance passed through the wall just below him.

Will remained perfectly still. When it was all the way through, the thing became silent and circled the room below him a few times. As it maneuvered, Will thought he saw human-like features—arms and hands—but he couldn't be sure. After a few passes, it stopped directly across the Exo from him. It moved a little to the left, then a little to the right, as if it were trying to figure out if something was there—at Will's "location" in the corner of the ceiling.

Then it stopped completely, transforming into a ghastly, ghost-like head and face, and screamed like a banshee—louder and more awful than anything Will had ever heard in his life. The face seemed to fix on him and then morphed into the most frightening, wicked thing he had ever seen. It was skeletal, evil, enraged, and it yelped its shrill screech through a wide, irregularly-fanged mouth. Long arms with giant claws grew out of the torso, and the lower part formed into a long, wispy tail.

Will was horrified as the thing tried to approach him, slowly, at first. Will adjusted his position to keep the Exo between him and the monster. It stopped, and then reversed its direction to match Wills movement. Will shifted slowly in the opposite direction. The thing stopped for an instant, seemed to coil itself up like a snake, and then exploded after him, wailing a deafening sound like that of twisting metal.

Will evaded in a panic, screaming in utter terror and desperation. He circled the room multiple times, barely evading the beast as it charged him again, and again in relentless pursuit. In a final act of desperation, Will fled back to his body, where he continued to scream.

Jonathan heard a knock, and watched as one of the large doors at the library entrance creaked open. He saw Denise push through and close the massive door behind her. The giant clock on the wall above the entrance chimed; it was eight AM. Denise set her book bag on a chair and took off her coat.

"Good morning," Jonathan said.

"You look tired," Denise said.

"We were up until 3:30 last night," Jonathan replied and rubbed his face with both hands. Sleep had become an annoyance to him; he had little time for it. "I think we've made some progress."

Julia turned from her position at the large window on the far side of the room, and walked out of the morning sun to join them.

Jonathan started the discussion in front of a large, portable whiteboard filled with notes written in blue marker. "A project called *Red Wraith* was first funded by U.S. Army Intelligence in 1947," he explained. "The details are scarce, but it seems that the project was based on a series of studies conducted by the Nazis in various concentration camps from 1941 to 1945. At least four events, or *incidents*, as they are referred to in the American documents, were cited as the basis for the Nazi project, which they had called *Red Falcon*. Hitler himself had allocated significant resources to fund it."

"I saw a seal stamped on some of the Nazi files that looked like a falcon carrying a strange, swastika-like symbol," Denise said. "Maybe that is the emblem for the Red Falcon project."

Jonathan continued, "We also have documents dating back to the early 1950's, from Army Intelligence to the Department of Defense, and later ones to DARPA and the CIA, that propose *scaled-up* research based on Red Falcon and the Nazi incidents. Other, more historical, events are also mentioned: paranormal activity in Russian gulags, strange happenings during the Spanish Inquisition, and unexplained events during the torture of witches in America. According to the records acquired by American forces during the second gulf war, minor incidents had also been observed at Iraqi torture facilities."

"So our government compiled all this information, and assembled a massive program over time," Julia added. "However, until recently, there were only a handful of small test programs scattered around the world."

"That's right," Jonathan continued, "some small-scale research was carried out by our government in secret military facilities in Guam, Mexico, and black CIA sites in Eastern Europe. Subjects for the scaled-up version of the research included military human resources—prisoners of war—and also citizens of foreign lands. With the help of the host countries' corrupt governments, it would only take money."

"The other option was getting people to *volunteer* through the penal system," Julia said.

"That's where the CP facilities come into play," Jonathan said.

"I still don't understand what it is that they're *researching*," Denise said.

"Neither do we," Jonathan said. "We only know it involves torture." He handed the blue marker to Denise. "Now, fill us in on the other Nazi incidents the proposals refer to so ambiguously. I filled Julia in on the first."

"The second incident was quite similar," Denise continued. "In that case, the Nazis systematically tortured *five* Russian spies. The men were kept in five separate rooms, and each strapped securely to a chair. The doctors would start by amputating half a foot, and cauterizing the wound. No anesthetics. The day after a *treatment*, an SS officer would come into the prisoner's room to ask some questions. After the interrogation, the doctors would remove either another few inches of an arm or leg, or start working on a new limb. The process continued until the men died. Some survived significantly longer than others."

Denise drew a rough schematic of the cell layout on the board; five boxes in a row. She then drew in some details: doors, windows and hallways, and the positions of the prisoners' chairs.

"One night, when there were just two of the five men left," Denise explained as she crossed off the three rooms in the center of the row of five, "an SS officer and two doctors entered the room of one of the prisoners, Vladimir Golmakovsky." She drew a circle around the room on the far right, and wrote *VG* next to it. "They interrogated him, and then proceeded to remove two inches of what was left of the man's upper arm, only *the man didn't scream*—in fact, he didn't react *at all*. His eyes rolled back in his head, but he did not slump over as if he'd passed out. One of the doctors left the room to call another to observe what was happening. When the two men were on their way back to the cell, they heard a high pitched, wailing sound, and men screaming. When they got into the room, the prisoner was still strapped to his chair, but the SS officer and the other doctor were *burned* beyond recognition. And what was also peculiar: the other prisoner, four rooms away, was found dead with a broken neck," Denise said, as she drew a circle around the man's room on the opposite end of the row. "Golmakovsky was dead by morning as well; he presumably died of cardiac arrest. Otherwise, none of it—not one death— was explained."

"It gives me the chills," Julia said and shuddered.

Denise continued, "The third incident I found has to do with the interrogation of a British spy. The woman was caught behind German lines, and was questioned for more than thirty days. They interrogated her in the mornings, and tortured her by night. They amputated fingers and toes, and told her they were sending them to her family in England. After about day twenty, the interrogators, including one doctor, began to report *telekinetic activity* during the torture sessions. They said the woman would occasionally become silent and unresponsive, and things would topple over by themselves—cabinets, tables, and on occasion, the interrogators... After day thirty, they had become very frightened of the woman, so they shot her."

"My god," Jonathan shook his head.

"I'm still searching for the fourth incident."

"Now, Julia, the CIA files," Jonathan said, and gestured for her to continue the conversation.

"First off," Julia spoke more towards Denise, "these files corroborate the information from Jonathan's DARPA files: Red Falcon *is* the Nazi precursor to the American Red Wraith project. The Red Falcon files were discovered by the OSS—the agency that would evolve into the CIA—before the end of World War II. Later, the CIA and other government agencies gave the project the highest security classification— same as that of the Manhattan Project. In 1960, DARPA, then known as ARPA, the *Advanced Research Projects Agency*, invested over fifty percent of its annual budget on a project called *Peripheral Biosensors*, and continued to fund it under various names until the present day. There are numerous private subcontractors, and my next task is to assemble a list."

Jonathan stood up and poured more coffee for everyone as he spoke.

"I suppose we should get back to reading: I have a stack of DARPA files to examine, Julia will continue with the CIA files, and Denise, you should find that last Nazi incident …"

"Actually there are *four* more," a man's voice echoed in from the direction of the entrance.

Julia reacted with a muffled gasp of surprise, and Denise whipped her head around to look at the man.

Jonathan stood silent for a few seconds before he could finally speak. "Who the hell are *you*?"

The man smiled. *"A friend,"* he replied, and walked towards them.

The two men looked down from the control room window and out onto the treatment floor.

"Did you feel that? Do we get earthquakes in Detroit?" the technician asked, confused.

"It's probably just one of the heavy machines on the next floor," the medic speculated. "But that screeching..?"

"Yeah, strange," the tech said. "After lunch we'll have to write it up."

Richard approached the three startled people, and tried to calm them with a smile. "I'm the one who sent you these files—I wrote the note and signed it '*A Friend.*'"

Jonathan nodded in recognition, then asked, "How did you find us?"

"You're not a hard man to find, Jonathan," Richard replied. "And I saw Ms. Walker going into the building—recognized her from our files." He turned to the face he didn't recognize. "But I'm afraid I don't know who *you* are."

"I'm Julia McDougal. Jonathan's wife. And what do you mean by 'from our files'?"

"My name is Richard Greene. I work with DARPA on the Red Wraith Project," he explained. "We've been monitoring your activities ever since you began snooping around the Thompson case… Forgive me, but there isn't much time—and we have a lot to talk about."

As Jonathan approached, the man took a step towards him and stuck out his hand. Jonathan hesitated, but shook it anyway.

"What do you mean 'there's not much time,' Mr. Greene?"

"I'll get to that, and please call me *Richard*," he replied. "There's a lot I need to explain... First, I am the head bioengineer of the project. I was initially responsible for the development and implementation of the Exoskeleton—but now I'm very much part of the management, and report only to the project head, Heinrich Bergman."

Jonathan was astonished. If anyone had enough information to take down the program, it was this man. "Why did you give *us* these files?'

"Because the project needs to be stopped," Richard replied. "It's gone too far and horrible things have happened. Many people have died."

"Why didn't you just report it to the authorities?" Jonathan asked.

"To *what* authorities? *The FBI*?" Richard scoffed. "I have no idea who is in on this, Jonathan. The only safe way to stop the program is to leak the information to the public. But it needs to be done carefully... Your name came up in our discussions of the Thompson case, and with your reputation and clout, I thought you might be able to help me."

"The people you work with—did they kill those women at the crime lab?" Denise asked, solemnly.

"Yes," Richard replied, and bowed his head slightly. "And many others, and more to come, if we don't move."

"More to come?" Jonathan asked.

"I believe Thompson is to be terminated within the next few days."

"What? Why?"

"Because his case is a risk to the project, once again," Richard answered. "Cynthia Worthington has come out of her coma."

Will was frightened enough that he had trembled uncontrollably for the full lunch period. He was now too afraid to separate—he couldn't risk running into that thing again ... *What the hell was it?*

The session restarted after lunch, and he knew he'd have to endure the pain the entire afternoon.

Stadler

Richard explained that the girl had emerged from her coma but had not yet spoken, and that Bergman wanted to preempt any assault on the program if she were to reveal Thompson's innocence.

"What could they be hiding that they'd kill to keep it secret?" Denise asked.

"The program implements various kinds of torture" Richard replied without hesitation.

"Dammit, I knew it!" Jonathan shouted.

"But it's more than that," Richard explained, sitting down at a table. The others followed suit. "It's a *carefully controlled* torture that's carried out by a high-tech, bio-interface system called the *Exoskeleton*. The patients are taken to their absolute limits, physically and psychologically. They skirt the edge of death."

"And you're an expert in this … *technology*?" Julia asked with a look of contempt.

Richard saw similar expressions on the faces of the other two.

"Please, let me tell you a little about myself. Just out of grad school, about fifteen years ago, I started working for a bioengineering company called SynCorp, a subcontractor of DARPA. They were developing a system to help severe accident victims—to aid in the process of rehabilitation. It would hold them together structurally, perform controlled movement, administer drugs, and monitor vital medical readings… I only learned that the research had a dual purpose after I accepted a position with DARPA... I started with a low security clearance—I only worked on functionality and performance, not application or implementation. I had no idea what they were doing with it until I was promoted to higher clearance levels."

"When was that?" Jonathan asked.

"About three years ago, when the previous person who held this position … disappeared," Richard responded. "My guess is she found herself in the same position I'm in now—in moral conflict—and was found to be a security risk. Bergman cleans up problems quickly."

"I still don't understand why they would go through all of this trouble just to torture someone. What's the goal?" Denise asked.

"They're after something very specific—you were revealing a hint when I walked in, Denise."

"What? The massacres—the incidents?"

"Yes," Richard answered, and shook his head. "I never thought I'd have to explain this to people on the outside." He stood and nodded towards the coffee maker. "Do you mind if I have a cup? I drove all night to get here." It was the second time in less than a week, he wanted to add.

Jonathan nodded, and Richard walked over to the coffeepot.

"Let's start with some background: the idea started with the Nazis …"

"The Red Falcon Project," Jonathan chimed in.

Richard nodded, and sat down again. "It was well known that Hitler was obsessed with the occult; if there were larger forces on his side, his army would be invincible—that sort of thing. But it was a German scientist named Gunther Nessler who convinced Hitler to create Red Falcon. He theorized that the next step in human evolution was to develop a quasi-physical presence *outside* of one's body. Nessler made two conjectures: first, that every person has this ability lying dormant; second, that the genetic evolution of this so-called ability can be coaxed to activate by extreme environmental conditions. He convinced Hitler that those who had the ability to *separate* would have unmatched power over the physical world—telekinetic abilities and beyond."

"What do you mean by *separate*?" Jonathan asked.

"It means the separation of *soul* and *body*." Richard waited for a reaction, but all three of his listeners appeared dumbfounded, and were silent. "I know it's hard to believe …"

"It's preposterous," Jonathan said, almost laughing.

"I understand your skepticism," Richard said. "As a scientist, I felt the same way, even after reading the horrific incidents reported by the

Nazis. I was skeptical right up until I found out that one of *our* subjects is *showing signs*."

"Signs that his soul left his body?" Julia asked, her expression doubtful.

Richard could tell that none of them were having it. "Well, he's showing preliminary behaviors identical to those that occurred just before the Nazi massacres." He pulled a folder from his briefcase and handed it to Denise, saying, "These are the incident reports that have been submitted in the last two days for Thompson; compare them to those you read from the Nazi files."

"*William Thompson* is the one showing signs?" Denise asked, shocked.

Richard nodded.

"Why did you come here, Richard?" Jonathan asked.

"I needed to relay the urgency to you. I didn't know things were going to move so quickly."

"I don't understand—because the man is *showing signs?*"

"Yes," Richard replied. "What you need to understand is that if Red Wraith has just *one* success—we will never stop the program. And if word got out, other countries would surely start their own programs just to keep up."

"Isn't it too late already?" Julia asked.

"I haven't passed the positive reports on to Bergman," Richard replied.

"But isn't it just a matter of time before he finds out?"

"By then I hope it will be too late... Either Thompson will be dead, or *you* will have found a way to blow the thing wide open... If I lead you to some particularly damning information..." Richard thumbed towards the mound of files. "Could you use your contacts to move on this immediately?"

Jonathan nodded. "Show me."

The pain of the dental treatment still coursed through Will's body and mind, but now there was something else he wanted to forget: the memory of the screeching phantom that had chased him.

Before the Exo went into the sleep rotation, Will sensed Landau's presence and spoke. "Landau, thank God you're here."

"You are frightened of what you saw this morning," Landau said.

Will had given up asking Landau how he knew such things, so he continued.

"I don't know what happened... It was so awful."

"Did you think it was going to harm you?"

"I certainly got that impression."

"I'm certain that it *looked* menacing," Landau said. "But let me assure you, no harm can come to you when you are separated... What you saw was the soul of a man a few rooms down. He was separated, like what you've been doing—but for his first time. He went into a rage, and was about to ..."

"About to what?" Will asked.

"I cannot say. Just know that everything has been resolved now."

"I have no idea what you are saying. What do you mean *resolved*?"

"He has moved on to the next world," Landau replied. "He won't be back."

Will thought he understood. If he separated, maybe he could just keep going further and further away, and never return to his body.

"Is that what *dying* is?"

"The body will die, yes," Landau affirmed.

Will couldn't tell if that was really an answer to his question, but Landau was already gone. His thoughts faded as the motors hummed, and the slow orbit of the Exo put him to sleep.

Jonathan and the others had sorted through the massive piles of folders and binders for hours, and it wasn't until the late afternoon that Richard found the file he was seeking. He handed Jonathan a thick folder labeled: *Compressed Punishment: Final Phase*, and told him to read it while he got a few hours of sleep—he needed rest for the long drive back to DC.

Jonathan took the file to his office two floors down, and read the report in a little over three hours.

It was half past eight when he returned to the library. Denise and Julia were sitting at a large table, and Richard was crashed out on a couch in a dark corner.

"Has he gotten up at all?" Jonathan asked, and thumbed in the direction of the couch.

"No," Denise replied. "Should I wake him?"

"First let me fill you in on the report," Jonathan said.

Jonathan felt exhausted. The report was filled with so many strange ideas that he'd had to read through some sections multiple times. It wasn't that he didn't understand the material; it was his disbelief in what was being stated: it was as if his mind simply refused to accept it. If it wasn't some kind of hoax, he was certain there was enough in the document to sink the CP program in one shot.

"So tell us," Julia said, looking weary but interested.

Jonathan nodded and began, "As Richard explained, the idea is to controllably force the very *soul* of a human being out of his body, and into a limbo state where it is capable of immense violence and destruction. To *separate* the soul from the body."

"They actually refer to the *soul*?" Denise asked.

"Yes... I know it sounds crazy."

"I agree," a voice came in from the dark.

Jonathan saw the silhouette of a tall, thin man, backlit by the evening lighting that shone through the windows on the southern wall. "Welcome back, Richard," Jonathan said.

Richard continued to speak, squinting as he came into the light near the table. "It sounds unbelievable, but the research actually has a crude foundation in science—or at least employs the *methods* of science. Based on the *incidents* reported by the Nazi's, they made one profound conjecture: if unbearable pain was inflicted upon the body, but it wasn't killed or damaged too badly, the soul might temporarily separate from it—to avoid the torment. When in this state, the subject's soul, his consciousness, would essentially be without physical limitations, and could wreak havoc on the physical world—as revealed in the Nazi files. Imagine what the military could do with this. Imagine a spy that could be completely invisible, have unlimited strength, pass through walls, and who knows what else. He'd essentially have *superpowers*."

Denise gasped, "I can understand the military's interest—but I can't believe our government is doing this right now, to *citizens*."

"It *is* the government," Richard replied, "but it's unclear who's in on it and who's not. The program runs independent of the administration— it's self-perpetuating, and hidden deep in the budget somewhere."

"If it didn't work for the Nazis, what makes our government think *they* can do it?" Julia asked.

"What makes you think it didn't work for the Nazis?" Richard replied. "If we had reproduced even *one* of their incidents, we wouldn't be having this conversation; it would already be too late—Red Wraith would be unstoppable. But from an application perspective, you are right, the Nazi program—Red Falcon—*did* fail. Even though a few of their subjects had been able to separate for a short time, they all *died*. None of them survived to retain their abilities—that's the ultimate goal."

"And the American program will be able to do this?" Julia asked.

"The answer to that is in the report I just read," Jonathan cut in. "The Red Wraith project is *different* than the Nazi program in some key aspects. The Nazi's made crucial errors. First, they mutilated their subjects. The Americans believe this was a mistake, as the soul might leave—go to the next place, wherever *that* is—rather than return to a severely damaged body. Second, the psychological state of the subjects in the Nazi project was an issue—they *knew* they were going to be killed in the end. No reason for the soul to stay... Third, the Nazi methods were too crude and impatient—the subjects died too soon. They made the incorrect assumption that, since the incidents they had observed occurred after thirty or forty days of torture, all of their subjects would either exhibit such phenomena in that amount of time, or they would die. They estimated that one in seven thousand were capable of separation."

"How does Red Wraith deal with these problems?" Julia asked.

Jonathan nodded to Richard to continue.

"There were a number of improvements," Richard replied. "First, the body is kept healthy—in fact, *very* healthy. The subjects are on healthy diets, the treatments they undergo actually supplement physical exercise, and they do no permanent damage. In fact they *fix* many things—although painfully."

"And I suppose the subjects don't believe they'll be killed, either," Denise added.

"They are made aware of the risks, but are assured a definite time limit on their torment—exactly one year—giving them hope... The torture methods have also been refined. The Exoskeleton is capable of holding a subject near death almost indefinitely."

"How did these improvements translate?" Jonathan asked.

"The Americans estimated that one in a thousand would transform, a factor of seven improvement over the Nazi estimate," Richard replied. "But Red Wraith has not produced one incident since its inception—*until Thompson, that is*. His case has not yet produced a confirmed *separation*, but it fits in perfectly with the statistical predictions for the new facilities. It will come soon."

"No incidents since the beginning; how many have they tortured?" Julia directed the question to Richard.

"Since 1947," Richard replied, "including all of the earlier experiments, around twenty thousand. To this day, we—*they*—are confused as to how the Nazis got so many incidents to occur using their unrefined methods, and in such a short time frame."

Jonathan changed the subject. "Why didn't you just send us this *Final Phase* report, rather than the entire crate?"

"Two reasons," Richard replied. "First, you're going to need all those files to back up the report in your hand. Otherwise no one is going to believe you... Second; I want you to expose everyone. There are names, and leads to other names in that pile. You can get them all."

"Aren't you mentioned in those files as well?" Denise asked.

"I am... But I don't care anymore... This is something that needs to happen."

"You'll get leniency," Jonathan assured him.

"I suppose we'll find out," Richard said, looking at his watch. "It's time for me to leave. What are your plans?"

Jonathan had already formulated a strategy. "Time is of the essence here; we'd like to preserve Thompson's life if we can," Jonathan replied. "I have some contacts at the state level, and I'll have the report formally disclosed through the DNA Foundation."

"You might be arrested," Richard warned. "The files *are* classified."

"It's a risk I'm willing to take. And I'll keep their source a secret as long as I can," Jonathan promised.

"How can I contact you?" Richard asked.

"You tell us," Jonathan replied. "What don't they have bugged?"

"I assume you all have cash-paid cell phones?"

Jonathan nodded.

"That will work," Richard said, and they exchanged numbers.

The large door creaked softly as Richard left the library. Jonathan didn't know what the man's fate would be, but he admired him for coming forward. He just hoped it wasn't already too late.

The halt of the Exo's rotation roused Will from a light sleep. He was transported into the next room, and given the usual offer for his confession. He was waiting for a possible announcement, but then remembered something: *they couldn't give him any more bad news.* They could tell him that the world outside had become a nuclear inferno, and he just wouldn't care. He had no connection to anyone or anything out there. They had taken away *everything* they possibly could. What else could they possibly do to him?

Will heard a click and felt a sharp jab in his left bicep. He knew that the injection was *not* antibiotics.

Before the drugs took hold, he recalled something he'd heard long ago: *the most dangerous man is the one with nothing to lose.* There was a dark freedom in that realization.

But it seemed to Will, even in his growing state of drug-induced depression, there was still *something* he still possessed that no human could ever touch... After everything else was stripped away, there was still something *inside*. The something he was when he left his body.

Will decided he would no longer tolerate the torture.

The next morning, Will still had a headache from the depressive drugs they'd pumped into him the day before. However, the conclusions he'd drawn while under their influence still remained valid: he was at the *absolute bottom*. They couldn't take *anything* else away from him—and now he would make the torture stop.

The Exo brought him to the next room, and a controller gave him the usual offer of relief, to which he replied with his usual response. A moment later a small iris opened in the ceiling, and Will heard a high-pitched hum. It took him only a second to realize what the noise was: millions of *mosquitoes*.

The insects smelled his nervous sweat, swarming him immediately. They filtered through the metal, tubes, and cables that made up the Exoskeleton, and attacked its sweet, fleshy innards. The itching alone was terrible, but the thought of millions of mosquitoes feasting on him was intolerable. Will summoned a pain memory from that now overdeveloped part of his brain. Even though he was still hesitant after being chased by the tortured soul of the man a few doors down, he exited his body, and was relieved of his suffering.

After a short time Will was drawn back, and awoke to a new feeling—a wooziness, like he was drunk, or poisoned. A loud click startled him, and a needle punctured his left arm, injecting something. He heard fan doors open, the air flowing rapidly, and he felt the mosquitoes being blown off of his skin.

After ten short minutes, the irises opened again, and a new wave of torment arrived: horse flies. Thousands. They bit as they landed, and their bites were by no means as gentle as the subtle injections of the mosquitoes. Will cursed in agitation, and separated once again. This time, when he saw his body black with flies, he swooped down, brushing them off. They scattered for a moment, but immediately returned. His frustration then turned to fury. He flushed them off again—only this time, while they were in flight, he *burned* them. Through his rage, *he burned them all.*

"What the hell just happened?" the tech asked, bewildered. "Was there an electrical short?"

The medic stood up to look through the one-way window. "Not sure—and what was that snapping noise?"

"Better get the foreman on the phone," the tech said, then noticed his partner staring out the window with his mouth hanging open. "What are you looking at?" He stepped up to the window as well. "Holy shit."

"They're all dead," the medic said with an expression of confused disbelief. "How are they *all* dead?"

"They're all fucking burned, man," the tech replied. "Call the foreman, now." He couldn't take his eyes off the thousands of burnt flies, some of them still smoldering, scattered over the floor. Not one was moving. Not one had its wings. A smell like that of burnt hair was coming through the vents.

The tech jumped when Wendler, the foreman, stormed into the control room.

"What the hell's the problem here? And what's that smell?"

The tech pointed out the window.

Wendler walked over to it and looked out. "What the fuck? Was there an electrical short, or a fire?"

"I don't think either one would kill *all* the flies, sir. And the patient looks unharmed," the medic said.

Wendler stared out the window for a minute. "Release the hornets."

"What? Sir, those aren't scheduled until this afternoon," the technician argued.

"Just do it," Wendler commanded.

The tech pushed a button and an iris opened in the room below them. Hundreds of hornets swarmed in. The Exo released a fine mist over Will's body, and the hornets attacked. A moment later, a light on the control panel indicated that the patient had received an injection on the right side of his neck.

"There goes the epinephrine," said the medic.

The hornets were all over the man's body and stinging *repeatedly*. A moment later they were in flight, and in that instant they all sparked like flash bulbs. Their burnt remains floated to the floor like singed dandelion spores.

Wendler stood perfectly still, staring out the window and mumbling incoherently to himself. He spun around and faced the controllers, his eyes blinking.

"I need to get the Warden—don't do anything—ANYTHING!" Wendler yelled. He rubbed his eyes, then almost fell over a trash can as he ran from the control room.

"We won't," the tech said, assuring himself more than Wendler.

Richard drove into the dark, underground parking structure, turned off his car and sat in silence. He was sure Bergman wouldn't be on his case for the delayed reports—the man was preoccupied with other problems—terminating Thompson and locating the missing project files. Richard got out of his car and walked to a secure elevator, which took him up to the seventh floor. Sunlight shone through the large windows in the front office area, and people bustled about; it seemed like a normal Monday morning. Once in his office, he checked his e-mail: a few meeting reminders, but otherwise nothing important. He'd hold onto the previous week's reports until the new batch arrived, in two days. With any luck, Thompson would be dead by then. He just hoped McDougal could deliver on his end.

Will didn't want to experience the invasive medical tests that were planned for the day, so he exited his body the minute they started. During his explorations of the room, and some of the adjacent rooms that included those above and below him, he had noticed something peculiar. While he was at the ceiling near the control booth, he saw a digital display screen on the support appendage of the Exoskeleton, about two feet from the insertion point on the small of his back. The screen was about three inches long and an inch wide, and displayed three digits: *761*. It hit Will immediately—*give us the number*. It was subtly placed, but he should have noticed it by now. He was intrigued: there was no way he could have seen the display from his body; it seemed they were expecting him to view it *another way*. He'd give them all a good shakeup when he felt the time was right.

Will felt the day's treatment had ended early. He didn't know for certain, since he'd spent most of the late morning and early afternoon separated. Action was something he could perceive clearly in that state, but *time* was a little skewed.

He sensed Landau after the evening feeding.

"You've been very active today," Landau said. "I know what you've been doing, and what you're capable of doing at this point... But I'm not sure you fully understand your potential."

"I'm not sure I really care," Will replied. Even with the development of his new abilities, he was still completely and utterly alone in the world.

"I know—because you've lost everything, everyone."

"Yes," Will replied. Again, Landau knew what he'd been thinking.

"Then you should feel *content*."

"What the hell does *that* mean?" Will spat back.

"You've already thought this out: there is nothing more they can take from you," Landau replied. "You have no possessions. No one can harm your family or destroy your career. No reputation or honor to worry about. They can't even inflict pain on you anymore—if you choose to remove yourself."

"You need to listen to me carefully," Landau said in a deliberate tone. "You are coming close to fulfilling a unique dichotomy—a link between two worlds. They have been conducting this experiment for over half a century, and many thousands of people have died. They have not yet succeeded—and this is probably their last chance."

"I don't understand what that means," Will said.

"You will soon face hard decisions—in the heat of rage and the depths of despair. And *if* you get out of here alive, you will have the responsibility to do something *good* in this world."

"What do you mean by *something good*?" Will asked.

"Trust your own judgment. It's the only reason you've lasted as long as you have... Now I will say good night."

"Good night, Landau." Will faded to sleep.

CHAPTER VII
Apocalypse

It was 7:30 p.m. on February 2nd when Heinrich Bergman got a call from Warden Halbreath.

"Your man, Lenny, is here," Halbreath said. "He's trying to set up the removal of Patient 523."

Bergman never liked Halbreath. The man was always asking questions he shouldn't be asking, disrupting things when it was not his place to do so. It was a typical case of an ex-military officer wanting to hold on to authority.

"When will it be finished?" Bergman asked.

"I think you should see what's going on here before you do anything drastic."

"Why are you delaying this?" Bergman was becoming agitated. "All you need to know is that this man is a security risk to the entire program."

"I'll admit I don't know exactly what's been happening, but I think you really need to come see for yourself."

Bergman sensed a pleading in the man's voice: he wanted to say more, but security protocol forbade certain things in phone conversations.

"You're telling me I need to come out there *personally*?"

"Yes," Halbreath replied, without delay.

Bergman was silent. *What could be going on?*

Halbreath continued, "And far stranger things have occurred since last week's report."

Bergman was confused. "Last week's report?"

"Yes, there were incidents reported for Patient 523."

Bergman was startled. If there had been anything in the weekly report, Richard would have told him. Then he remembered that Richard had been out sick. "Tell Lenny to hold up until I get there," Bergman ordered. "I'll get the first flight out tomorrow."

Bergman hung up on Halbreath and immediately called Richard. "Get up to my office, and bring last week's CP report."

What a quandary he was in now, Bergman thought. The longer the termination was delayed, the more time the girl had to start communicating—and possibly to claim Thompson's innocence. Whatever was happening at the Detroit facility, it had better not be a false alarm. Otherwise he'd have to seriously consider removing Halbreath from his post, in the most permanent sense.

Jonathan hung up the phone, got up from his desk, and sat down at the large table in his office. Denise was sitting across from him, and seemed anxious to hear his report.

"The Governor will see me as soon as he has an opening—they said within the next twenty-four hours," Jonathan replied. "I'll show him the report, and some of the supporting documents we've found. He's a good man, and may be able to expedite a move on this."

Richard was much calmer than he expected to be when he got the call from Bergman. He knew it was just a matter of time before word of the incidents got out, but he'd hoped it would be a few more days.

Bergman was on the phone when Richard arrived at his office, but waved him in and pointed to a chair. Richard took a seat, opened the reports and tried to look interested in its contents. He'd play it off like it was news to him as well.

Bergman got off the phone, and sat at the table. "You look like shit," Bergman said.

Richard was suddenly grateful for his lack of sleep; it helped him look the part.

"Well, I feel like it too."

Bergman nodded. "Evidently, a lot has occurred while you were out."

"Yes?"

"*Halbreath* requested that I come out to the Red Box to see a patient."

"What's going on?" Richard tried to look surprised.

"No idea," Bergman replied, and pointed to the binder in front of Richard. "Those are from last week?"

"Yes, and this week's reports should be in tomorrow."

Bergman grabbed the binder, and turned it sideways on the table so both men could see. "Let's have a look at Thompson—*523*," he said as he thumbed his way through the tabs. "Here it is." He opened it up to the tab for *523*, and began to read.

Richard already knew what it said, but pretended to read anyway. From the man's breathing alone, he knew Bergman understood the implications of the report. Thompson was clearly exhibiting the precursor signs of an *incident*: no reaction to pain, and talking to himself in muffled gibberish.

"Holy shit," Bergman said. "We nearly lost this man! And Halbreath implied that more incidents have occurred since this report. This could have been a disaster—I was having him removed from the system."

Richard wished it had been done—just one more day might have been enough. He had taken huge risks, and all for nothing. Now, even if McDougal got the files to the right people, the government would shield the project instead of disowning it.

"Pack your bags, Richard. You're coming with me to Detroit," Bergman said almost gleefully. "I'll get us on the 5 a.m. from Reagan International."

Richard nodded and forced a smile.

He could see only one option now, considering the circumstances. He'd have to pack his gun.

Richard sat down on the couch, and looked at the clock above the fireplace; it was 10:30 p.m. He was in the house where he and his wife had made their life together, and now, even though all of the furniture was still there, it seemed like an empty shell. It saddened him deeply, but he knew he'd done the right thing sending her and the girls away.

He programmed Jonathan McDougal's number into his pre-paid temp phone. He then put the phone, some files, and his snub-nosed .38 Special in a lead-shielded, steel case. During the flight, the case would be put in a special compartment along with Bergman's, and they'd pick it up as they disembarked. He knew Bergman carried a gun regularly, but it would be *his* first time. It made him nervous; he hadn't even fired the weapon in more than three years.

Richard reached back into the case and retrieved the phone. He dialed McDougal's number, and he heard the man answer after two rings.

"Who is this?"

"I made a visit a few days ago," Richard replied. They wouldn't use their names. "My boss already knows about the incidents—he called off the hit on the subject. The supervisor of the facility requested we go there in person. Evidently there have been more incidents. What's the status on your side?"

"I have a meeting with the governor of Illinois tomorrow. He will have some immediate influence, if I can convince him that this is real."

"If anyone is going to take action, let me know," Richard said. "You can reach me safely at this number. If I don't hear from you, I'm going to assume things aren't moving forward, and I may have to take drastic steps... Is there anything else?"

"I also sent one of my people, the young woman you met, to try and communicate with the girl," Jonathan informed. "We're doing everything we can on this end."

"I wouldn't have expected anything less," Richard said, and ended the call.

After an unusually long wait following the morning feeding, Will was startled by a loud click, and felt a needle stab into his right upper arm. He immediately felt a warm sensation spread from the injection site, fluming through his blood-stream. It wasn't unpleasant at first, but then, in a split second, it felt as if he was burning from the inside out. He screamed uncontrollably, and felt another hypodermic needle jab into his left inner thigh. Again ... warm ... warmer ... fire. The pain was too intense, and he left his body. All he could do was watch it quietly suffer.

Richard thought the control room had to be beyond its recommended capacity; everyone had to contort their bodies so they didn't accidently push a button or hit a switch. All the important people were there: Bergman, Lenny, Halbreath, Wendler, and the two treatment controllers.

"What am I supposed to be looking at here?" Bergman asked, looking out the window.

The tech explained as he pushed a button, "I'm injecting him with a chemical we call *fire fluid*—it's horrible. The patients usually scream until they pass out, then wake up screaming again. The process just repeats and repeats."

"Okay, okay," Bergman said quickly. "Are you sure it's working?"

"Don't know for sure," the tech replied. "But it's from the same batch we used on the last guy. Seems this patient isn't responding—he's not passed out, but he's not in pain either... In fact, his face even looks calm—see the monitor?"

Bergman glanced at Halbreath. "I'm hoping we didn't fly out just for this... There's more?"

"Let's go to the conference room," Halbreath said. "I'll show you why I asked you to come."

As they headed for the door, Richard couldn't take his eyes off Thompson, first from the window that overlooked the treatment room, and then from a monitor on the wall. The man's eyes were closed most of the way, the narrow slits showing only white. *He could be in the wraith state right now,* Richard thought.

"Intriguing, isn't it?" Bergman said. "Let's go see what else they have."

Despite the situation, Richard couldn't help being fascinated by what else might be in store.

Will watched the men leave the control room. There was only one person in the group he thought he recognized—it was the man who welcomed him to this hell on that first, horrific day. He wanted to know who the others were—something was happening.

Will saw one of the two remaining controllers scan some sensor readouts on the wall, and heard him say to the other, "His pain level is at eight point one—he should be screaming his lungs out."

"Let's up the dose a little," the other replied, turning a dial and pressing a button labeled *INJECT*.

After a few seconds, Will sensed an increase in his background agitation—his suffering body—and went back into the treatment room just in time to see the Exo eject a spent needle cartridge to the floor. The clanging of the metallic cartridge on the tile set off a tidal wave of emotion within him; an anger rising, eclipsing all else. He decided it was time to do something about it.

Will pressed through the glass into the control room once more, and examined the two people there. Their nametags read: *Paulson, Technician 34;* and *Schmidt, Medic 34.* He then went back into the treatment room to read the three digit digital display behind the head-cage of the Exo.

Oh yeah, Will thought. *This should shake them up all right.*

"Looks like he's back," Schmidt said. "About time."

"Wait," Paulson sat up. "He *said* something." Both controllers listened for a moment. It became clear: the man was repeating a number.

Schmidt looked at his computer monitor, and then turning to Paulson said:

"Jesus... He's right."

"Really?" Paulson leaned over to look at the number on Schmidt's screen. "Have you ever heard of anyone getting it right?"

"I'm sure it has happened, it's just a one in a thousand chance," Schmidt said and turned to the keyboard. "There's protocol for this." He pushed a button that activated the intercom in the treatment room. "Patient 523, what's the number now?"

After about ten seconds came the reply, "311."

Schmidt nodded, typed, and called to the treatment room again. "And now?"

After a short delay, the patient replied, "172."

"Holy crap," Paulson said, walking to the window. "It would be impossible for him to see it in that position. Do it again.

Schmidt put in a new number and called once more. "And how about now?"

"879... How long are we going to play this game, Schmidt?"

Schmidt looked to Paulson with an expression of confused fear. "But how ..."

"I don't know," Paulson replied, just as confused. He went to the intercom and spoke. "How do you know his name?"

"It's on his nametag, Paulson," the patient replied.

Both controllers stared at each other wide-eyed.

Finally Schmidt said "Let's get the warden—right now."

Richard, Bergman, and Lenny sat down at a large conference table as Halbreath and Wendler set up a computer and projector. Bergman was trying to remain calm, but his excitement was obvious. For some reason, Richard thought of something an old physics professor from his college days had said. He said that if something was *possible*, referring to science or engineering or whatever, humans would eventually *do it*, even if they destroyed themselves in the process. Richard knew the idea applied to Red Wraith project: it had already cost too much.

Wendler dimmed the lights and Halbreath narrated the presentation.

"This is the video of Thompson in the insect room," Halbreath explained and pushed the play button. A view of one of the treatment rooms appeared with Thompson and the Exoskeleton at its center—the date and time appeared in the lower right-hand corner: January 31, 9:36 a.m. EST.

They watched as black flies swarmed in on Thompson's body, crawling on top of one another to get to his flesh. The audio was clear: the buzzing of thousands of flies, and intermittent screams. Then the screaming stopped, and a few seconds later the flies all took to the air as if they'd been blown off by a breeze—only to return to the body. After another few seconds of gorging, the flies went airborne a second time, but before they could return, the screen flashed white multiple times—making it impossible to see. The flashes were in unison with crackling sounds— like those of thousands of flashbulbs igniting. A few seconds later, the picture recovered, and the full view was restored.

"What the hell just happened? Where are the flies?" Bergman said, his eyes bulging.

"They burned up. See the floor and the burnt parts floating in the air?" Halbreath said as he pointed to the screen.

Richard was overwhelmed; he had never seen anything like it. He turned to see Bergman's expression, which was like that of a child on Christmas morning.

"Let's look at the hornets now," Halbreath said as he fast-forwarded.

"There's more?" Bergman asked, elated.

"Yes. The hornets, and also the dental assistant."

The video showed the hornets flying out of an iris and attacking Thompson voraciously. In just a few seconds, an event occurred that was identical to that of the flies, and the camera was again saturated with bright flashes.

Bergman sat down. "This might be the real thing... A *real* incident... And what about the dental—"

The door to the conference room flew open and slammed into the wall as Paulson and Schmidt burst into the room. Richard nearly fell out of his chair.

"He's reading the *numbers*," Schmidt said, out of breath.

Richard could hardly believe what he'd just heard. *The numbers.* It wasn't uncommon for patients to report a correct number from time to time—a one in a thousand chance is not difficult when over three hundred guesses are made each day. What really mattered was the *number of times* a patient would give the correct number. Nobody ever got *two* correct.

"How many times did he get it right?" Richard asked, knowing the protocol.

Paulson looked to the Schmidt, who shrugged. "*At least four times*," Paulson finally replied.

Richard was astonished.

"That *has* to be real. Let's get down there," Bergman said, looking at Richard with wide eyes.

Richard knew the odds of guessing a number between one and a thousand four times in a row was miniscule—one in a *trillion. It had to be real.*

"But wait," Paulson said. "He also knew our *names.*"

Bergman put his hand on the man's shoulder.

"You're sure of that?"

"Yes sir… When he gave us the numbers, he used our names."
Bergman turned to Richard once again. "Let's get down there."

Back in the control room, Paulson sat at a computer terminal and checked the treatment parameters. "The pain level indicators all read zero, and there is no active treatment right now," he said as he turned up the volume for the room microphone. The treatment floor was silent.

"Can you talk to him?" Bergman asked.

"Here, *you* can," Paulson said, and handed him a portable mic.

Bergman hesitated briefly, finally saying: "Thompson."

There was no response.

He waited a few seconds and said it again, this time louder, "Thompson."

Again, no response.

Bergman turned to Halbreath. "Is he unconscious?"

"I have no idea," Halbreath replied, "but the medical crew is already on their way down there—they want to try a direct injection of concentrated fire fluid."

"Can we go down there—on the floor?" Bergman asked.

"Yes, follow me."

Richard didn't know if it was safe to go down to the treatment room, but then he remembered his contingency plan. Personal safety was not a factor anymore—it couldn't be. This might be his only opportunity to get close to Thompson. He pulled his left arm tight against his body, and pressed the hard object against his chest to reassure himself: the gun was loaded and ready.

Will watched the warden and all but two of the other men leave the control booth. He knew they were on their way to him. He listened in on the controllers' conversation.

"What the hell's going on?" Paulson asked.

"No idea," Schmidt replied. "But I am *freaked out*."

Will needed to know who he was dealing with. He went back to his body, and said "Paulson, who were those men?"

He waited ten seconds for an answer.

"Better answer me before they get down here."

Paulson and Schmidt stared at each other, frozen. Neither man replied.

Schmidt's coffee cup suddenly smashed against the wall, seemingly of its own volition, spraying him with coffee and ceramic chips. The door handle made a horrible screeching noise as it spontaneously ripped itself from the control room door, leaving a gaping hole surrounded by shards of jagged metal.

"Who are they?" Will screamed.

Paulson pushed the intercom button, shaking. "They're government guys—some research agency. The boss is Bergman, his partner is Richard—I don't know his last name. The tall guy with slicked hair is the warden. That's all we know for sure."

"What's the warden's name?"

"Halbreath, Jack Halbreath," Paulson yelled hysterically.

"Now go away—get the hell out of there," Will commanded.

After a brief moment of hesitation, Schmidt rushed for the door and tugged at it frantically. He kicked and strained, but it was thoroughly jammed.

Paulson ran over and tried to help, only to be thrown across the room by an unseen force—the same thing happening to his partner. The door then ripped itself from its hinges with a deafening screech, and flew into the hall.

The two men ran out.

Stadler

Will waited for the men from the control room, but was confused when he saw three different, yet familiar faces enter through the access door. The doctors strode in, Poliakov assembling a hypodermic needle and filling the syringe with a yellow fluid. He then approached Will.

"I'm afraid I'm going to have to decline treatment today," Will said. "I'm just not in the mood for more needles."

Poliakov ignored him and continued his approach.

Will exited his body and advanced upon the man. From the perspective of the other doctors, Poliakov suddenly thrust the needle into his own thigh, plunging its contents into his bloodstream.

Will returned to his body to watch Poliakov's reaction: he thought the doctor deserved a taste of his own medicine.

"Why did you do that?" Dr. Noh yelled at Poliakov.

"I didn't ... I ..." Poliakov trailed off as his eyes bulged.

His face distorted into a terrible grimace, and he burst into a blood-curdling scream. He then dropped to the floor, convulsing wildly. Dr. Johnson approached to aid him, but took a wild kick to her midsection. Poliakov suddenly went silent, no longer moving.

Johnson's face was pale as she cradled her stomach. "We better get him to the lab."

Will watched as the two doctors dragged Poliakov out of the room, leaving a double trail of dark streaks from the heels of the man's shoes. Will knew he didn't have to let them go, but he did—there might be bigger fish to fry.

The access door swung back slowly, but didn't close completely. A few seconds later Will heard Poliakov's screams recommence: it was a relentless chemical.

Now he'd wait for the others.

Richard followed Bergman and Halbreath down the narrow service channel that led to the treatment floor. Lenny followed closely behind. Without warning, there was a horrific scream about fifty feet in front of them that echoed down the corridor. Halbreath and Bergman both stopped suddenly, and Richard peered around them to see what was happening. He saw two people in white coats struggling to drag a third, who thrashed for a few seconds before falling limp and silent.

"What's going on?" Halbreath asked as he approached.

"Not sure," Johnson replied. "We'll explain in the medical lab."

When they got to the med lab, Poliakov was laid on one of the exam tables. For the half hour that followed, the man repeatedly awoke, then screamed and thrashed himself back into unconsciousness.

Johnson recounted what occurred in the treatment room—what Thompson had said, how Poliakov injected himself with the chemical.

Halbreath took a call on his cell phone out in the hall. When he came back in, he told Bergman that the two controllers had fled their post, and described what they reported witnessing in the control room.

"Okay," Bergman took the lead. "I want to have a meeting in one hour. Halbreath, you set it up."

Halbreath nodded.

"I want *all* of the relevant personnel to be here," Bergman added, "that means the controllers who are responsible for the *next* treatment room, the engineers—and the entire medical staff. I don't care if they aren't on duty—get them here. One hour."

Bergman dialed his cell phone as he left the room. Richard knew he'd want all of the project contributors there to witness the first controlled event. This was Bergman's moment— what he hoped to be remembered for. But Richard wasn't sure it was going to work out the way he hoped.

At 9:00 p.m., Richard sat at a large table in a conference room with all of the other personnel that Halbreath had gathered. Bergman sat at the head of the table.

"What room is he in tomorrow?"

Halbreath answered, "He was supposed go through a surgery prep routine. He has a precancerous cist... Just maintenance, really."

"We'll need something else," Bergman said. "Something more severe."

"The electrical dental stimulation has been the most effective treatment thus far," Halbreath replied. "But if you want him to talk, then the bone-bending program would be best."

"Does the room, or the Exo, have a mechanism for *terminating* the subject if the need arises?" Bergman asked.

"Why?" Halbreath seemed confused.

"A safety precaution," Bergman snapped. "There's potential danger here. I'll be carrying a weapon, but we'll need a backup plan."

One of the engineers, a thin, balding man in his late thirties, cut in. "We could load sodium pentothal into one of the injection chambers... The program is designed to keep the subject alive for as long as possible, but we could override that interlock with the warden's access code."

"Good," Bergman said. "Set it up so it can be activated with the push of a button—there might not be *time* to do anything more, understand?"

The man nodded.

"Now," Bergman addressed everyone, "you must understand that everything we've talked about here, and everything you see tomorrow, is strictly classified... This might be the most important discovery in recent times, but it needs to remain a secret." His phone rang in his jacket pocket.

"I have to take this. I want all of you here at 5 a.m. tomorrow." He turned away and answered the call. "Admiral Sparkes, yes, you should get here tonight if possible …"

Will was exhausted but could not sleep. He sensed Landau's presence.

"I'm aware of your activities today," Landau said.

"Yes, it seems I have the tools to survive—if I *want* to... But I can't find much to live for here..."

"What has happened to you is something that usually takes a complete lifetime to occur," Landau replied. "It is the *purpose* of this life. You are now fully *stripped*."

"It's the *purpose* of this life to be stripped?" Will asked. "I don't understand."

"Everything you lost you were going to lose anyway," Landau said. "*All* of it... People try to forget that by clinging to the people around them, their careers, physical belongings, youth ... but it will *all* be lost... *You* no longer have to live through that long, tortuous process."

"Those are things that bring people happiness," Will replied. "How can *losing* them be the purpose of this life?"

"All the things that make you *think* you're happy in this world do *not*," Landau replied. "It is a façade. *Not one thing* in this world is permanent. A hundred years from now, everyone you have ever seen or heard of will be dead. *Everyone*... There is only one objective of this life—to strip you of your desires, lies, and misconceptions. Real life starts after this is accomplished."

Will couldn't speak.

"Is it really such a dark idea?" Landau asked. "When a man thinks he is happy in life—with his job, wife, family, health—he immediately starts to fear the loss of these things, and feels his own mortality by proxy... The purpose of your life, of everyone's life, is to shed the *real*

Exoskeleton—*fear*," Landau said. "Fear of losing youth, loved ones, material belongings—fear of pain, fear of death and what lies beyond... You have already shed all these things."

"It feels like something big is happening," Will said. "I can't sleep."

"You're right, Will. Something big *is* happening... And I've taken you as far as I can. You will be on your own from here."

"I understand."

"One last thing," Landau added. "You've experienced first-hand that you are not limited by the physical world—even the Exoskeleton cannot contain you. But let me remind you of something else: you are not limited by *time*, either. That was the purpose of my question: *where were you in 1952?* The correct answer to that question is *somewhere... You have been, and always will be somewhere.*"

Will was silent.

"Goodbye William."

"Goodbye Landau," Will replied with a meek voice. He would not hear from Landau again—but he was at peace with the thought; it seemed he no longer needed him.

The Exo started its rotation.

"What the hell was he saying?" Bergman asked Richard. They'd been sitting in the control room for an hour, listening intently to Thompson's muffled gibberish.

Richard shrugged. He had no idea—it sounded like someone speaking in tongues, but with *two* different voices, alternating like a conversation. From the camera trained on the Thompson's face, Richard noticed that even his facial expression changed as he switched voices.

"All I can tell you is that he's *not* sleeping," the night tech chimed in, pointing to a brain-wave monitor on the control panel. "Seems to do this a lot." He handed Richard a ringed binder labeled *Nightly Reports*.

Richard paged through it—there were a dozen such reports of Thompson carrying out garbled conversations. "Do the other patients do this?" Richard asked, and handed the binder to Bergman.

"Some, yes," the tech replied. "But they're usually talking in their sleep, or crying to themselves; nothing like this, and not nearly as often... Guy might have a split personality."

Lenny walked into the room with a hot cup of coffee, and Bergman asked the night tech and medic to step out for a few minutes.

The controllers obliged, and closed the door behind them.

"As you both know," Bergman began, "our Thompson problem has not changed, but the solution to the problem obviously must."

Richard didn't understand.

Bergman continued, "Thompson *is* the program right now. And, therefore, a threat to him, is a threat to the *entire project*." He looked to Lenny.

Lenny nodded. "I'll get the first flight out," he said.

"Where's he going?" Richard asked.

"Southern Illinois," Bergman answered.

It took Richard a few seconds to process the information. When he realized what Bergman meant, his guts twisted, and he felt sick.

He had to contact McDougal.

Richard got to his hotel room a little before 11:00 p.m., took off his jacket, and unstrapped the shoulder holster for his .38 Special. He pulled out his temp phone and called Jonathan.

"I have some news for you," Jonathan said immediately.

"Go ahead."

"I went to Springfield and spoke with Governor McGuinness today. He's going to help us get the ball rolling on this."

"It might already be too late," Richard responded. "There's going to be a test tomorrow. Everyone is convinced that Thompson is transforming—I'm convinced, too."

"We'll keep pressing—we're doing everything we can."

"I believe you," Richard responded, "but that's not why I'm calling." There was only silence on the other end, so Richard continued, "Bergman ordered a hit on the victim—the girl that just came out of a coma. She's a threat."

"My God!" Jonathan shouted. "Denise is there with her."

"The assassin's name is Lenny Butrolsky," Richard explained. "He's flying to St. Louis from Detroit Metro early tomorrow morning. I don't know any other details."

"Okay, I have to make some calls immediately. Thanks for the info," Jonathan said and hung up.

Richard hung up his temp phone, and picked up his permanent one. He stared at it for a minute: it occurred to him that the upcoming conversation with his wife might be their last.

Denise plugged her phone into the car charger and turned it on—seeing she had missed calls, she then dialed her voicemail. There were eight new messages. As she listened to the fifth, she almost drove her car into a ditch. The clock on the dashboard read 10:07 a.m. She searched frantically through her purse, and quickly resorted to dumping it out on the seat. She grabbed the Glock 40 and put it in her jacket, pushing the accelerator to the floor. *She had to get to the hospital.*

When the Exo halted its rotation, Will knew immediately that something was wrong. It didn't place him in the feeding position, and there was no maintenance routine.

A few minutes later, the access door opened and a dozen people walked in—some in suits, others in military uniforms and lab coats. A tall man in a dark suit walked over, his hard-soled shoes making loud clicks on the tile floor. It was one of the men from the control room the previous day.

He walked under Will, who was suspended about ten feet above him, and opened his mouth to say something.

"You're Bergman," Will said, cutting him off.

Bergman didn't respond, but closed his mouth and turned to the others with a serious look.

"I *am* Bergman," he finally replied. "Have we met?"

Will ignored the question.

"All these people are here to observe your new abilities," Bergman said.

"What *abilities*?" Will asked. "Did you come to hear me *scream*?" He could sense this man was somehow responsible for everything he had gone through.

Bergman reddened. "I think you know *exactly* what I'm talking about."

Will did not respond.

"I only want you to do something simple," he said, nodding to a technician who set down a bottle in the corner of the room. "I want you to tip over that bottle, Mr. Thompson," he said and then walked back to join the others. "If you do, you'll get the whole day off—no treatment today."

"Let me out of this thing," Will said. He couldn't hide his anger any longer.

"We can do this the easy way, or the painful way, Mr. Thompson. Your choice. I thought you'd appreciate a break after thirty-four days of treatment."

Will had lost count again: had it only been *thirty-four days*? He shook it off. "If I were you, I would think *very carefully* about my next move," Will warned.

"Well then, it looks like you have chosen," Bergman said and then turned to Halbreath. "Is everything ready up there?"

Halbreath nodded to Bergman, then spoke in the direction of the control booth. "Load the bone bender program, the right femur, and start on my mark." He turned back to Bergman. "Give it a minute, then tell me when you want to start."

Bergman walked up to Will. "This is your last chance."

"Actually, it might be *yours*," Will whispered back.

Bergman backed off and nodded to Halbreath, who motioned "go" towards the control room.

The program started a few seconds later, and Will felt the Exo exert pressure on the middle of his right thigh. After a few seconds he felt his femur start to flex, and the dull pain quickly began to sharpen. It finally reached a level where he had to scream. The people in the room covered their ears and looked away.

Will soon had enough, and he separated. He watched from above as everyone slowly took their hands off their ears and looked at each other. A military man walked a little closer. "Look at his eyes." The others walked up to have a closer look as well. Will's anger increased exponentially as he watched them.

Halbreath suddenly noticed a new sound; like screeching static. "What the hell is that?"

Bergman grinned and looked around. "Now we're talkin'..."

Will saw Bergman pull a pistol out of his coat, and release the safety.

Denise screeched to a halt near the emergency entrance and rushed into the hospital. She ran to the elevator and hit the button for the eighth floor. It stopped twice on the way up, during which she was crawling out of her skin with anxiety. She finally got to the eighth floor and ran past the nurse station to room 822, stopping short a few steps past the threshold. There was no one there.

She ran out and went straight to the nurses' station. A woman was on the phone, and Denise interrupted. "Where's the girl from room 822?"

The nurse held up her hand, and continued to talk.

Denise snatched the phone from the woman's hand, and hung it up. "This is important, where the hell is she?"

"I'm going to call security," the woman said, picking up the phone again.

Denise grabbed it, and held on to it as she walked around to the other side of the station and looked at a computer monitor. "You can call security after you tell me where they moved Cynthia Worthington."

"Yes, I'd like to know as well," a man said from behind Denise.

Denise spun around and saw a large man pull a gun with a silencer from his pocket, aiming it at the nurse.

"Tell me, please," the man said with a subtle accent.

Denise froze. Her gun was in her pocket, but there was no way she'd be able to pull it before he could turn on her.

The nurse's eyes widened with confusion for a second, but she quickly came to her senses.

"She was moved last night, but I don't know where."

"Last chance," the man said.

"I don't know where she is!" the woman screamed.

Denise heard a muffled shot, and the woman fell to the floor, holding her shoulder.

"Okay, now *this* is your last chance," the man said, and aimed the gun at her head.

The woman whimpered, "They moved her to the secure wing,"

"And where's that?"

"Fourth floor, east wing," the woman replied, crying now.

"Thank you," the man said, shooting her in the head. He was turning the gun towards Denise when she jumped over a desk on the opposite side of the station, knocking down a computer monitor in the process. She landed heavily on the tile floor, and fumbled around in her coat for the Glock. She found it, removed the safety, and aimed in the direction of the man as he walked around the station. As soon as his head came into view, she fired, missing far left.

The shot startled him however, and he ran in the direction of the elevators—headed for the fourth floor.

Will watched his body suffering below him, and observed all of the people *watching* it suffer. This enraged him to the point where he heard a ringing sound build in his mind. The people in the room covered their ears and tucked their heads into their chests—he knew they must be hearing it, too.

He had to fight the strong urge to destroy them, and thought maybe he should try to depart—to leave his body behind before something awful happened. There was nothing left for him in this world now.

He passed through the wall into the next chamber where another inmate, presumably *Number 522*, was undergoing a "treatment." The man's voice was hoarse from screaming. A doctor Will hadn't seen before was operating on the man's lower abdomen. He wanted to stop it, but in this case he couldn't; a disruption in the middle of an operation might kill the man. For a split second, Will considered killing the patient himself to end his misery. But then he thought it was not his place to do so—this man might *want* to live.

The next room was *empty,* and he knew that that could only mean *one* thing; 521 was part of the twenty-seven percent that didn't make it out alive. He wondered if 521 was that horrible aberration he saw—the *wraith*. The thought made him feel an overwhelming sense of guilt, both for his own suffering body that he was abandoning, and for the man who was 521. He looked back in the direction from which he came. Maybe he could do *something* before he left. Maybe he could stop the compressed punishment program himself—all the important players seemed to be within his reach.

He would go back.

He would become the wraith.

Denise ran for an exit she hoped would lead to a stairwell. It did, and she leapt frantically down the stairs, two or three at a time. She twisted her ankle on the final landing, and limped to the door leading to the fourth floor. Through the window to her right, she saw the man exit the elevator, and turn right down a hall.

She had two choices: she could take a route opposite that of the man's and hope to find the girl first, or she could turn right, and intercept him before *he* found her.

Denise opened the door and turned right, towards the elevators, then left to follow the direction in which the man had gone. She walked as quickly as she could without making a scene, dodging patients and nurses, until she came to a large door with a sign that read: *Have Security Pass Ready.* It was the secure wing. She opened the door slowly, and saw a security guard slumped over a desk, dead. She walked quietly around the desk, and proceeded down the hall, navigating smaller, tributary halls to the left and right. She realized she had to move faster—she had to get to him *before he got to the girl.*

Denise started running, no longer worried about being quiet. She came to the end of the large hall, and turned left, down one of the narrower passages. After a few strides, she heard a deafening blast behind her. It startled her so badly she fell down to her left side, and slid against the wall. Having dropped the Glock in the fall, she scrambled to pick it up, and spun to see what was behind her.

The image was seared into her memory, and would frequently haunt her nightmares. The assassin was facing her, but he'd fallen to his knees, his gun beside him on the floor. Another thirty feet behind was

Jonathan, weapon in hand, running towards the man. He pushed the man down, and kicked the gun down the tile floor, towards Denise.

"It was a good thing you turned left," Jonathan said, breathing heavily.

"What? What are you...?" Denise asked, shocked and somewhat dazed.

"I got here an hour ago," Jonathan replied. "I left at 3:30 a.m., after I'd convinced the local police to at least move the girl to the security wing."

Security guards rushed in, disarmed Denise and Jonathan, and called the medical staff for the wounded man.

"Is he going to live?" Denise asked.

"Looks like he took it in the shoulder," Jonathan said, looking over the now unconscious Lenny. "No better place to get shot than in a hospital."

"Did you see the girl?" Denise asked.

"Yes, she's fine," Jonathan said. "There is a lot happening. Let me fill you in ..."

Will pressed through multiple walls and returned to his treatment room. He heard Bergman instructing the controllers to increase the pain level, and observed the extreme distortion of his right thigh. Then something happened that put him over the edge.

Will actually *heard* it—it *broke*. His body shook violently in response. He saw his upper thigh bent at an unnatural angle. The femur had snapped.

Will felt an anger surge through his being that was far beyond anything he had experienced in his life. He knocked Bergman to the floor. Someone made a move for the door, and he smashed it closed; the steel door buckled, and the frame warped as though it were hit by a truck. He ripped off the door handle, and dragged the would-be runner back to the middle of the room. He smashed the one-way window of the control room and dragged people through it down to the chamber floor. He attacked the Exoskeleton. It was all happening *simultaneously*.

Richard was completely disoriented. He tumbled and rolled up against the walls. The room was a vortex of smoke, and smelled like burning electronics and plastic. Sparks flashed like lightning in a storm cloud, producing images in strobe: pieces of broken metal, torn wiring, bodies strewn about—all in a constant whirlwind of motion.

Through the smoke and intermittent flashes of light, Richard saw Halbreath struggle with the access door, but manage to squeeze through a gap in its warped frame. He heard Bergman screaming to the controllers to initiate the injection, but nothing was happening. Bergman pulled himself off of the floor and raised his gun to shoot Thompson. Richard anticipated the shot, but it was never fired.

He saw Bergman's expression change to panic and then to pain: he was trying to pry his hand from the pistol, but couldn't. His panicked cries quickly turned to shrieks. Richard was confused until he saw threads of smoke rise from Bergman's hand: the gun was getting hot, but he couldn't let go. His screams grew even more frantic as the gun began to glow, a dull red at first, but it quickly turned orange, and got brighter and brighter until it was practically white. The sickening stench of burnt flesh diffused through the room, and Richard flinched and ducked as the rounds in the gun exploded— the weapon deforming and melting, glowing lumps of molten steel splattering onto the floor.

Suddenly Bergman's entire body went up in flames. His screams faded as he collapsed to the floor, after which the only sounds made were the crackles and snaps of his smoldering corpse.

Richard's thoughts quickly shifted: *this would be his only chance.* He navigated through the kinetic chaos to get a clear shot.

Halbreath barged into the control booth and understood immediately why no one had pushed the injection button: the room was *empty*. He ran to the window opening and looked out: below him was a whirlwind of dynamic activity. The Exoskeleton was in the center of it all, with long strands of electrical discharge spraying in all directions, seemingly probing the space around it. People tumbled in the air, and then disappeared back into the smoke and debris.

Halbreath ran over to a control consol and pushed a small red button. A moment later, he heard a computer-generated voice say, "*Injection initiated*." He almost made it to the exit before he felt something wrap around his entire body. He felt himself being dragged through the window, and then landing hard on the treatment floor.

Will seemed to be sensing and acting upon multiple threats simultaneously. When Bergman had pointed the gun, Will's anger seemed to *automatically* channel toward the threat—first, through the man's gun, then through the man himself.

Now he heard the Exo's injection hatch open, even through the background noise. He ripped the offending mechanical component from the Exoskeleton before it activated. His fury increased—his responses becoming involuntary—they were becoming natural reactions. It was a snowballing effect, and he felt a great power building up inside of him.

Richard struggled to avoid the flurry of debris—human bodies and mechanical parts—as he made his way across the experimental floor. A body hit him from the side, knocking him down. He got up and limped to the wall in front of the Exoskeleton, trying to find some sort of cover.

He had to fire without hesitation. That way there would be no time for Thompson, or *the wraith*, to react.

Richard waited for a clearing in the whirlwind of debris, aimed and pulled the trigger.

Will heard the shot from all places at once. His reaction was instinctual, although he wasn't sure what that reaction *was*: it was as if time had stopped... Or maybe he was reacting so quickly it only seemed like time had stopped.

He saw the muzzle flash, and saw the bullet halt about two feet along its projected path, which he intuitively traced to the head of his body, just above his right eye. Will's anger had reached the point of no return—now a cascading wellspring of fury. His entire field of vision turned to white, and a deafening blast drowned out every other sound. An instant later he felt a giant mass press him down. He pressed up against it, but he felt himself fading away. He was in his body again, and that was his last thought.

Will knew he was no longer inside the Exoskeleton, but he had no point of reference to the physical world. He tried to look at his hands, but they were not there. He couldn't determine whether or not it was a dream, but he thought he was talking to Landau.

"What happened? Where am I?" Will asked.

"Everything is going to be okay now, William," Landau said.

"Is it over?"

"It is over…You are free."

Will heard whispering voices, and the light was blinding white. With much effort, he forced his watering eyes to stay open, and human-shaped silhouettes began to form. One of them spoke louder now. It was calling his name.

"Will ..." it said. "Will ... you there, Will?"

He recognized the voice. "Dad?"

Other voices acted up, but he couldn't tell if it was crying or laughter that he was hearing. The silhouettes slowly turned into blurred images, and then cleared. Will couldn't believe all that stood before him: it was his mother and father, his sister and brother-in-law, and a few other people he didn't recognize.

"Dad?" Will asked again. He was in disbelief.

"Yes," Dale Thompson said and smiled.

"Where am I—am I in Heaven?"

Will heard a loud bout of laughter.

"No, Will," his father said and laughed with the others. "You're not in heaven. At least I don't think so."

"Am I in *Hell*?"

This brought on a longer and louder bout of laughter.

"You're here on Earth with the rest of us," Dale replied.

"But you were all *dead*. You're *dead* ..."

"No, Will, no," Dale said, his face became very serious. "They *told* you that. But it's not true. They pumped you full of drugs that made you hallucinate. They made you believe all kinds of things that weren't true."

"How did I get *here*?" Will asked. He noticed now that his right leg was in a cast, and his body was riddled with other bandages and patches, covering smaller wounds.

"You almost *died*—there was an explosion, and a part of the building you were in collapsed on top of you," Dale explained. "That was three days ago—you're in Chicago now."

"I … I don't remember … did anyone die?" Will asked. Bergman's face entered his mind.

"Over twenty people died," Dale replied. "You were lucky. If it weren't for that metal contraption they had you in, you would have been crushed too."

The *Exoskeleton* had saved him. The thing that had caused him the most pain in all of his life had, in the end, saved him.

Will glanced up at the ceiling-mounted television above their heads. It was on a news channel, but the sound was turned off. The lights of fire trucks and ambulances flashed, and people were scurrying about. The camera panned up to the Red Box: about a third of the way up the building was a huge hole, fifty feet in diameter, Will estimated. Wires and rebar splayed out from the vertical crater, and pointed to the massive debris on the street below. He could see that some of the floors had collapsed, and was sure the damage extended well into the interior of the building. He was starting to remember what had happened—*he* had caused the explosion.

"They thought it was a terrorist attack at first," his mother said.

"What do they say about it now?" Will asked.

"Nobody knows. But there are all sorts of wild speculations."

"Yes," Dale cut it. "And the truth is coming out about the place." He shook his head slowly. "We had no idea, son... To think those bastards were hurting you..."

Will didn't want to think about the Red Box anymore. "Did they really sell my house?"

"Yes, but I have a feeling that you're going to get all of that back," his mother replied.

A voice boomed unexpectedly from the doorway. "You bet he is, and much more."

Everyone turned to look at the man who had walked into the room. Will thought he was about his dad's age.

"I'm so happy to meet you, Dr. Thompson," the man said.

Two women followed behind him, one about the man's age, and the other much younger.

"Who are *you*?" Will asked, confused.

"We're from the DNA Foundation," Jonathan said. "This is Julia, my wife, and Denise, my intern... My name is Jonathan McDougal."

"They were working on your case, Will," his mother added. "And now they're going to shut down that awful program."

Will realized something at that moment: *Out of* the Exoskeleton meant back *into* prison. "So, I'll be going to jail now?" he asked.

Everyone became silent until Dale said, "I think Mr. McDougal can answer that for you, son."

"You're going to be exonerated," Jonathan explained. "Cynthia Worthington came out of her coma about a week ago, and has been regaining her faculties steadily since then. She still can't speak, but she can write."

Will wanted to stand, but was only able to sit up a little taller. "What did she say? What happened?"

"It wasn't you," Jonathan said. "She was attacked by *two* high school boys from a town over."

"She'll testify to this?" William asked. He was in a state of cautious disbelief.

"We already have a written statement," Denise said, and smiled. "You're as good as free."

Will didn't know how to react. He closed his eyes and felt an emotion that he could not define—a paralyzing elation. He had no words, only tears.

The McDougals and Denise told Will all about the Red Wraith project, and how the government sought to develop people like him for their own purposes. Will was astonished, but not entirely surprised; the program had a strange air about it from the beginning.

Dale Thompson left, and came back a half hour later with a half-dozen fully-packed paper bags of fast food. "I bet you're hungry for some real food," Dale said to Will as he put a hamburger and fries on his hospital tray.

Will nodded. The last time he'd had real food was when he was fed through the head cage of the Exoskeleton—it seemed like a lifetime had passed since then.

"What day is it?" Will asked.

Denise replied, "Thursday."

"No—the *date*."

"Oh, February seventh."

Will counted back; it had been *forty days* since he'd been dropped off on the roof of the Red Box. *Only forty days.* So much could change in forty days.

"I still feel like I might be hallucinating all of this—it just seems too good to be true," Will said. "I'm really here? I'm really free?"

"I think you are, William," Jonathan affirmed.

"Thank you, Jonathan. How can I ever repay you?"

"You don't owe us anything," Jonathan replied. "Be we would like to do one more thing for you; we'd like to represent you in the multitude of lawsuits that are going to result from this… We'll get you back on your feet and then some."

A doctor came in and asked Will if he was in any pain. Will shook his head and laughed: *he could handle a little pain.* The doctor then told everyone to leave for the night—they could visit again tomorrow.

After everyone had gone, Will turned the TV to CNN—they cycled through the Red Box story about every ten minutes. Bergman and Halbreath were dead, as were many others he recognized. Two of the doctors were dead—Poliakov wasn't at the final event, so he was alive. Colby, the dentist, was killed. His assistant survived, but was in critical condition; *Hatley*—he'd never forget her name, or her smirk.

He learned the name of the man who had fired the last bullet: Richard Greene. He'd been blown through the building, and what little was left of his body was found in the street, and on the walls of the adjacent building... Will didn't know he was capable of such extreme violence. He believed he could never have *consciously* gone through with such an act. It had been an automatic response—a matter of self preservation.

There were many names mentioned that he did not recognize, but apparently none of the other patients were killed. Their Exoskeletons had saved them, as well. The structural integrity of the building had been compromised by the explosion, and the attempted evacuation of the facility had been quite revealing.

The FBI was now investigating the entire CP program, and operations at both the Detroit and New York facilities had been halted. They'd begun extracting inmates from their Exoskeletons, which evidently took at least a day for each patient. Additional engineering teams were being assembled to expedite the process.

At ten o'clock, the "Lance Gates" show came on, and the guest was psychologist Amy Walte.

"Dr. Walte, what kind of people will be coming out of a program like this—where will they be at, emotionally?" Gates asked.

The camera switched to Walte, an attractive blonde woman with large, super-white teeth, and square, black-rimmed glasses. "It's difficult to say," she explained. "They've been through a horrific ordeal… The majority of them will most likely be transferred to mental health facilities. The limited information we've gathered so far indicates that these men have essentially been turned into monsters… But let's not forget that there are already more than a thousand former CP patients walking the streets as we speak…"

Will wondered if *he'd* become a monster as well.

From the ceiling of his room, just above the door, Will watched the two men enter. It was 3 a.m., and he was on edge. One of the men turned off the TV while the other turned on the light beside his bed. His eyes were wide open, and completely white.

"Holy shit!" the man shouted and jumped back.

Will went back to his body and looked up at them. "Who are you?"

"I'm Agent Scott, and this is Agent Carver. We're with the FBI."

"What do you want?"

"We won't be able to keep you a secret very long, Dr. Thompson."

"What do you mean?"

"It was all recorded," Agent Scott replied. "Everything you did during your treatment, and what happened during the final … *incident*."

Will figured they'd recorded everything. Just because that part of the building was destroyed didn't mean the video data had gone along with it.

"So what do you want from *me*?" Will asked.

"We want you to *work* for us," Agent Carver answered.

"I don't think so," Will replied without hesitation.

"Dr. Thompson," Agent Scott cut in. "I can't blame you for not trusting us. But you must understand that the FBI had nothing to do with Red Wraith. It was exclusively a DARPA/CIA project."

Will was silent. He just wanted to be left alone.

"All of the people involved with this project need to be tracked down," Agent Scott explained. "But there are more pressing matters to be dealt with first... Namely the former patients of the program—they're banding together, dropping off the grid like flies. We believe they may be planning something, and thought you might be able to help."

"I don't understand how I could help with that," Will replied.

"It might be a stretch," Scott replied, "but we thought you might be able to provide some insight into how these men think… And, of course, your abilities might be of use to the bureau along the way."

Will nodded, but remained silent.

"There's one more thing we can offer you," Carver said. "Anonymity and protection."

"And why would I need that?" Will asked.

"You're a weapon now, Dr. Thompson," Scott replied. "A very *unique* weapon. And it is highly unlikely there will ever be another like you. Governments and extremist groups will either want to possess you, or destroy you."

Will considered this for a moment. *They were right—he was a walking, talking psychic weapon.*

"Maybe we can talk more next week, when I'm out of here."

The two agents glanced at each other.

"That's good enough for me," Scott said, grinning.

The two men shook Will's hand and left, closing the door behind them.

Will sighed and closed his eyes. Life was going to be even stranger than he'd originally thought. Now it seemed he'd have to live his life on the run, or in hiding. Even so, his outlook remained positive.

He found himself wondering: if he could go back in time and sidestep the whole mess—the false accusation, the public humiliation, the torture, the Red Box—would he? He knew the answer almost immediately: *no*. There was no way he would trade the experience. It had been horrible, yes, and he'd never want to do it *again*—but it truly was his most powerful experience. It had become his greatest asset. He was completely stripped; all the worst things that could ever happen in his life already had. It was the *fear* of these things that was the *real* Exoskeleton.

There were many consequences of the transformation—but the most profound, Will discovered, was that he'd shed his most basal and deeply hidden fear: the fear of *death*.

About the Author

Shane Stadler is an experimental physicist. He has worked at numerous government research and defense laboratories, and is currently a professor of physics at a major research university. *Exoskeleton* is his first novel.

Dark Hall seeks to promote a diverse body of quality works,
advancing the tradition of Horror storytelling as well as
providing exposure for up-and-coming writers.

Visit us online at

www.darkhallpress.com

Printed in Great Britain
by Amazon.co.uk, Ltd.,
Marston Gate.